Given

by

Ashlynn Monroe

Given

ISBN: 978-1-937325-62-6

Copyright © 2013, Ashlynn Monroe

Edited by Leigh Lamb

Cover Art by Fantasia Frog Designs

Published in the United States of America by Beachwalk Press, Incorporated

www.beachwalkpress.com

Dedication

I'd like to dedicate this book to the amazing staff at Beachwalk Press. My incredible editor Leigh Lamb is absolutely my hero. I'd also like to thank my Facebook peeps who've shown me love and support throughout the writing process. You guys rock! **HUGS**

Chapter 1

"I'm going to run away," Cina said.

Kristannie Damiani looked up from her book to stare at her best friend and roommate silently.

"I know I've said it before, but I mean it. You'll be gone next week. I can't stand it here anymore. Without you, my incarceration will be unbearable!"

"I'm trying not to think about leaving. You'll survive, we all have to." Krista didn't mean to sound unkind, but she was the one who should be freaking out, not Cina.

"Sorry. I get how much it sucks to be you right now, but at least you'll be getting out of this place and away from Frau Bitchenstein."

Kristannie chuckled. She hated Miss Ramstein as much as the rest of the girls. They'd dubbed the evil woman Frau Bitchenstein because of her German accent and bad attitude. But no matter how hard she made their lives, it was hard not to pity her. She was just as much a prisoner as the girls were. "You'll be okay without me, Cina. You'll see."

"Like hell I will. You've been the closest thing to family I've had since I was ten. I had my brothers and dad, they really loved me, but then I was ripped away from my home. It was hard for me. You're lucky all you had was your mom. You never had to hurt like I have."

Gaping at her friend with open-mouthed shock, it took Krista a moment to respond. "Lucky? How is orphaned at three years old lucky?"

"You don't remember what it's like not to have a family."

"I remember my mom. I also remember being alone for days in our apartment with her corpse. None of us are lucky."

"Sorry." Cina had the courtesy to look contrite. "It was hard when my mom and my older sister died. I was so little, I don't even remember them. I just remember my dad crying and keeping me inside the house. He made my older brothers take turns staying home from school with me, he was so afraid I'd get sick too," Cina said, shrugging sadly. "Then they still kept me home because they were afraid I'd be taken." Cina walked over to her dresser and picked up her only photo of her father and brothers. She rubbed the glass lovingly.

"When my mom's boss finally called the police, because she hadn't gone into the office for days, they came to the apartment and broke down the door. I remember holding her body and screaming as they took me away from her. I don't even know what they did with her body. She's probably in one of the mass graves. I can't even remember the name of the town I'm actually from. They brought me here, and I've never left. I can't remember much about my dad. Maybe he was just a man in Mom's life. I know he didn't live with my mom. I've been here since this was a tent city. I don't know why I was immune, but my mom wasn't."

Cina had a faraway look on her face. "I heard that if your dad had immune female relatives, you're immune. I don't think it's true, because my sister died. She was fourteen, so maybe she didn't make it because she'd hit puberty already, but I wish they had a real answer for us. If it comes back, I want to know I'm safe."

Krista nodded to her friend in agreement.

Cina let her hand fall away from the photo. "Who knows, maybe it's all randomness. So, are you scared?" she asked, turning back to look at Krista.

"I told you I'm trying not to think about it," Krista whispered. She opened her book again, hoping Cina would give her some peace.

"I'd be happy."

Sighing, Krista closed the book again. She knew Cina well enough to know she wouldn't drop the subject until she was satisfied. They'd have to have this talk at some point before tomorrow, so she gave up on ignoring her pending doom. "Why would you be happy? Do you really think there's anything out there for any of us anymore?"

"Yes. Freedom. I don't care who my six are. I just want out of here. They aren't stupid enough to hurt us. If they did that, we'd be back in the lottery. Women's Social Services will be checking up on us regularly."

"Oh goodie, more people like Frau Bitchenstein coming 'round to tell us how to live. You talk about freedom as if it still exists for those of us with the double X chromosomes. Cina, we are all prisoners for life. Even if you get the kindest, wealthiest six, do you think they'll just let you hop on a plane and travel? Do you think the day after they Give you, you'll be able to learn to drive a car or just skip down the street unaccompanied? Hell no! You'll be even more of a prisoner, and you'll be raped every night on top of it. Only they won't call it rape—they'll call it repopulation."

Kristannie shook with the anger inside of her that had been building for the last eighteen years. She'd watched the tent city grow into a massive secure complex and seen more and more girls arrive against their will. Unlike herself, these girls had fathers and brothers who loved them. It wasn't fair that women were the most valuable commodity on the planet. She just wanted to be human and live life. Cina had gone too far this time. Krista couldn't put the cork back in the bottle.

"Fuck you, Cina! You get to stay here another year. At least you have control over your body while you're here. Me—

six men will rape me—very soon. I'm going to have a goddamn monitor implanted in my arm so they can track me if I decide to run. Freedom, my ass! Oh, they'll say it's to protect me from those who kidnap women of childbearing age and sell them to wealthy men who can't participate in the lottery, but it'll only be for my six to know where the hell I am all the time. There are apps for it. Apps! They'll just pull out their cellphones and see where I am all day long. They'll also have private security to 'guard' me. This place is heaven compared to what I'm going to be dealing with."

Krista was trying not to cry. Saying what awaited her aloud escalated her growing panic. A deeply imbedded terror she'd been trying to control for the last six months clawed to the surface of her consciousness.

"They don't tell you any of this crap until the last few months. You know why—so you don't freak out. If the girls here knew what was going to happen to them on their twenty-first birthday, they'd have a riot on their hands. I look at the little ones and want to cry. Think about it, Cina, our moms died when we were two and three. They died with almost every other woman on the planet, and the few female survivors hadn't had girls after the epidemic. The teens who survived were Given, and the children being sent here now are their daughters. That's what will happen if we have daughters, they'll be taken away on their tenth birthday and we'll never see them again!" She paused. Her rant left her emotionally drained. Krista put her hands over her eyes, as if she could block out the terrible truths. "They'll tell us it's to protect our daughters from those who would take them from us to sell. They'll tell us they have to preserve the human race and our sacrifice is an obligation to our country, but do you think those words will make it hurt less?" Kristannie took her hands off her face to look at her friend. Cina said nothing, which was unusual for the emotional and bubbly twenty-year-old.

"I didn't know. God, I'm sorry, Krista. We have to get out of here."

"And go where?"

"Who cares as long as we don't get a six pack?"

Krista shook her head. She loved Cina like a sister, a sister she'd never see again after tomorrow night, but the woman didn't have a practical bone in her body.

"I'd rather have my six than be taken by human traffickers. At least I know my six are healthy, economically solvent, and have to treat me right. If they step out of line, even a little, I have the right to request a new six, and it doesn't take more than one request to be up on the lottery board for the evening drawing. Last week, three out of seven nights there weren't any birthdays in our region. Men aren't foolish enough to risk losing their woman. It's not as it was. A woman can't just walk down the street, have a job, and make her own choices. Even with the constant guard, restrictions, and red tape, I'll be safe. I might not like this, but I'm not running. The women who do run end up sold or selling themselves, no thanks."

"How do you know that, about them selling themselves?"

"Think about it. You'd be a fugitive. It's not as if you could go rent an apartment and get a job. You'd have to live underground the rest of your life."

"I heard there are hidden communities in Canada where it's like it was before the pandemic."

"Nowhere is really safe anymore."

"You have a point. See how much I need you around to be my common sense? I'm scared." Cina's lip trembled.

Krista put her arm around her friend. "So am I, but at least when you're Given, you might be allowed to have a visit or phone calls or Skype with your dad and brothers. Look forward to that, seeing them again is something. I'd rather just stay here, but that's not possible."

They sat silently for a moment. A bell rang. "I guess free period is over. What activities are you scheduled for now?" Cina asked.

Krista could hear the weight of the new knowledge in her

friend's voice. She hated that she'd been the one to tell Cina the hard truth. The guardians in the protection center tried to make being Given out to be the holy grail of good days, but the oldest girls knew the truth and were sworn to silence. Some of the girls were genuinely happy and excited for The Giving, but most weren't.

"Self-defense, my favorite. Just don't say anything about what I told you or I'll get demerits and lose privileges. I only earned the right to stay in the room instead of going to the half-year dorm because of my behavior credits. The truth is why they take the twenty-and-a-half-year-olds out of the general population. You have another five months before you have to go there, don't speed that up. The crazy things they make us watch and read make me feel icky about the idea of sex. The place is as depressing as a funeral home. I heard two girls are currently under guard in their rooms for trying to escape, others have had to go on depression meds, and one even tried to commit suicide. Finding out our guardians lied about everything we're looking forward to is devastating. Anyway, I'm going to SD so I can blow off a little steam. The instructor only lets me practice on dummies now, because I'm getting so good she's afraid I might hurt one of the other girls." Krista smiled, relishing the moment of pride. "Where are you going again? I can't remember the schedule."

"Home Ec. What's the point? Aren't we just supposed to lie on our backs all day? Most of these guys can afford a cleaning service and cook." Cina looked pale. Krista wished she could take the truth back, but that wasn't possible.

They stood up and left the tiny bedroom they'd shared for nine years. "I wish I could take you with me," Krista whispered.

Cina hugged her friend. "I'm so sorry. I really didn't know any of that."

"They mess with our heads here. Sometimes it works. I've been here since I was three. Maybe that's why it doesn't work on me. I've seen this place built and I saw the turmoil when girls started coming here after the laws changed." Krista shrugged. "The younger girls are the ones who they'll fully brainwash, unless their mothers tell them the truth. If I have a daughter, I'll just make being Given sound great and try to make her all patriotic. At least I'll know she's happy. I hope I only have boys," Krista said, then sighed.

"Me too."

"I wish I were sterile, then I'd be able to stay here as a guardian. They've got it the best," Krista said wistfully.

Cina had to turn down a different hall for Home Ec, so Krista walked the rest of the way to her class in silent contemplation of her mysterious future six. She couldn't help wondering if they'd all be older and ugly or young and hot. The lucky girls ended up with a bunch of trust-fund babies in their early twenties.

She walked in the door and immediately began practicing her round kicks on the first dummy she saw. Losing herself in her favorite activity, she let her mind go blank. Krista used the dummy hard, kicking and punching like her life depended on it.

"Are you all right, Kristannie?" Miss Blake asked quietly near the end of the hour.

"Yes. Tomorrow's my birthday."

"I know. I'm going to miss you. It'll be all right. You know they do a very careful screening. The men aren't older than thirty-six, and they have to be able to afford to keep you safe. I've heard many women find a favorite among their six, love even. I hope you find love."

Tears threatened as the heartfelt words registered. "Thank you, Miss Blake. You've been very good to me, and I'll always treasure what you've taught me."

"I know you will. I don't normally teach half-years. Very few earn the right to stay in the regular population classes. You should be proud of yourself. Your six will be lucky men. Email me at the school anytime. I was once in your shoes. It was before they tested fertility. I cared very much for one of my six. The required removal, so that the men could reenter the lotto again, was difficult. I wanted to stay. My favorite was outvoted. The others wanted the chance to have a child. If they'd gotten a lawyer, they could've dragged out my stay, and possibly kept me, but that's not what happened. I watched the drawing every night, just to see if they received a new girl. Last week, the last of them hit the age limit. They're ineligible now. They are as doomed as I am. I still email with the man I loved. They regretted letting me return not long after they let me go, but it was too late to get me back. They'll never have another woman in their bed again, but I lost the man I loved. Returning is far worse than leaving, I promise."

"I'm so sorry. I didn't know."

"I'd appreciate it if we kept this between us. I was one of the first girls to experience The Giving."

"No worries, my lips are sealed."

"Thank you." She smiled as she replied, but the sad look remained in her eyes.

"I won't be in class tomorrow," Krista whispered sadly.

"I know. It's been my pleasure to teach you."

She gave her favorite teacher a small wave and left the room as the bell rang. The next class was Social Responsibility and she hated it, but at least it was all lecture and simple. She could zone out if she wanted to. She went in and took her seat.

"So tomorrow you actually get to leave here? What do you

think it'll be like?" whispered a younger girl she didn't know well. Kristannie didn't know how to respond.

The intercom beeped. "Kristannie Damiani, please report to the half-year dorms," crackled a voice over the speaker.

She slid out of her seat, relieved that she didn't have to answer the curious girl's question. In truth, she had no idea what it would be like. Six men who'd share "custody" of her was a daunting future to contemplate. No sex education in the world would be enough to prepare her for The Giving. Marriage was outdated; men had custody of women now. After your childbearing years were over, they could keep you or return you to the state. There wasn't a woman old enough to have reached menopause since the pandemic, but that would be changing in just a few years. She wondered just how many aging women would end up working as guardians. The government pushed baby production so strongly that they forgot people still wanted human contact. The idea of The Giving being for anything but procreation was discouraged. Would she find herself in an old folk's home for breeders some day?

She walked down the long, cold, white corridors until she reached the restricted half-year dorm. A guardian opened the door and she went around the corner to the administrator's office. Each dorm had a separate administrator. Miss Neal was wonderful, but she had a very sad job. Seeing the girls leave every six months had to be hard for the kind woman.

"Hi, Miss Neal."

"Oh good. Please sit down, Krista. Tomorrow is your birthday, but you know that. I'm afraid you won't be able to return to the general population before you leave. I've arranged for Cina to pack your things and meet us in the morning so you girls can say your goodbyes. The drawing is happening right now due to the unusually high number of birthdays for tomorrow, but there were none for today. I thought you might like to listen with me."

"Listen?"

"Here." She turned up the radio on her desk.

"Welcome, gentlemen. Today sector three has four birthdays to celebrate. One is in Wisconsin, two are in Iowa, and the final young woman comes of age in Michigan. Each state in the sector has an equal opportunity for selection. Let the randomizer generate our first lucky six."

"I'm the first one to be Given, aren't I?"

"Yes."

Krista bit her nails, the pause was excruciating.

"Blue zone," another man's voice said; blue zone was Minnesota. "One alpha nine delta seven tango bravo eight." The number meant nothing to Krista. There was applause on the radio.

"Is that it? My six are one A nine D seven T B eight?"

"Yes, let's take a peek to see who they are." Miss Neal began typing furiously on her keyboard. "Here we go. I'm happy for you, honey. They're young, and they're all from Bloomington, Minnesota. That'll make it easier for you, no bouncing between cities. They have already drawn up the legal papers required. There will be no bickering and it will be an easier transition for you. They're friends and filled out the twelve-forty-seven form to be a unit, you can't ask for a better arrangement. I'm so glad you've been Given to a group that's both prepared and amicable, it doesn't get much more ideal than that!" She paused, giving Krista a hard stare. "Do you have any questions for me? Is there anything that you might not want to ask general instructors or guardians?"

"How does the 'sharing' work? Do I go to six houses every night?"

Miss Neal smiled sadly. "Unfortunately, every contract is different. In some cases that might happen, in others, everyone shares one house. It's very complicated. There is legislation about women's rights and the need for consistency, but, the repopulation act really stripped any say in this from women. I'm sorry that I can't be more help. I will tell you that, in a situation like this, the men usually live close by. These men have been planning for today for years, hoping for you. You are the thing they've wanted most in the entire world. I hope you'll think about how much they've done to ensure this day came, and how desperately they surely want you. If any of them hurt you in any way, besides the protected act of penetration, you'll be free to request a new six immediately." She pushed a small box toward Krista. "This is a panic button. It reports to our system here. If you activate it, we'll send a retrieval unit to you. The implant you'll be getting this afternoon has a GPS locator."

"Do you know they use the same type of GPS for pets? Am I someone's pet now?"

Miss Neal frowned. "I care about my girls, Krista. I know this isn't the romantic future young girls used to dream of, but in these times, we must be practical. There was a time when the government talked about artificial insemination and just housing you girls here for life. I think 'given-to-six' is a much better arrangement. The government realized men needed hope to have a woman, and women wanted to have a relationship with the fathers of their children. No matter what you think right now, things could be darker. Focus on the good in this situation and you'll have a much easier life. I've heard from girls, who felt much as you do right now, that they've fallen in love with one, if not all, of their six after being Given. Give it time before you decide you're unhappy. Give these men who worked so hard to earn you a chance for happiness."

Miss Neal was a wise woman. Krista nodded. "Okay, sorry."

"Oh sweetie, don't apologize. You aren't the first girl to experience this anger and you won't be the last. This isn't easy for you, but it is for the best. We aren't supposed to have favorites, but you've been here for so long, many of us feel like you are our own little girl. I'm going to miss you. You might be motherless, but you have far more mothers than you realize."

Those words choked Krista up a bit and she swallowed the lump in her throat. "Thanks."

Miss Neal reached out and patted her hand affectionately. "Keep in touch. Six months from now, I can't wait to hear about how much you care for your six and how good they are to you. You are already precious to them, I'm certain of it. Everything will be all right, I promise."

Kristannie wished she could be as confident as the older woman sounded.

"Now, let's see." Miss Neal flipped through some paperwork. "We have several agenda items for you this afternoon. The implant first, and then you'll have a special video to watch with Miss Stanley. Afterward, you get to enjoy

the afternoon by tending to yourself in the spa room. Shave
your legs, take a bubble bath, paint your finger and toe nails,
just relax, and remember you'll be all right. Go to Miss
Stanley's room for a physical and the implant first. I'm told it
doesn't hurt much at all."

Krista nodded grimly. Miss Neal's words didn't take away
the butterflies fluttering in her stomach or her dread of Miss
Stanley. She stood. The older woman grabbed her hand and
Krista turned in surprise.

"You're stronger than most girls I've seen leave, Krista.
Remember, a woman's power has always been strongest over
men who adore them. Make your six adore you." The stark
honesty in the woman's expression gave Krista a moment's
pause.

"How?"

Miss Neal smiled slowly. "I hope the video may shed
some light on the subject. You girls are very sheltered here, but
I know you talk. I was once one of you before it was
determined I was sterile. Be bold, Krista, don't let fear rule
your actions tomorrow. They will love you if you remember to
trust yourself."

Krista nodded and the other woman let go of the hand
she'd captured. "Thank you."

"There's more to the world out there than the whims of

men, you'll see. I've been here far too long. You are lucky, even if you don't realize it."

Krista gave the guardian one final glance as she went out the door. Miss Stanley's office was just around the corner and Krista ducked her head in the door. The woman looked up, her usual sour scowl etched deeply into her features. When she saw Krista, her eyes softened just a bit. "Hello there, birthday girl. I hate to see you go."

The uncharacteristic kindness of the woman's tone made Krista's eyes widen. When the guardian stood up chuckling, Krista realized how her expression must look and managed to pull herself together.

"I know what the girls think of me. You've always been a good girl, and I'm sad to see you leave, but I'm happy for you. There's a great, big world waiting for your spark, Kristannie, but before you can leave, I have to sign off on your medical evaluation and show you the instructional video. I'm sorry, this is basically government-approved porn. Let's get your implant and exam out of the way first." She handed Krista an alcohol swab. "Rub your upper arm, the left one, with this."

Tearing open the package, Krista did as requested. A movement out of the corner of her eye was her only warning. "Ouch!" She jumped and covered her aching upper right arm with her left hand.

"Sorry, it's easier if you don't see it coming." Miss Stanley moved to place a band-aid over the small drops of blood where the implant had gone into Krista's arm. "I learned a long time ago never to tell a girl when it's coming. Don't worry about infection. This device cleaned your skin just before the implant went in. If everything goes well for you, the device will function for a least a decade before it needs to be replaced."

"You mean I have to have it taken out?"

"Yes, and a replacement put back in, but you have many years before you have to worry about it. Put on this gown and hop up on the table." Miss Stanley left the room.

Krista lay nervously on the table. A moment after she situated herself under the paper sheet, Miss Stanley returned.

"This won't be pleasant. I'm afraid I have to break your hymen."

"My what?" Krista glared at the woman, her lower lip trembling. Her eyes were watering, and she tried desperately not to cry.

"This will actually be better for you. I know it seems strange, but it's official protocol before I can sign off on you medically. After interviewing some of the first girls to leave these institutions, the government decided to remove the hymen in a medical office to avoid unnecessary emotional duress after The Giving. This way, you won't associate sex with pain, or at least that's the male theory." She handed Krista a tissue. "Please don't cry. I've done this often, and I promise to make it as quick and painless as possible."

Krista nodded, but she was shaking uncontrollably. She lay back and closed her eyes tightly. The woman gave her no warning. It was painful, but over quickly. Krista cried silently as Miss Stanley finished the rest of the exam.

"You can get dressed now, Krista. You were brave. I've had girls faint. Others scream and thrash until I must call security to have them restrained. I'm sorry. After you dress, press play on the remote sitting on top of the television. The video will help you understand your role and what will be expected of you soon."

Krista shrugged, unable to look at the woman who'd stolen something from her. She knew the guardian was just doing her job. Miss Stanley was no more to blame for the state of the world or idiotic government decisions than she herself was, but deep down a bitter anger rose in her very soul.

The woman left and Krista started to get dressed. Clothing made her feel slightly better. She was sore and felt violated, but she did win the victory over her emotions and managed not to break down sobbing. Taking a deep breath, she wrapped her arms around her middle and focused on trying to see the positive aspect of what she'd endured. Now she only had to fear the act, not necessarily the pain that awaited her after The Giving.

Relief that the exam was over and everything checked out well and the anxiety over the "educational videos" battled within Krista as she finished dressing. At least Miss Stanley had given Krista privacy to watch the awful footage. She sat down, remote in hand, and pressed play.

Scenes of a man and a woman disrobing awkwardly and the woman laying down and spreading her legs began playing. They'd given her enough sex education to make the video only mildly shocking. Neither of them seemed happy or in love. Passionate wasn't the word she'd use to describe what she was seeing, painful was. The woman wore a faraway, zombified gaze and the man kept glancing nervously at the camera.

The next scene showed the woman letting two men take turns. This time, at least one of the men looked happy, but it was more of the same for the poor woman. After the men had left the room, the woman stood and cleaned herself. A narrator explained the importance of cleanliness before the woman went back to the bed and lay down again. Three more men entered the room. They didn't kiss or caress her. Each man waited in line at the foot of the bed as if they were waiting for the bathroom to open up or to be served dinner in the cafeteria.

They all essential raped the empty-eyed woman before politely leaving.

After they'd left, the woman sat up and said, "I'm doing my duty for my country. This has been the best day of my life, a baby is a treasure." She spoke woodenly. Frankly, Krista thought she looked insane and it creeped her out completely. When the horror show ended, she happily turned off the TV.

Miss Stanley returned. "I heard the television shut off. Do you have any questions about the video? I know you girls live sheltered lives here. Please remember, sex is a beautiful and completely natural act. Without sex, the human race won't survive. They Give you to six to increase the odds of conception."

"What happens when I get pregnant?"

"You are carefully monitored. A live-in doctor will stay with you until you give birth."

"What about the baby?"

"It depends greatly on your six. Most men allow the male children to stay with you, however, after six months you will be required to begin the breeding process again."

Breeding process. The words caused a shudder to run through Krista. She said no more and stood to leave. Having seen the graphic depiction of the future awaiting her only heightened her anxiety.

Chapter 2

After a fitful night of tossing and turning, Krista awoke in the half-year dorm feeling discombobulated from the strange bed. *Happy Birthday to you, Krista. Today's going to be a hell'uva long day.* In the not so distant past, she'd probably be a college student, happily anticipating her first night of buying alcohol and excited about a big party. In this other reality, Cina would have a fake ID so they could go to the bar together and look for hot guys. She'd be looking for Mr. Right, not given to Mr. I-can-afford-you. But that world was long gone. Six men awaited her in Madison. They would pick her up after signing some papers and shaking the governor's hand.

She stood up and walked quietly into the bathroom for a quick shower. She was happy to see the jeans and sweater fit. It had been years since she'd dressed in anything besides the protection facility's uniform, so the clothes felt odd against her skin. She applied a light coat of makeup and left her hair loose. She made big, soft curls with the curling iron she'd borrowed from Miss Neal. Satisfied, she left the bathroom just as the morning bell rang. The other girls began to stir.

"Are you scared?"

"Do you know what they look like?"

"Did you see the video?"

She looked at the eight half-years who were sitting up in bed and staring at her curiously.

"Yes. No. Yes," Krista answered the questions then quickly left the room before they could ask more. She hurried past several offices.

"You look beautiful, Kristannie," Miss Lane said, looking out into the hallway and smiling.

"Thanks," Krista muttered, stopping and turning to look at her teacher.

"Come into the guardian's lounge for breakfast. You can order anything you'd like. A few of us would like to say our goodbyes properly."

"But we aren't allowed in…"

"Pfft." The older woman made a disgusted noise. "We've been planning your sendoff all week. You're the closest thing to a daughter most of us will ever have. I remember rocking you on my lap and reading you books."

Krista followed the woman down to the guardian's lounge.

"Surprise!" screamed most of guardians. Krista jumped and Miss Lane laughed.

"You should see the look on your face. Oh, I'm so in heaven, cake for breakfast, yum!"

"Birthday cake!" Krista said, smiling widely. "I haven't had birthday cake since I was little. I can't even remember what it tastes like."

"Well, have a bite, and then you'll know." Miss Neal laughed, handing Krista a huge piece. "I know we aren't supposed to celebrate birthdays, but what the heck. Jory made this herself last night. Oh crap, we forgot the candle. You were supposed to make a wish."

"I'm eating cake! What more could I wish for right now? I do wish I could stay here. This is my home," Krista said, frowning and looking down at her feet.

"No. This is where you grew up, but it's not really a home. Love your six, raise your sons with them. Then you'll feel what it's like to be home." Miss Neal said.

Krista took another bite of the white cake with colorful dots.

"Don't forget to open your present." Miss Neal's voice trembled slightly.

Krista set her cake down as they slid a big box into her lap. When she pulled off the lid, a gasp escaped her. She picked up a beautiful dress; it was dark, navy blue and made of soft, shimmering fabric. The front was low-cut and the dress was sleeveless. Underneath was a pair of matching pumps and a headband made of the same material as the dress. Heat rose to her cheeks when she saw the risqué black lace bra and panties. She looked up at the women sitting in a circle around her smiling and eating cake for breakfast.

"Think of this as your wedding dress. We can't very well send our girl out into the world without anything special to wear," said Miss Neal.

Kristannie's eyes misted. "Thank you."

"Keep looking," Miss Stewart suggested.

Krista saw a hardcover book. She carefully set the dress aside and picked the album up. Inside were pictures, drawings, and even report cards from when she was small. The women had used a combination of officially documented photos and candid snapshots to illustrate her childhood. She'd forgotten how much the teens had played with her as a child. One picture was of her sleeping, all cuddled up with a rag doll one of the other girls had made for her. Another showed her jumping rope with Cina not long after her friend had been ripped away from her family. She could still see the haunted look on Cina's face.

Krista giggled when she saw the picture of the little dog the older girls had found and hidden when the camp was nothing but a tent city. They'd gotten away with hiding him for almost three months. She'd enjoyed the dog more than anything else the wretched place had to offer.

"I didn't know anyone had a camera."

"We weren't supposed to. Just like you girls hide contraband now, we did too," said Miss Stanley.

"Who dug up all these old report cards and awards?"

"They were in your file. We had a wine night and put this together for you. I won't lie, there were tears. You'll be missed, Krista. All of our email addresses, our personal ones, are on the back page. Don't forget us," said Miss Blake quietly.

"How can I forget my family?"

The teachers swarmed her. She was smothered in a comforting, but crushing, group hug. Cina came into the room, looking around fugitively. "Come in and order breakfast with us," Miss Blake told Cina.

"Oh cake, I found my breakfast!" She set Krista's bag by the door and hugged her friend. Both girls started to cry.

"Okay, no more tears. Let's eat!" Miss Neal said with false cheeriness.

* * * *

The drive to Madison, the state capitol, took several hours. Krista's nervousness increased with each passing mile. Looking out the window at the beautiful scenery, she realized just how much she'd forgotten about the world. Watching as the miles of open, rural countryside rushed by caused her to feel small and afraid. The high walls of the Young Women's Educational Protection Facility of the Northern Quadrant made her feel safe, but this expansive space was too big. The rolling hills and corpses of trees were beautiful, but there was just too much…freedom.

She thought about all the horror stories she'd heard from the girls with family who were forced into government protection; stories of men taking young girls and women against their will and selling them to the highest bidder. Were men like those waiting somewhere, planning to seize her before she arrived to her six's private security?

Shaking off the morbid fear, Kristannie focused on trying to remember the time before her mother died. She'd ridden in the back of her mother's car and looked out at the big world beyond the glass. She could remember her mother singing to the radio and laughing while she drove. She thought her mother's name was Alicia, but she couldn't remember for sure, and her records were sealed. The new laws prevented her from knowing anything about her past. She was property after all, government issued. A tear trailed down her cheek.

* * * *

"Stop fidgeting, Jared."

"Christ almighty, Max, calm down. We're all nervous, lay off the kid," Brax said.

"He's only a year younger than I am, it's not like twenty-two makes him a child. We need to pull it together so they don't decide we can't handle this," Damon growled gruffly, defending his younger brother.

"I, for one, can't wait to feel her. Finally, boys, we lose our virginity tonight! A real living woman—and she's ours." DeAnthony gave a joyous whoop. His friends chuckled nervously. The two bodyguards they'd hired stood armed and silent, watching the assembled crowd. Giving Day always brought a crowd of curious men and protesters.

"Women have rights! God gave Eve to Adam, not to six!" shouted a protestor who came too close to the waiting men. A police officer ushered him back behind a barrier.

"Equality for all men!" The angry man stepped back toward the waiting six. Two police officers escorted the outraged man back behind the line again.

"You can't blame them." The other five men turned to look at Braxton with horrified expressions.

"So what are you saying? You want to give up your share to that guy?" Malcolm joked.

"How would you feel if you didn't qualify, Mal? We've never had the chance to touch a woman. Old porno is the closest we've ever gotten to having sex with one. Most of these protesters probably don't qualify for the lottery. If they're not gay, they'll likely die without having sex. The old guys who lost wives or girlfriends have been without for almost twenty years. Granted, they sell some very lifelike devices, but I've heard they don't compare to the real thing. I guess we'll find out soon." Braxton's tone was serious as always.

Mal shrugged, playful as usual. "There are so many girl-boys—you know, the passers, the guys passing themselves off as girls—moving here from economically poor countries, these angry assholes might as well spend their time at the airport waiting for planes. That'll get them a lot closer to sex than wrecking the happiest day of our lives. Remember when these things were full of clapping and handshaking instead of tension?"

"Those days are over. Let's just be glad we were drawn and let the other guys worry about lifelike rubber and passers," Max grumbled.

"She's here." Jared's words came out in a whoosh of anticipation. They watched the black SUV with tinted windows as it pulled up to the front of the building. They stood in front of the grand capital tense, quiet—waiting.

A uniformed solider opened the front passenger side door and stood, surveying the crowd. He opened the back door. Max sucked in a deep breath and the sound broke the spell the other five men seemed to be under.

The crowd suddenly began shouting and the rabble of voices grew chaotic. The six men turned to watch a tall, grubby-looking man sprinting across the green grass of the capital lawn, running toward the SUV and their woman. A police officer tackled the man and the two rolled onto the ground. More officers swarmed the desperate man.

"I just want to touch her!" the wild-eyed man wailed as they cuffed him.

* * * *

Krista stepped out, and the screaming men frightened her. She saw a police officer tackle a man only a few yards away. She started to get back into the SUV, but one of the soldiers grabbed her arm gently.

"It's time, miss."

"I'm afraid."

"We'll protect you. It'll be all right. It's always like this on Giving Day. Don't worry. We will see you safely until you are under the guard of your private security."

This was everything she'd feared, only worse. She hadn't expected the protesters. Someone shouted the word "whore"; she knew the man's hateful word meant her. How any of them could think she'd asked for this was beyond her imagination.

Six young, well-dressed men stood in front of the steps of the large, white, domed building. They were looking at her with…possessiveness. The moment she saw them she knew that these men were her six, or more accurately, she was theirs.

Everything had been sort of slow motion, but then as the crowd grew more agitated, the soldiers quickly ushered her up the sidewalk. The governor didn't come out for the official ceremonial signing of The Giving right, too many threats to his life and ugly behavior had changed this day. As men who couldn't qualify grew angrier with the government, The Giving ceremony became less pomp and more circumstance; and the circumstance was, until they had the woman away from the crowd, they were all in danger. A secretary rushed out and handed the men the last of the paperwork to sign.

There wasn't a single introduction as the security, soldiers, and six young men surrounded Krista and rushed her around the corner and into a waiting limousine. They all hurried to get inside as the soldiers held back the men running toward them. Even inside the car, Krista could hear the angry shouting. The trunk slammed shut. Krista saw the driver slide into the front seat and the engine roared to life.

Feeling the vehicle lurch forward was a relief, but the sensation was short lived. Six pairs of eyes stared at her, each reflecting stark emotions. Some looked hungry, while others appeared wary. The handsome, tall, black man reached out and ran his hand down her arm. She squeaked and shrank back, afraid they'd decide to claim their rights to her there in the car while the driver and security guards watched. One security guard sat next to her and the other sat next to the driver. Both guards were armed and looked a bit edgy.

"For God's sake, DeAnthony, can't you see she's terrified?" The speaker was also tall. His complexion was very tan—too tan for spring in the North, clearly indicating an exotic ancestry. He wasn't as handsome as DeAnthony, but she thought his dark eyes were exceptionally beautiful. His black hair was a little shaggy, as if he might be overdue for a haircut. He gave her a small, friendly smile, but said nothing more. This man was trying to give her space, and she appreciated his thoughtfulness.

"My name is Max Barker. I'm twenty-six and I own a construction company. My company does a lot of work for the government and some high profile private corporations. My overly-friendly friend, DeAnthony Billings, is my business partner, he's thirty."

She bit her lip and gave him a quick nod of acknowledgement.

"Yes, ma'am, I'm the old guy in the group," DeAnthony said casually. He smiled at her and his straight white teeth flashed.

At least he has good genes to give Uncle Sam lots of babies that don't need to worry about seeing an orthodontist, Krista thought randomly as hysteria threatened to overwhelm her. These men would all be using her soon. What they did for a living didn't really matter. She was just something valuable they'd won. While Max's gesture was nice, Krista doubted any of the men cared if she even remembered their names, let alone occupations.

"I'm Jared Reynolds. I just turned twenty-two. I'm in med school." The speaker had reddish-brown hair and many freckles. He looked as nervous as she felt. His green eyes were friendly and she couldn't help liking him. "That's my brother Damon." He pointed to a man who looked very much like him. Damon nodded, but remained silent. "He's vice president of our father's manufacturing company. Our company makes building materials. That's how we met DeAnthony and Max."

"I'm DeAnthony's twin brother," a very short, pale, albeit handsome, blond man stated with a straight face. Krista raised her eyebrow at him and he laughed.

DeAnthony laughed and reached over to put the man in a headlock. "Oh yeah, he's a brother from a different mother. The funny guy is Mal, Malcolm Jones. He's been my bro since high school. Mal's a stand-up comedian. Do you get cable in the Quad?"

"No cable," Krista answered quietly.

"Well, Mal, looks like you've got fresh ears for all those old, terrible jokes."

Mal's expression seemed to light up as he smiled and his face became extraordinary. His blue eyes twinkled. She'd never heard a comedian before, but she loved a good joke. The realization that she wanted this man to make her laugh gave her a moment of surreal contemplation. She'd lived in fear of her six—unknown and demonized in her fearful, sheltered imagination—and now she was curious to know more about them. *This whole meet and greet is just too weird.*

Only one man said nothing. Krista glanced at him nervously. He appeared to be studying her, which made her feel an instant distrust toward him. The others must have noticed her focus, because Jared cleared his throat. When she turned to look at him, he gave her a small, boyish grin. "The guy you're staring at is Brax, Braxton Bray. He's a writer. Fiction. The guy writes stories about a world where the women are free to live and it's the men in high demand. Very sexy stuff, he's a best seller. He's Mal's cousin," Jared said.

"Oh," Krista said, staring at Braxton again. She didn't like the way he was staring at her, as if she were an alien.

"Don't worry. He's cool, just quiet," Mal assured her casually.

She nodded, unsure as to what to say to any of the men. Brax was one of the most handsome men she'd ever seen. He seemed to be studying the events in a way that made her think he was distancing himself from them all.

Everyone sat quietly for a moment. The interior of the limo was feeling a bit claustrophobic as the awkward moment lengthened. "We won't hurt you," Braxton said, breaking the silence.

Krista stared at him for a moment. She could see the honesty on his face. "Thank you," she replied tightly.

"I mean it. Okay, we've told you a bit about who we are. Who are you, Kristannie Damiani?" His tone was so genuine, it surprised her. There was something in his eyes, something she couldn't put a name to. Intensely, he gazed into her face. He leaned forward and rubbed his hands on his thighs. "I want to know you, Kristannie."

The words made Braxton her favorite. His contemplative expression changed to curiosity. DeAnthony was the tallest, but Braxton was a close second. His blue eyes were vivid, unique. His hair was a light brown and it was a bit shaggy, she wondered if it was as soft as it looked. Clamping her hands together, she held them in her lap to make sure she wouldn't be tempted to reach out and touch him. Even if she was supposed to have sex with him, he was still a stranger, after all. She looked down at her feet, and she felt the heat of a blush creeping into her cheeks. When she glanced back up at him, Braxton grinned.

"I want to know you, really," Braxton said quietly.

"There's not much to tell," she replied. "For starters, you can call me Krista, if you like. I was three when the plague came, and my mother died. I miss her, even if I don't remember much about her."

"We lost mothers too, I understand. What do you do for fun?"

"I like to read. The classics are my first choice. Bronte, Dickens—those are my favorites. Does it really matter what I like? I'm just property now, aren't I?"

The men all looked uncomfortable. "I know this isn't the most romantic situation, but I hope you'll find comfort in the fact we've been waiting for you for years. We've built a home for you, Krista. You'll complete our arrangement, and I hope you'll make it more than just a structure. The seven of us will be living together. You won't have to bounce from place to place. We're good friends and, I know the reality of this arrangement is far from ideal, but I hope you'll be able to make the best of things. I don't want you to be afraid." Braxton took her hand and stared into her eyes. "I'm not the kind of man who'd use you, and my friends are all good men, we'll protect and cherish you. There isn't the luxury of time to build a relationship before sex. We all know it. If you aren't pregnant in six months, they'll take you away. I hope you understand the need for expedience."

Krista flinched. "I know. I knew I'd be raped today."

It was Braxton's turn to flinch. "Please don't think of what we'll do as rape. I promise you that even if we aren't experienced, we'll be considerate."

Krista looked away. The other men sat sullenly. Braxton was making an effort to comfort her and she was being ungracious. Her six could've been less attractive or careless with her, but so far, they were better than she'd expected. "I will try," she said, squeezing Braxton's hand.

His surprised expression became a grin. "That makes me very happy, Kristannie. I want to make you happy. I want to give you a Giving Night you'll remember fondly the rest of your life."

Her breath caught in her throat and she felt as if all the oxygen left the limo's interior. Braxton was definitely her favorite.

"So you write about a world where my situation is reversed? The library where I grew up contained materials approved for suitability. I've never read you, but I'd enjoy seeing what you think my world is like."

"It's our world too, Krista. I hope my years of imagining things through the eyes of someone highly prized, but without choice, will meet your expectations."

She couldn't help her grin. "I promise to be extremely critical and demanding in my review."

Braxton grinned back. "You won't be my first scathing review, sweet lady. I can take it."

She felt a connection, and the sensation filled her with relief. Maybe everything would be all right. *God, I hope it'll be all right. Please don't let them hurt me.* With at least one, she felt the stirring of real emotion. It wasn't lust or love, but it was better than being a mindless sex slave. In the instant of realization, her gratitude for Braxton overshadowed her resentment of him and his five cohorts. They were as much prisoners of circumstance as she was. It wasn't as if they selected her any more than she'd chosen them.

"Are you disappointed with what you received? It's not as if you were able to specify body type or hair color." She maintained eye contact with Braxton the entire time she spoke, even though it was hard for her.

He flushed. "I've always thought blondes were more my type, but right now I'm pretty sure I have a thing for brunettes. Krista, you're a woman. That fact alone makes you perfect, but you are beautiful. Sweet, fresh…believe me, we aren't going to be picky."

She frowned. It's not as if she was asking for grand, love poetry, but his raw honesty was a bit hurtful. *Well, I asked*, she reminded herself. "Thank you for being honest."

"I've always thought brunettes were sexy." Jared spoke up. She turned to see him flushing and grinning. "I'm a bit jealous right now. Braxton is hogging your attention. I think you're beautiful and, if I had a choice, I couldn't imagine not picking you." His exuberant words made her grin.

She bit her lip, trying to cover how pleased his words made her. Even if he was just saying it to get into her good graces, she needed to hear just that type of pretty lie. Glancing at Braxton, she noticed he didn't look very happy.

"How about you? What do you think of us, Krista?" Braxton looked at her hard, daring her not to lie with his expression.

"I'm relieved. I'm glad you're all young and attractive. I'm glad you live in the same house, and I'm glad you are friends. I've heard stories of how awkward the sharing can be." She blushed fiercely. "I've only seen propaganda about what it is to be with six men, but have you talked about the reality of how we'll accomplish this?" She glanced over at the security guard and her embarrassment grew. Krista reminded herself the guard knew why they'd picked her up. She turned her attention to *her* men again.

"We've spoken about this often, usually after one too many beers, but yeah we've got a rough idea." Max was the one to speak. "We all have our own rooms, and you also have a room of your own. We thought tonight we'd give you your choice, and then after that we'll use an order determined by drawing lots," he said. He turned to look at Krista again. "Everyone wanted to be first. It sucks to be the guy who has to wait." He winked. "Unless you'd like to take on more than one of us at a time, baby, what do you think?"

Her mouth dropped open. His words were too horrifyingly close to the creepy propaganda film she'd seen the day before. Braxton slugged him in the arm.

"Geez. You've just traumatized her again, and we were making progress," Brax chided.

"I don't hear you saying all the right things, blondes— Jesus," Max retorted. He glared at his friend.

"He's kidding. We don't expect anything that'll make you uncomfortable," Jared said, and she could tell he was trying to sound soothing.

"Umm, okay. I—I want this to work. So far you guys aren't as bad as I'd imagined. I understand the practical need for order in this arrangement. Sorry, I'm so…absolutely terrified." Her voice trailed off, so the last two words came out as a whisper.

Braxton reached out and cupped her cheek with his hand. He ran the pad of his thumb over her skin softly. She froze, unaccustomed to being around men, let alone being touched by one. "Sex can be pleasurable for a woman, Krista. I don't know what they taught you at that school, but I promise you, we aren't going to forget to see to your mutual satisfaction." The way he said satisfaction made her shiver. She liked his voice.

"Can I touch you too?" DeAnthony asked, and she liked the deep rumble of his voice as well. He sounded unsure, and she realized just how much this had to mean to him, to all of them.

Krista reached out and took his hand with her free one. "This is so strange, all of it," she told DeAnthony.

"I know. We'll make it work," he replied.

Chapter 3

They pulled up to an extravagant home in a gated neighborhood just outside of Minneapolis. The geography here was so much flatter than the bluff country she'd grown up seeing glimpses of on the other side of the compound walls, but the small community was beautiful. The security guards got out first.

"Why do you have two guards?" Krista asked.

"Because we aren't taking any chances," Damon replied. "They live on-site twenty-four seven in a private guesthouse and work twelve-hour shifts. Yesterday was their first day. Living with security will be new for all of us. These gentlemen are Carl and Timothy, both are gay and both come from an elite company that provides services to men who've won the lottery." The others began getting out of the limo. Damon helped her out of the car. "You're safe, Krista."

She gazed up at the house. The building looked fairly new. Brick walls stood three stories high. There were large windows, and the design was very modern and geometric. The lawn was perfect and the gate to their property looked impenetrable. The driver used a call box to have it opened. Trees obscured the fence, but she could still see it. They'd built a compound. She frowned at the thought that she'd left one fenced home for another.

The driver got her bags from the trunk, and DeAnthony took her arm. His touch was warm and she saw the gorgeous contrast between his dark skin and her fair flesh. He smiled down at her and her stomach did a little flip. He was so handsome, and she could feel how hard his body was just standing next to him. Jared ran up and took her other arm, and DeAnthony rolled his eyes at the younger man.

The two men led her up the stairs and ushered her into the house. The design was open and everything appeared spotless. The art was cold, modern. The furniture looked new and unused. It looked more like a showcase than a home.

"We aren't here often, most of us travel frequently for work. I'm sure that'll change now," Malcolm told her as he took her bags from the driver. The man nodded and left. "Let's show her to her room."

They all followed Malcolm up the stairs and down a long hallway. Her room was very large. A king-size bed with fresh, white, plush bedding sat in the center of the room. Malcolm set her bags at the foot of the bed. There was a walk-in closet, as large as the room she'd shared with Cina. She had a private bathroom with a garden tub and personal vanity table. There was a big, white couch and television in the corner. Everything looked new and untouched.

"This room has been waiting for you for four years, ever since we began the process to participate in the lottery. This is your home now, Krista. When you finish unpacking, come back downstairs, we want to show you around," Brax said.

They left her alone. She sat down on the bed and air whooshed from her lungs. She shook a little due to nervous anticipation. *Oh God, who should I pick?* Choosing felt so very wrong to her. She may belong to these men for a long time, and the idea of alienating any of them, or getting off on a bad start, twisted her stomach in knots of nervous anxiety. She stood up and unpacked her few belongings. The closet looked so empty after she'd put her scant possessions into it. She began walking down the stairs and she heard their voices. Krista paused to listen, feeling a bit evil for eavesdropping.

"It's only right that she pick."

"We've all waited so long, shouldn't we draw straws or something?"

"For God's sake, she's a human being, not a new toy. Let the girl have her pick. We'll all have a chance."

"What if we all share her tonight? Then it's fair to all of us."

"It wouldn't be fair to Krista. If she was your new bride, would you want to pass her around to five other guys?"

"There's no more marriage, so the question isn't valid. The world isn't nice and romantic. The fact is, she'll have to sleep with all of us."

"For tonight, let her have some peace. I say no one should touch her."

"Are you fucking kidding? Hell no, she picks at least one of us and that's final!"

"Shh, she'll hear you."

"It's not like it'll hurt her the first time, they have their cherries popped by the doctor. I say we ask. She seems understanding."

She'd heard enough. She finished walking down the stairs, one squeaked. They all turned, giving her guilty looks.

"Yes, I heard. I was thinking about the same thing. I don't know if I can pick. I don't want to cause infighting here, and I don't want anyone to feel hurt. I don't know what to do," she finished miserably.

"We won't force you to do anything you don't want to do, but you should sleep with at least one of us tonight," Damon said.

"If you want to pick more than one, that's okay too," DeAnthony amended. Krista blushed.

"Let's show you the rest of the house and have some dinner," Mal said, his tone quiet and even. He took her hand

and led her through the house, showing her the other bedrooms, the numerous bathrooms, and the game room. She could tell they used the game room most often. It was the only room that felt lived in. In the kitchen, a man stood at the stove stirring something. "This is Steve, our housekeeper."

The man looked at her with intense longing, but quickly cleared his throat and wiped his hands on a dishtowel. He held out his hand and she took it; they shook awkwardly. "Do you have a favorite food, miss?" The housekeeper wouldn't look at her.

"I'm not picky, but I'm a huge fan of strawberries."

"I'll remember that," he said, still not looking at her. "Supper will be ready in a few minutes, if you'd like to have a seat in the dining room."

"Thanks," Malcolm said as he took Krista's arm. "I want to show you the garden. It's been my personal hobby when I'm not on tour." He led her out the side door onto a big outdoor patio. Everything was magical. The garden was huge. She noticed a koi fishpond too.

"It's perfect," she said honestly.

"Thanks. It's how I've dealt with my celibacy," he replied tongue-in-cheek.

Krista giggled. "You are funny."

"Yep, that's what my agent tells me." He smiled.

"Soup's on, come in," Jared called out the door.

Malcolm walked her back toward the house, but before they went in, he turned to look into her eyes. "Will you chose tonight?"

"I don't know. I don't want to hurt any of you."

"I won't lie. I want you to pick me. Krista, can I kiss you?"

He was holding the door closed. She stood trapped between his arms as he leaned in, putting his weight on the door. They were alone. She wet her lips in anticipation of her first kiss. The shade trees near the house obscured the late afternoon sun. Looking into his face with intensity, she swallowed nervously. "Yes."

Malcolm smiled and leaned closer. His lips brushed hers gently and then she was in his arms and he was pressing her against his body, hard. Something poked her in the side. His erection. Her heart pounded with the realization that his body was ready for sex. She hadn't realized men could become erect while still wearing clothing. Her cheeks heated. For a fleeting moment she worried he might try to claim his right to her immediately. There was no doubt Malcolm wanted her. When he didn't start ripping her clothing off, she relaxed enough to enjoy the kiss. Instinctively, her arms wrapped around his neck. His lips moved over hers and she moaned, leaning against him.

His hands moved through her hair and she heard him growl as he pushed away from her.

"Damn it, you taste so good." He was breathing heavily. Desire was evident in his expression. She saw him struggling for composure. "You have no idea how badly I want you right now. The next time I kiss you, I won't stop at your lips." His face flushed. He opened the door and she ran past him, rushing inside.

Jared turned and his expression darkened. "What happened?" the youngest of her six queried angrily. When Malcolm came in, looking disheveled, Jared glared at him. "What did you do?"

"Let's eat." Malcolm brushed past the other man, bumping him with his shoulder. Krista saw Jared's fist clench.

"It's fine, Jared, really. It was just a kiss that I gave permission for."

"You kissed him?" Jared looked hurt. "He got the first kiss? That son-of-a-bitch, we agreed no sneaky stuff. If I'd known we could just ask for a kiss, I'd have asked first."

"I'm sorry." She blushed and looked down at her feet, feeling odd.

"God, I'm sorry. Don't look like that, Krista. I'm just so afraid they'll push me to the side because I'm the youngest. I have the least to offer. I'm still a student. If it weren't for my father's money, I'd still be waiting to apply for the lottery. I'm afraid of losing my chance with you somehow. This whole process has made me a little crazy."

She stepped closer to him and put her hand on his cheek. It was so weird, but she felt sorry for him. It was nice to feel sorry for someone other than herself for a moment. Krista leaned forward, closing her eyes, and brushed her lips lightly against his. When she opened her eyes, he was staring at her.

"Thank you," he said tensely. They walked down the hall and Jared opened the door for her.

The others glared at Jared suspiciously and he flushed deeply. He held her chair for her and she sat down, quietly thanking him. Steve served them in courses. She couldn't remember a meal she hadn't eaten cafeteria style from a rectangular plastic tray. The meal was tense. She noticed them giving her longing looks, and glaring at each other. By the time a dessert sat in front of her, she'd had enough.

"I won't pick," she stated flatly. She heard a few forks clatter and the men all looked at her with varying degrees of anger and horror.

"We've waited so long. Fuck," Max mumbled.

"Tonight, I want you all to join me in my room. I don't know what will happen, but I can't stand this…whatever this is!"

"Are you sure about this, Kristannie?" Braxton asked, raising his eyebrow.

"Yes. I can't live with you all fighting over me. I want everyone to be as happy as this terrible situation allows for. I refuse to live in a house filled with intrigue, designed to get in my pants. Just promise me we can go slowly, please. Okay?"

"As slow as you need," Max reassured.

The dessert sat on the table, forgotten, as they all looked awkwardly at each other.

"So were any of you...you know, sexual with each other?" Krista asked, and immediately she heard choking. She turned to see Damon struggling to swallow his water. Jared patted his brother on the back.

Malcolm snorted out a laugh. "When I was younger, I used to get a lot of blowjobs from fans. I'd close my eyes and pretend they were female, but no, I'm not attracted to guys, so it's been rough on me."

"We aren't that kind of friends, and worse, some of us are related. I've been with men, but it wasn't what I wanted," Damon told her.

"Dude, you never told me that," Jared said, looking pale.

"You got a problem with it?" Damon asked his brother.

"No, it's just—you're my big bro and I guess I never thought you'd be with a guy."

"Deal with it, Jared. I had needs and found a solution to my problem. I cared about the man I was seeing, but the relationship felt empty. We were both lying to ourselves. Both of us knew we wanted a woman. We're still friends, but it just wasn't what either of us truly wanted. Does that disturb you, Krista?"

"No. If the situation reversed, I might have done the same thing. No one wants to be lonely. I didn't mean to cause more drama, but I was curious."

"Well, I'm finished. Anyone else finished?" Jared said. He wiped his palms on his pants nervously.

"I think we should just get night number one over with. I'll be upstairs and you can *all* come to me as you please, *together*."

"Wait just a goddamn minute here! No fucking way! Just because we share you doesn't mean I have to see all their asses naked!" Max shouted at her. Krista flinched.

"You, calm down. Now. She's offering this for us, not for herself, you asshole. I'm in, and I bet everyone else is too. If you don't want to see my ass naked, then go to bed. I'm going to her room!" Damon shouted at his friend. The two men glared darkly at each other. Max threw his napkin on the table, but didn't make a single move to leave. No one said anything else.

She stood and the sound of every man in the room scooting back his chair was loud and conclusive. She couldn't watch as they stood graciously for her to leave. She didn't blame them for being eager; none wished to be her last. She just couldn't choose, or make them do it. As scared as she was, the idea of them all being there the first time was actually slightly comforting.

Krista went quickly up the stairs to her room. Hastily, she shut her bedroom door and looked around at the unfamiliar setting. Everything felt so strange. Outside her window, evening was beginning to darken the sky and the room had a dreary, purplish cast as the natural light died. She flipped on a small table lamp. The cheerful glow chased some of the shadows away, but Krista still wrapped her arms around herself, trying to calm down.

Panic contrasted with the resignation she felt over the situation. These men would all, at some point in the near future, have intercourse with her. Now seemed like just as good of a time as any to get over the awkwardness of them all vying for physical release inside of her. She'd never have a flowers-and-candy romance, but she wasn't without common sense. Having every one of them participate the first night avoided her concerns over jealousy and infighting. These men would be keeping her in the beautiful prison they'd built to house her, and she wanted to live as peacefully as possible. Her destiny didn't belong to her, but that didn't mean she wasn't wise enough not to know subtle ways to shape it to her liking. She was glad to have such a lovely home, but it still didn't excuse the fact she may never leave here again. With the dangers lurking beyond the gates, she wouldn't have let herself leave if the decision had been hers.

Krista knew her situation could be worse, but right now, everything felt bad. Knowing some of them had some sort of sexual experience was both disturbing and reassuring. She worried that perhaps her inexperience would make them feel she wasn't as good in bed as the men they'd been with, or worse, they wouldn't know what to do. She didn't really know what to do. Someone had to lead, and she knew it wouldn't be her.

Slipping out of her navy blue dress, she looked down at the lacy, black bra and matching panties. They contrasted nicely against her pale skin. She pushed her hair off her shoulders and took a deep breath before looking in the mirror. Her face was grim. Krista thought about how different her first time would have been with a single man who'd taken her on dates as love had slowly built between them. No woman would ever experience that again.

She was as ready as she'd ever be for them. Krista lay on

the bed awkwardly. She pulled her legs up, and then stretched them out. She spread them a bit, but it all felt too weird. Huffing with exasperation, she stood again and began pacing the room. Six men would have her tonight, and she'd have to endure it all. *What if it hurts me, what if they're rough? I don't care what Miss Stanley said, this could be painful.*

Glancing at the couch, she sighed. Krista sat down on the pristine, white cushions and tucked her legs under herself. The lamp's light surrounded her. Darkness chased the dying daylight away completely; she forced herself to look away from the window and forget there was a world beyond the walls of this pretty cage. This house was her world now, and the population of her new world was six men who had every right to her body. No one was coming to rescue her from this duty.

Startled by a noise outside the closed door, she jumped. She could hear feet in the hallway and whispered voices. She turned her attention to the white, wooden door. Such a minuscule barrier between who she was right now and whom they'd create in the next hours. If they were rough or cruel they might destroy her, and that's what she feared the most. Her six were coming to claim her. A soft knock sounded on the door.

"Come in," she called out hoarsely.

Jared, Max, and Mal vied to be the first in the door. The

sight would've been comical if she wasn't feeling sick from nervous fear. DeAnthony followed them and then Damon. Finally, Brax brought up the rear of the group, he looked pensive and his lips were pressed into a hard line. They all stopped and gazed at her with lustful and excited expressions. Brax was the only one who didn't ogle her with open desire.

The heat crept down her cheeks, neck, and chest. For an awkward and extremely uncomfortable moment, they just stood silently, unmoving. She didn't know what to do. This didn't feel natural. She'd heard of women overcome with need who enjoyed sex, but she just felt uncomfortable. Krista nibbled at her lower lip, fighting tears. *What if I'm the other kind of woman, the one who doesn't like sex?* She knew she'd be having sex at least six days a week, possibly more often. The thought that intimacy would be a chore was terrifying. *If only I had time to get to know them. I should've chosen one, this is so much worse. Why did I think I could handle this?*

The men all seemed content just looking at her mostly nude body. She felt so dirty. "What do we do now?" Krista asked quietly, looking away from them. "Do you want me to just lie on the bed and close my eyes until it's over?" Her voice was the merest of whispers. Her face was so hotly uncomfortable, she put her chilly hands on her cheeks to take away some of the burning.

"No, Krista, we don't want you to do that. We want you to enjoy this," Brax replied quietly. She glanced up at him in surprise and she saw the intensity of his look. His face was so different from the others, she believed him.

"Speak for yourself," Max grumbled. Then remorse filled his expression. "It's not that I don't want you to enjoy it, but damn it, seeing you like this has my cock so hard it's killing me."

Krista swallowed around the lump in her throat. *I just hope it doesn't hurt.* She tasted blood from where she'd worn the skin raw on her lower lip.

Jared was the first to move. He sat down on the couch next to her. "Can I touch you?" he asked.

She didn't trust herself to speak, so she just nodded. Jared's hand slowly began to caress her back. Light strokes skimmed her body so gently that his soft touch caused her to relax a little. With the eyes of so many men on her, she couldn't enjoy the tender caress as much as she might have in private.

"Your skin is really soft." Jared's voice sounded strained. He began brushing the hair off her forehead. "Can I unhook your bra?"

Krista jumped. The question took her by surprise, which was ridiculous, but still the query shocked her inexperienced sensibilities. She gave him a single, tense nod. She heard the subtle sound of the stays unhooking as he pushed the small hooks apart one-by-one. Jared was infinitely tender as he pushed the lace straps off her shoulders and arms. The insignificant bit of fabric fell to the floor unceremoniously. She heard a moan and a gasp from the group of men, but she wasn't sure which ones had made the noises.

Krista managed to look at Jared. His reverent gaze made her flinch; no one had ever looked at her like that before. Prickles tingled inside her core. The first hint of excitement caused her heart to pound. Jared leaned close to her and placed a delicate kiss on her shoulder. He sat up and looked into her eyes. "You have beautiful breasts. May I touch them?"

Her heart was beating so ferociously it hurt. She couldn't speak, couldn't nod. She wasn't sure if she was ready for such an intimate touch. Her back was one thing, but her breasts were entirely different. She cleared her throat. "Start slow," she uttered quietly.

Another groan came from the voyeuristic group still huddled in the doorway. She heard the cracking sound of one of the men hitting the groaner. "Quiet," Max commanded in a loud whisper.

Krista's cheeks were burning again. She refused to let herself look at the other men and focused her attention on

Jared.

"Let me know if you want me to stop, okay?" He tilted her chin so that she'd look into his eyes. "I want you to like what I'm doing. If you don't, I will stop."

Her lips pressed together tightly and she nodded, holding her breath. His fingers skimmed the flesh of her nipple so lightly she wondered if she'd imagined his touch. Then he pressed the pads of this thumbs against her skin with more pressure. She groaned.

"Do you want me to stop?" Jared asked quickly.

"No," she croaked out the word with effort.

He gave her a small smile and knelt on the plush carpet in front of her. His precise movements and quiet voice reminded her of someone trying to tame an animal. *Am I becoming a tamed creature, a wild thing that needs to be broken for them to ride?* Before she could let her mind go to some place dark, Jared's voice interrupted her introspection.

"Thank you for letting me touch your breasts. Can I kiss them?"

Once again, the escalation of his actions caused her a moment of panic. This time she glanced at the group standing in the doorway. They were still dressed, but she could see the evidence of their erections in the bulges of their pants and the hungry looks in their eyes. She turned her attention back to

Jared, who was gazing at her anxiously. Reaching out, she touched his face softly. "Okay," she whispered, then took a deep breath, which she held.

He took her small breasts into his hands, and this thumbs swirled around the areolas and nipples gently. The sensation built inside of her and she let go of the breath she was holding. When he leaned forward and placed his lips very softly against her left nipple, she gasped, and then he sucked it into his mouth. She felt the hot wetness against her skin, and as he suckled, he varied the pressure until she cried out again. She looked down, watching his face pressed to her chest. His eyes remained closed, and she reached out to trace his eyelids softly. She ran her fingers over his cheekbones and finally allowed her hands to come to rest on his shoulders. He began tweaking her other nipple with his fingers. Krista closed her eyes and a quiet, albeit slightly primitive, noise issued from her.

She felt heat and her body seemed to hum with need. She realized she wanted more and liked the sensation. "Jared, you're wearing too much clothing," Krista told him, and she could hear the huskiness in her own voice. He glanced up at her and she saw surprise in his eyes.

He pulled away. "Are you sure?"

Shyly, she looked at him through the veil of her eyelashes. "Yes," Krista whispered.

He stood and took off his shirt without finesse. Then he paused and glanced at the group of waiting men. Damon gave him a nod of encouragement. The younger man flushed very red. "I'd feel better if I wasn't the only naked man in the room." His hands went to his fly.

The others shifted uncomfortable. They all looked at Krista.

"Okay." She didn't know what else to say. The sound and sight of the men disrobing made her breath catch and she stared at the group, transfixed by the image. DeAnthony's body was lean and muscular. His dark skin was flawless, and he had the least amount of body hair. Jared was thin, lacking DeAnthony's muscle tone, but she didn't find him unappealing. His chest and arms, except for a sprinkle of freckles, were very pale. Her eyes scanned for Braxton, for some reason she wanted to see him naked most of all. She tucked the factoid away in the back of her brain for later examination, when she could think clearly again, but searched for him now.

Her eyes caught his and he paused. They just held the silent communication for a moment before he straightened and stepped around the others who were still shedding clothing. Brax's penis stood erect; she liked how he looked without his clothes on. His body was hard and he had natural definition to his muscles. She noticed a dark birthmark on his abdomen. The splotch reminded her of the inkblot she'd seen at her final evaluation. She'd said it was a butterfly.

He raised an eyebrow at her, and she realized she'd been staring at him for far too long. She didn't know why she wanted to see him so badly, or why looking at him naked gave her a jolt right through her core. She ignored the nibble of worry her need caused her to feel and just enjoyed Brax's nudity. For someone with a sedentary occupation like writing, his body didn't show any sign of a butt-in-chair lifestyle.

He looked away from her and she saw something she couldn't name flicker across his face. For some completely irrational reason, the expression crushed her feelings; this experience had caused her to be far more delicate than she'd expected. His opinion, above them all, mattered. There was something about the quiet man—he stirred up complicated emotions inside of her.

Mal had something on his flat stomach. Krista craned her neck, frowning as she squinted to read red writing on his skin. Her head cocked slightly to the side. "Enjoy here?" she uttered. She burst out laughing. Hard. Mal had written the words and drawn an arrow pointing south. The others all turned to look at him, giving him varying looks of amusement, annoyance, and anger.

"It's edible!" he announced, far too proudly. Krista

couldn't stop her bubble of chuckles from rising up and out. The massive emotional pressure had been crying out for an outlet, and Malcolm's prank was delightfully ridiculous. She'd needed something other than cock and chest hair to focus on to chase away her terror.

"For Christ's sake, go wash that shit off," Max growled at the shorter man.

Mal shrugged and looked Krista in the eye, his expression still filled with playfulness. "Do you want a taste first? It's strawberry," he said with a wink, wiggling his eyebrows suggestively.

She rolled her eyes, still chuckling. She pinched her lips together, trying to keep a straight face. "I'll take your word for it, but strawberry is my favorite."

His expression softened toward her very subtly. "I know. I heard you tell Steve."

She couldn't take the grin off her face. "Mmm, I appreciate your thoughtfulness, I think."

This time it was Mal's turn to chuckle. "I'd better go wash this off before Max decides to take a bite."

What happened next came so completely out-of-the-blue, Krista scrambled back, almost falling off the back of the couch. Max swung, hard and fast, hitting Mal in the face. Blood spurted from Mal's nose and he held his face, rambling off a string of profanity so profound it made Krista's ears burn.

"Why did you do that? Jesus, it's Mal, we know how his sense of humor is, and frankly I'm surprised he didn't do something even more outrageous," DeAnthony said. He looked as confused as Krista felt. She feared Max's volatile temper and didn't relish the idea of ever being alone with him. However, she knew it would be impossible to avoid that happening at some point in her near future.

"I... Fuck!" Max grabbed his clothes and rushed out of the room.

"I'll talk to him," Damon said, going after the angry man.

Krista jumped up and hurried to the bathroom, returning with a cool, damp towel, which she handed to Malcolm.

"Thanks," he said, and his voice sounded funny. Jared was already looking at his face. She was worried that his nose was broken. She should hate him, all of them, but she couldn't bring herself to feel that way.

"It's not broken," Jared said, alleviating her fears. "It'll hurt like hell, and you'll have a nice matching set of black eyes, but it'll heal before your next tour."

"Damn, I could've made some great 'you should see the other guy' jokes," he teased, but held the towel to his face.

"Go put your head between your legs and keep pressure on it to stop the bleeding," Jared prescribed.

"Yes, doctor," Mal teased, but he followed Jared's orders.

DeAnthony's hand began rubbing her back. "Don't worry about this, Krista. Max has always been a hot head. Mal should've known not to make a joke at his expense when he was already tense. Come over to the bed and relax." His voice was pitched in a way that told her the fight hadn't dampened his lust. He kept rubbing her back in slow sensual circles, and she allowed him to gently lead her to the bed.

"Shouldn't we go check on Max?" she asked nervously. Her earlier sexual interest was gone.

"He'll be fine. Let us make this up to you," Jared quickly spoke, there was a desperate quality to his words. Krista realized just how desperate the men were for this and she forced herself to remain where she was. She tried to stop her body from trembling. It was slight, but she felt embarrassed by her weakness. She'd had years to prepare for tonight, but she didn't feel ready.

Braxton came over and sat next to her on the bed. He took her hand in his and she couldn't stop her eyes from glancing at his erection, only inches from her hand. "Are you sure you want all of us here tonight?"

"I don't want anyone to hate me. I may have to live with you for a long time. I'm afraid. I won't lie."

"We talked about this earlier. We think having all of us

inside of you might be too much for you, but there are things we can do to alleviate your discomfort, and ours. Would you like me to tell you how I see this working the best for everyone?"

She wasn't sure if she wanted to hear the words spoken. Doing it was one thing, but hearing it felt…strange. Curiosity won and she nodded, not trusting herself to speak.

"There are more things that a man and a woman can do than just the act of him—penetrating her. A woman can use her mouth to release a man's natural tension. She can also use her hand. I'd like you to lie back and just allow us to touch you, explore you, and when you feel ready, you can let us know what you need. Let us make tonight one that'll show you just how good it can be. Afterward, you can decide if you are willing to allow more than one of us here, and we can make a rotation. I don't want you to feel used, but there's only one of you and six of us. I wish we had the luxury of time, but we don't."

She nodded. He was right, getting her pregnant right away was the only way to ensure she remained with them. Even Max's anger didn't make her want to leave these men. Realizing she wanted to remain here, for now, was a shock. If she had to be Given, she was glad it was to this group of men.

"Lay back and close your eyes," Brax whispered.

She did as he'd asked. Then his hands were touching her hair, shoulders, and face. She shivered, feeling as if this was a dream. Thinking of it that way helped her to relax and gave her an analytical distance from what was actually happening. Someone pulled her panties off her hips and down her legs.

She knew which one of them was touching her, even if she couldn't see. She could smell Jared's over-saturation of body spray to her left; he was touching her hair and face tenderly. DeAnthony had the largest hands, and she sucked in a quick breath when he touched her thighs. His touch was gentle, but the location was most uncomfortable. Malcolm wasn't touching her, and she knew he was sitting on the couch, bleeding in agony. She wanted to say something to him, but she was afraid to move or open her eyes. The experience was leaving her on the verge of panic, so she lay still and just did her best to relax by taking deep, calming breaths. Brax's fingers traced her collarbone, and then his fingertips trailed over the curve of her shoulder. Slowly, she started to relax under the soft caresses of the men.

"Damn, you're beautiful, woman," DeAnthony uttered. "I'd love for you to part those legs. I want to see you, Krista. All of you."

She was shaking, but decided to give him what he wanted. That feeling from earlier, the one that promised she might actually like this, returned. She knew she wasn't beautiful, but a sweet lie was forgivable. She opened her legs, just a little.

"Oh baby, give us a little more," DeAnthony requested huskily.

Heat warmed her cheeks. She only opened her legs a little wider. She doubted they could see much, but she was still nervous.

A gentle touch against her nipples made her hiss. She knew two different men were touching her breasts. One was a little rougher than the other was, but the sensation was wonderful and she parted her legs wider for the men. The slow growing flame of want began to burn hotter and she unclenched her fists. She hadn't even realized she was doing it until she relaxed a little.

She heard a moan and knew it was DeAnthony getting a good look between her legs. "I want to touch your pussy, Krista," DeAnthony whispered.

She nodded, her eyes still closed. The first touch made her jump. He ran his fingertip against the outside of her pussy, but then he flicked the little nub that hid there and she bucked her hips.

"Shh, baby, you'll like this," DeAnthony promised. He began rubbing there and at first, it was almost a violation, but then warmth began to fill her and arrows of excitement struck her core. Her stomach muscles became taut and tight. Brax and Jared were rolling her nipples with more pressure, and she realized she liked it, all of it.

Cautiously, she opened her eyes. Jared smiled down at her, but Brax wore his typically serious, contemplative expression. She smiled at both men.

DeAnthony dipped his finger into the slickness that was forming at her entrance and when he returned his fingers to her clit, she cried out softly. "Mmm, you like that, baby?"

"Y…yes, oh, yes," she answered, finding her missing voice. "I want…"

"What do you want, Kristannie?" Brax asked, his focus so completely on her that she had to swallow around the lump in her throat. His eyes had the power to captivate her unlike anything she'd ever experienced. She just needed him to keep looking at her like that to find the courage to voice her pleasure.

"I want to learn…how to make you feel good, all of you." She never took her eyes from Braxton as she spoke.

"I don't think you could do much to make us feel bad, baby," DeAnthony answered.

"Jared's dick is the smallest." Brax paused to look at Jared. "Nothing personal, dude," he said, and Jared just shrugged in response. "We thought you could learn to take a man in your mouth on him. Would you like to take Jared's cock in your mouth?" Brax asked, and his voice had an instructional tone that made her feel strange. She realized hearing him ask such a sexual question in such a casual tone, he might as well be asking if she wanted the last cookie, but his question heightened her building sexual curiosity.

"Yes," she replied, and she bit her lip, afraid of making a mistake.

Jared stopped playing with her nipple and knelt on the bed beside her. She glanced at his erection. He wasn't that much smaller than the others were, but she thought she could do it. Rolling to her side, her lips were just an inch or so away from him. Krista licked her lips. She leaned in and took his cock gently into her mouth. He made a low sound and she gasped, pulling away.

"Did that hurt?" she asked shyly.

"Hell no. You're doing fine," he replied gruffly.

She leaned forward again and took more of him in her mouth.

"Put your lips over your teeth, Krista. That's it. Now slide over him. Press the bottom of him with your tongue," Brax instructed.

"Stop…ordering…her around. She's doing just fine. Ahhh," Jared ground out between his moans.

Krista gasped against his cock as a new sensation of warm heat settled on her pussy. She pulled away from Jared to look down and DeAnthony's dark head was between her pale thighs. The sight was beautifully erotic and, for a moment, she watched him as he licked her. She turned and took Jared into her mouth again. She'd never have imagined it, but she didn't want to stop. A peculiar power surged through her. What should have been degrading was instead uplifting. The realization struck her sharply as she glanced up at Jared's face. She had the power to give or withhold pleasure from this man. He was lucky—she was in a giving mood.

Feeling the position of her newfound knowledge, she quickened her pace, all the while enjoying the growing sensitivity in her pussy as her clit swelled from all the attention DeAnthony lavished on it. When Jared cried out loudly, DeAnthony stopped licking her and the bed dipped where he was lifting himself up to get a better look at what she was doing.

"Oh God, I…I'm going to come, Krista. I…Ahhh!"

Something hot filled her mouth. She forced herself to swallow, not sure what else to do with the strange, sour flavor. She pulled away.

"Go get her some water, now," Braxton ordered Jared, who stumbled away toward the bathroom. She heard the soft hiss of the sink and then Jared rushed back with a paper cup.

"Sorry. I should've pulled away." He looked flushed, and she wasn't sure if he was embarrassed or if it was from his gratification.

"Shouldn't I have swallowed that?" She glanced at Braxton, since he seemed to be the conductor of this orgiastic symphony.

"You did great. It's your choice if you swallow, but Jared should've shown a little more restraint and given you warning enough to be able to make a choice."

She took a drink of the water, not sure what to say or do.

"Her mouth felt so damn good. I'd like to see you try not to come if she was sucking your cock."

"I'd love for her to suck my cock," Mal said, and his voice still sounded funny as he held the once white, and now red, towel to his face.

Krista felt uncomfortable, used. She wanted them to like her, to keep her, but this was a bit like she was trading herself for security and peace.

"Are you sure you're up for it, Mal?" Jared asked. "You are injured."

"I'd have to be dead for this hard-on to go away, and even then it'd probably get rigor mortis and they'd have to bury me in a tall casket," he replied, grinning.

Jared snorted and then coughed to cover his amusement. Krista put her hand on his arm and gave him a shy smile. He grinned like a Cheshire cat at her attention.

Mal came over to the side of the bed, and Krista's lips parted obediently. Mal thrust himself at her and she sucked him into her mouth. She could hear moans from the voyeurs watching her. He slid in and out of her lips and she sucked him back in. Mal groaned a long, low sound of satisfaction and took a fistful of her hair in his hand.

"Be gentle with her, you asshole!" Braxton growled.

"Damn it, I can't help it. This is so fucking good. I've imagined a woman's soft face pressed up against me like this— her hot, little mouth…oh God! Lord Jesus, yes!" Mal's warm, salty cum shot into Krista's mouth, and she did her best not to gag.

"Don't take the Lord's name in vain, man," DeAnthony chastised his friend, but glancing up into Mal's face, Krista knew he wasn't paying any attention. Mal's eyes stayed closed, his head tipped back and she could feel his body shudder where it pressed against her cheek. He gasped out another small groan as his cock slipped out of her mouth. She swallowed his ejaculate, and Jared held the water glass to her lips. She took a quick sip, gratefully.

"I think it's time we show Krista what she can expect

from us before she practices any more of her new skill. Lie on your back and spread your legs for us. We aren't just about taking from you," Brax uttered in a husky voice.

She obeyed without hesitation. She wanted to feel the sensations she'd enjoyed earlier. She noticed Jared was growing hard again already. This time Braxton was the one between her legs. DeAnthony and Mal took the places Jared and Brax had occupied earlier.

Brax placed a tender kiss on the nest of hair between her legs, then rolled his tongue over her already sensitive clit. When he dipped his fingers inside of her pussy, she arched her back, unprepared for the intimate invasion. His touches, both inside and outside, felt wonderful. When the two men sitting next to her on the bed began to fondle her breasts, the combination of sensation made her body buck. Krista gasped, crying out loudly.

The door opened and she glanced sharply at it. Her lust-clouded vision registered Damon coming in. He no longer had a hard-on and looked upset. After a moment of watching the spectacle on the bed, she saw his cock growing. Her eyes widened a little, it was amazing to see, the others had been hard before they'd undressed.

Brax sat up, but his hand found her clit and he continued to rub her, driving her wild. She moaned, closing her eyes. Her head rolled to the side and she pushed her hips up, pressing her body more tightly against his hand. He chuckled warmly.

"All right, boys, let's get this party started. Who's first?" Krista heard Braxton's words, but they didn't register until she felt the bed dip between her legs. Opening her eyes, she glanced up to see DeAnthony's big smile. She smiled back, but it felt tight and unnatural. Nervousness made her clench her teeth.

"Relax," Braxton, said still rubbing her pussy, only his pressure increased, as did the speed of his concentric circles against her clit. DeAnthony was so big; she feared it would hurt as much as what Miss Stanley had done.

Jared smoothed the hair out of her eyes and moved a strand from between her lips. Krista glanced up at him and she saw tenderness in his eyes. Her body did relax a little, but she was still afraid.

"Let Damon go first," Brax ordered.

"Who the fuck died and made you the boss of fucking around here?" DeAnthony demanded. He glared at Brax. "What, she's got a problem 'cause I'm not white?" He gave Krista a very angry look.

She felt terrible. She wanted to avoid conflict, but it seemed no matter what she was willing to do they were determined to fight over her. "No," she replied quietly. "You're big—really big. Sorry. It hurt when the nurse, umm, you know. Anyway, please just get it over with." She turned her head to the side and closed her eyes. The weight left the bed and her eyes flew open. Krista turned her head and saw DeAnthony backing off.

"I don't want to hurt you, but I'm going to have you, so get used to the idea of my big, black cock in that tight, white pussy." He sounded bitter, but she could see he wasn't as angry as he'd been a moment before.

Damon blocked her view of DeAnthony, and the bed dipped again. Damon was the smallest of any of them, even Jared. He didn't touch her or kiss her, but without preamble, his cock poked at her slick cunt. She glanced up at Jared, her eyes widened. He smiled down reassuringly, running the pad of his thumb over her cheek.

"He won't hurt like that. Trust me, I'm almost a doctor," he whispered, grinning.

Something inside of Kristannie cracked and she smiled back. Damon slid inside of her, and Jared hadn't lied—it didn't hurt. There was no amazing pleasure either, Brax's hand felt better. She sighed, and the tension completely left her body. It wasn't going to be as bad as she'd thought. Damon began slowly sliding in and out, and Brax never stopped rubbing her clit. A new tension began building inside of her. She moaned, closing her eyes. Then came the hot sensation of Damon's release. He grunted. It was over. He slid off the bed, picked up his clothes, and left the room without a word. Deep disappointment surged inside of her. His abrupt departure left her feeling slighted. She knew there was more, if he'd just held off a moment more...

The bed dipped again. DeAnthony was between her legs. This time she wasn't afraid, and to her secret shame, she wanted what his cock could give her. The feeling building within her was wonderful. Brax's hand continued its magical motion, and her body wanted more, as if she were on the verge of something amazing.

"Are you cool with me?" He sounded worried.

"Please, DeAnthony, I want..." She didn't know what she wanted, but his beautiful wide smile told her she'd said the right words to alleviate the tension between them.

He lowered himself and placed a kiss on her stomach. She groaned. His eyes looked up into hers. Mal began to play with her nipples, and Brax's hand pushed her higher and higher toward the pinnacle of the sensations her body reveled in. She knew there was more, instinctively. This was so much better than she'd hoped for, this was great.

DeAnthony kissed her stomach again, and then the tip of his hard cock nudged her pussy. She tried to widen her legs, but they were already as wide as they'd go without pain. He pushed inside her, widening her tight, slick sheath. He didn't just stop as Damon had, instead, his hips began trusting back and forth. She felt his hardness slam all the way to the deepest place inside of her.

"Ah, baby." He moaned. "I didn't hurt you, did I?"

"No, please don't stop. I'm just so…damn it, please I need it!"

He grinned. His hard, fast pumps made her feel exquisite. Brax moved his hand away, and she vaguely wondered if he'd lost feeling in it, then her mind thought of nothing as sensations washed over her from head to toe. Bliss, real and good—she came. Screaming.

"Yes! DeAnthony! Yes!" Her hips bucked up to meet his thrusts. "Damn!" She never swore, but whatever filter she possessed fled as she bore down on her scream making a primal cry that startled her. She couldn't believe she was making those sounds, or relishing Giving Day. Krista whimpered as the tidal wave that'd sweep her out to sea began washing her back onto the shores of reality.

Jared continued to brush her hair out of her face and off her sweaty forehead tenderly. She'd have to give the young doctor props on his bedside manner. Mal had removed his hands from her breasts, but she couldn't remember when.

DeAnthony's body stiffened and he cried out, and then collapsed on top of her. He laced his fingers through hers and they lay panting companionably for a moment.

"You should get off of her. You've got to be heavy." Brax mumbled the command half-heartedly. The boss man seemed deflated. Krista glanced up at him.

"Are you—"

"No," he cut off her question.

She felt hurt, but couldn't pinpoint the reason. The other men gave him curious looks. She could see he was still hard, and a droplet of fluid even leaked from the tip of his penis. She bit her lip.

"Are you mad?" She hated asking, but she wanted harmony. Airing a grievance immediately would avoid a repeat occurrence.

"No." His eyes softened when he looked at her. "You've had enough. You've been satisfied, and for now, it's time to give you a break. Hell, I don't want to try to follow that performance anyway, I'd never be able to read the reviews later."

"What reviews?" Krista panicked. Did men report the results of Giving Day somewhere?

Brax chuckled. "Never mind, no real reviews. I just don't want these knuckleheads thinking I can't make you scream like that. I can wait my turn. I want…I guess I'm feeling a little old-fashioned all of a sudden. I want to be memorable."

"Damn, I'd say this whole night has been memorable," DeAnthony interjected. "I'm going to remember this fondly for the rest of my life." He placed a kiss on Krista's forehead, holding his lips against her skin for a lingering moment. When he pulled back, his eyes stared deeply into hers. "Thank you," he muttered.

She gave him a half-smile. "You're welcome. I think I should be thanking you." All the men laughed, but she noticed Brax's didn't sound genuine. They all stood up and began collecting clothing.

"You have as much privacy as you want. If you ever want to invite one of us to your bed, or stay in ours, I'm sure I speak for all of us when I say it'd be welcome. Tonight, I think you'd probably like some private time, right?" There was a strange hopefulness in Brax's voice.

"Thank you, I—yeah, it's just all so weird. I feel like I'm in someone else's bed and life. It's so hard to accept…goodnight." Heat rose up her neck and cheeks. How could she explain the surreal adjustment her government and these men expected of her?

Brax walked over and sat down next to her on the bed. "I know. I mean, I think about it, what women go through now.

I—just don't feel like we don't care. I care, and I'm sure the others do too."

She doubted Max and Damon were in the caring category, but the other four men had treated her well, better than the poor woman from the educational video received, that was certain.

"I want to read one of your books," Krista blurted out. Curiosity filled her and she suddenly wanted to see if he'd gotten it right. The idea of a book about her plight, even if it starred a man, was appealing. There was nothing like it in the library at the protection facility.

Braxton grinned. "The whole series is on the bookshelf in the game room. Help yourself. You just have to promise to be perfectly honest."

The worry on his face made her smile. He wanted her to like his work and it made her feel pleasantly surprised. "I promise to give you a tough, uncensored review."

He leaned down and kissed her cheek. "Thank you." His deep voice rumbled as he whispered in her ear and she shivered.

Knowing he wasn't going to have sex with her was both a disappointment and a relief. She'd wanted to experience him the most, but she was glad he'd waited too. Somehow, the idea of it being special with him made her feel better about losing her technical virginity only to be thrust into the middle of what was essentially the most immoral, government endorsed morality she'd never imagined in her wildest dreams. She wished she could talk to Cina. She needed the comfort of a friend and more importantly, a female ear.

The men left and she sat alone in the dim room feeling jittery. She wasn't tired, despite the late hour. She stood up, realizing she was a bit sore, and went into the extravagant bathroom. The towels were so soft. She'd picked a couple off the pile on an antiqued iron wall rack. Holding them to her nose, she took a deep breath and sighed. Krista had become used to thin, small pieces of cotton that smelled of bleach. These towels were so plush they reminded her of blankets, and they smelled fresh. She set them on the vanity and turned on the shower. There were bottles of shampoo and some fancy soap bars shaped like flowers.

The boys had really been thoughtful in the design of her domain. A small spark of hope lit inside her soul and grew, becoming a small flame. Maybe, if she could just accept that the world was what it was, she could be happy. Then she thought of her teachers, women who'd let themselves love and found themselves returned like purchased clothing that didn't fit. She didn't want to be someone's return.

Shaking off the dark thought, Krista stepped into the shower. Sighing, she let the warm water caress her skin. Using the apple scented shampoo and the floral soap, her body began to feel clean again. She washed the scent of sex away. As she watched the water swirl down the drain, tears filled her eyes and she leaned against the wall, sliding down the wet tile to sit on the floor.

For a moment, she gave into tears and cried for the woman who'd never go out on a first date or give a nice boy who'd brought her flowers the gift of her virginity. There'd be no fairytale wedding. She wouldn't find a husband who'd give her a picket fence, dog, and two point five children. That life was gone forever. She had six men to navigate, all of them vying for her sexual favors. She'd have to be very careful if she wanted to keep the peace and her sanity.

Krista stood. One last sob wracked her body and then she turned off the water. She stepped out onto the chilly tile and grabbed one of the humongous towels. If she had to be a prisoner, at least she was in a comfortable cell. Drying off, she went out into the bedroom. There was a box on the foot of her bed. It was big and wrapped in a red ribbon. She pulled off the lid after loosening the ribbon. Tissue paper covered the contents and there was a card on top of the paper. She picked it up.

Krista,

*Thank you. Please accept this small token
of our appreciation. Sleep well, knowing you
have our esteem.*

B and the boys

Braxton had left her a gift. She smiled. She barely knew
them and yet this gesture just felt like his solo handiwork. He'd
certainly had no time to go the store, and the idea of him
anticipating her need for some sort of reassurance spoke well
of his thoughtfulness.

She moved the tissue paper aside. The transparent barrier
crinkled loudly in the quiet room. She picked up a fluffy, white
robe. It was soft, one of the softest things she'd ever touched.
There was a plain, white, silk nightgown. It wasn't something
she'd consider "sexy" lingerie, but it was sexy in a
sophisticated and understated way.

She smiled, sure now that Brax had picked this out on his
own. He seemed one step ahead, and that told her he thought,
not just acted. This was so him. To see seduction as something
with layers instead of just physical parts of a woman's body
was something she hadn't anticipated from men who didn't
have to "work" at a relationship, but had received her as a
prize. She ran her hand over the silk and the temptation to go

around knocking on doors looking for him was great.

She knew it wasn't a good choice, and deep down she wasn't ready for emotional sex, physical sex had been enough for her for one night. She did put on the nightgown and then the robe. Krista glanced at the bed, frowning. She wasn't tired. Quietly, she opened her bedroom door and decided to find a copy of Braxton's imagined world. Reading would help pass the time, unless sleep finally caught up with her. When her mind was racing, as it was now, she never had luck getting into a restful state.

Krista was down the stairs and near the glass patio doors when a shadow made her jump. She looked around frantically for a light switch, but the house was so large she had no idea where she'd find one. Normally, there was one by doors, but she didn't see one anywhere within reach. The shadow moved again and she squinted, holding herself still in the shadows. Then, as her eyes adjusted to the darkness, she realized Max stood alone on the patio, pacing.

Krista began toward the room where she'd find the book, but paused. Glancing back at the door, she felt guilty for having let Max run off and not stopping him. She feared for her safety, but she also wanted to understand him. He was part of her strange, new household, after all, and she needed to know what had set him off. It had to be more than the joke.

She turned the knob slowly and pushed open the door. "Hello, Max, it's me," she whispered. The glow near his face told her he'd just taken a puff of something to smoke. "Are you okay?"

"Go away," he said quietly. There was sadness in his voice. Against her better judgment, she didn't go back inside.

"It's just me. What are you doing out here?"

"I could ask you the same question." The words weren't snarky, but she had a feeling that'd been his goal; something kept him from being truly nasty to her. She peered at him in the darkness, but couldn't see his expression very well.

"I couldn't sleep," she replied honestly.

He grunted. "Me either. Want a cigar?" This time she heard humor and decided declining the challenge wasn't going to fix the tension between them.

"Sure."

He stepped closer to her and took a small cigar from his shirt pocket, bit off the end, then lit the tip. Max handed her the glowing stogie carefully.

"Thanks," Krista said. "This is my first time smoking." She took a puff and began coughing hard. "Ugh!"

"You okay?" She could hear the humor in his voice, and it was both annoying and a relief.

"A...Ah, I—gross." She took another more delicate drag,

coughing again.

Max chuckled. "Here, drink this, it might help."

She took the glass from him and the moment the liquid hit her throat she began choking. Gasping loudly, she coughed again. "Are you trying to kill me?" She managed to spit the words out between coughs.

"A little brandy will fix you right up, besides a cigar isn't the same without quality booze." One of the security lights flipped on, illuminating his amused face. For a grumpy man, Max had a beautiful smile, Krista decided.

"I'll take your word for it." Krista sat the cigar down in the ashtray and then placed her hand on his back. He flinched and his face twisted in revulsion. The look stirred a memory.

There'd been a girl brought into the Young Woman's Educational Protection Facility about a year after the government had mandated all females not in a Giving contract live in custody for their own protection. This girl was used in propaganda about how great it was to live in the safety of the center. She'd been repeated raped by her uncles who'd kept her hidden away in a basement. She'd suffered for years. During one of the assemblies, they'd brought her up to speak about how much happier she was to be safe, and a caregiver had inadvertently touched her arm. The girl had jumped and turned, wearing the exact same expression as Max had on his face now.

"Who hurt you, Max?"

His eyes widened, and then narrowed. "What are you talking about?" She'd seen the honesty of his surprise. He wasn't going to fool her.

"I won't tell the others. Who hurt you?" She repeated the question quietly. Krista knew any sexual abuse in his past would've made him ineligible for the lottery based on the stringent restrictions for participation. She knew why he'd hide it. "Your outburst, it wasn't about what Mal said, right?"

"Don't play head games with me. Go to bed."

"I just want to understand." She genuinely did want to help him, and not just to keep the peace in her new household.

Krista cried out sharply as he literally picked her up, crushing her against the wall of the house. They were out of sight, deep in the shadows now.

"You want to understand? This is what it feels like to be helpless and afraid. Need me to show you how it can hurt worse?"

"N—No, please, I'm sorry, Max," she stuttered, afraid of what she'd unleashed in him. "I just want to understand, really. I don't want you to be in a situation that makes you uncomfortable, like earlier. I didn't know. I swear, I won't tell the others."

He relaxed his grip on her, slightly, glaring into her face. While he wasn't her favorite person right now, he might someday father one of her children, she needed to help him. "Let me help you," she pleaded.

His lips descended and he kissed her with punishing force. Max let go of her arms and she wrapped them around his neck, trying to show him comfort. She didn't know what he needed, but he'd instigated this kiss for a reason and she wasn't about to risk destroying the tenuous connection they had. He pushed away from her as abruptly as he'd grabbed her.

"Go to bed, Krista."

"If you would like your turn, I'd understand. I promise I won't call for another group session again. I just want us all to get along. I want to help you."

He put his hand against the wall and leaned down, very close to her face. "Don't pretend a good fuck fixes anything. Sex is as much a weapon as it is anything else. Never forget that. I won't let you use sex to control me." He pushed away from the wall and ran his hand through his hair, turning from her. Then he looked back, and in the dim light, she could see remorse on his face. "Don't say anything to the others, please. I'm sorry if I hurt you. Just forget it. I'm fine. I'll take my night when it's my turn. Don't worry about it."

"I'm here if you need to talk. I didn't mean to upset you."

He snorted, shrugging. "Smoking and drinking with me won't make you less a prisoner or me less an ass for participating in your slavery. I think you've had enough vice for one night. Go to bed."

She knew the shock had to be all over her face. He saw her as a prisoner, worse a slave; was she a sex slave? Less accepting girls had said similar things about what a Given girl was, but hearing it from a man—one of her men—it shocked her. She didn't want to be a sex slave; she wanted a life, maybe a pseudo family, if that was even possible. She didn't like feeling as if he was ordering her around, but she wanted to get away from the unstable man and the misery he stirred inside of her. Krista rushed inside, went right to the bookshelf, grabbed the book she wanted, and hurried back up the stairs.

She sat down on the small sofa. Tucking her legs beneath her, she looked at the cover. The image of a man in chains, surrounded by beautiful women made Krista roll her eyes. She turned the book over and read the blurb. It talked of Sperm Production Facilities where the men lived that forced them to donate their sperm three times a day and punishment rooms where men endured rape for bad behavior. Krista scowled. This was the first book in a series. She wondered if the rest were as twisted as this one. Still, curiosity made her want to read. Krista opened the book and began.

My name is Samuel Johnson, and I haven't left this prison since the year I hit puberty. Ripped from my mother's arms at fourteen, I've learned women only want two things: sex and compliments.

Chapter 4

Krista jumped at the sound of her door opening. The book fell off the arm of the couch and she sat up, feeling stiff. The leg she'd been sitting on had gone numb.

Jared peeked his head into the room cautiously. "Good morning, or should I say afternoon. I was worried about you."

"Sorry, I stayed up late reading." She motioned him to come in.

He wrinkled his nose as he entered. "Why do I smell smoke and brandy?"

Krista blushed. "I decided it was time to grow up."

He raised his eyebrow. "That stuff is bad for you. If they come for inspection and smell booze and smoke, you'll be removed so quickly you won't even have time to say goodbye."

She grinned at his the-doctor-must-lecture-you-now voice. "Yes, doctor, I'll quit immediately."

Jared grinned back. "I brought you a muffin and some juice. Do you drink coffee? I could go make you a cup."

"I've never been allowed to have coffee, they were pretty careful about what we were allowed to eat and drink. I've heard it's bitter, but someday I'd love to try a cup."

"I forgot that was on the no-no list."

Krista frowned. "What do you mean?"

Jared looked like he wished he could take back the casual statement. He blushed and the red stain made his freckles stand out even more noticeably. "I...don't be mad, but we have a list of what you can and can't eat, as well as a list of things we can and can't do with you. Steve has the food list, so I'm sure this muffin and juice are fine. They have specific items they want you eating, for fertility or something. From my standpoint, it's ridiculous. There's really little or no science to back up the nutritional benefits of some of the food, but there are a few things on the list that would be great for you if you do get pregnant."

She felt the stranglehold tightening around her life. She'd thought she'd be mostly allowed to just live, without the protection facility interfering. "I'm still going to try that cup of coffee," she grumbled.

Jared gave her a small nod. "I'll personally make it for you. I don't think it will hurt a bit before you're pregnant."

She liked him; it was unavoidable. As much as she didn't want to like anything about being here, she saw the benefits.

Jared handed her the muffin and juice.

"Thank you, this is very thoughtful. What time is it?" Krista began yawning as soon as she'd asked the question.

"Almost one. I wanted to make sure you were okay. After

last night I… How are you?" She thought his flush was adorable.

"I'm fine. Thank you for checking on me. Would you like to sit with me while I eat?"

He nodded exuberantly and plunked down next to her. "You look pretty this morning," he said.

She didn't feel pretty. Her mouth felt sticky, and he was right, she reeked of cigar smoke. "Thanks. So what are you guys up to today?"

"We all took our two Giving weeks off. Most of us work or study so much we aren't used to having this much time on our hands. I'll be working on my homework this afternoon, but otherwise I'm just hoping to spend time with you. Everyone is going crazy downstairs waiting. We made a rotation—unless you want to p…pick who gets what nights." He rubbed the back of his neck and looked away.

So far, nothing he was talking about was making her feel happy she woke up. "Whatever," she replied and then realized just how terrible her single word reply actually sounded. "Umm, sorry, I—dang it, my neck hurts."

"I can help you," he said cheerfully, pulling her so that her back faced him. He slid the robe off her shoulders.

"So now you're a chiropractor too?" She really didn't mean to be so snippy, but all his talk of food restrictions and rotations had put her in a terrible mood. She just wanted to explore her new world.

His hands began rubbing her neck and shoulders. His pressure was firm, but not painful. "Tell me if I'm hurting you."

"No, it feels good."

"I'm sorry, Krista. I know this isn't easy for you. It's not easy for us either. If the world were different, we wouldn't find ourselves having to share. This is going to be harder for some of us than others. Sharing a woman doesn't come naturally. I'm pretty easy going, but hell, it's still hard for me to know tonight you'll be in Braxton's bed."

Krista held her breath. Braxton's bed. She didn't know if she was ready for him. She wished she'd saved the nightgown now. "Where's your washing machine?"

"Steve does all the laundry. Do you have something for him to wash?"

"I don't have many clothes. I'd love to have what I've worn washed today. I can do it if you just show me where the washer is."

"Right now?" He sounded a bit pouty.

"Yes, please."

"All right, let's go."

"Wait, I need to get dressed." She opened the closet and

took out her last set of clean clothing.

"Wow, that's all you have, huh?"

"They didn't give us much at the protection facility. We wore uniforms, like prisoners. This is everything I have that's not standard issue from the facility. I'm lucky to have as much as I do. Most women leave with just the clothing on their backs, some have to leave in uniform even. I guess they figure we'll spend most of our time naked anyway, so why waste tax dollars."

"I don't know if you realize how hard the world was hit economically. Since women worked, they paid taxes too. When everything went crazy, the economy crashed. Just think about industries that make tampons and cosmetics, sure there are boy-girls who need a new lipstick or blush, but what about the tampons?"

"Yes, let's feel sorry for the tampon manufacturers. Oh, the humanity!"

Jared grinned. "Okay, maybe not them, but I'm serious, the government isn't hoarding money, it just doesn't have any."

"Not to get all political here, but I did read, a lot. They weren't doing all that great before the world went to hell. If they can go into debt over heated toilet seats, they can afford to give a girl more than the use of communal uniforms and a single Giving Day outfit. I was gifted the dress I wore, or this would be what I'd shown up in." She held out the simple white cotton sundress. "It's the only thing I have besides jeans and a sweater. They don't even shell out for new shoes, you have to wear the same plain, Velcro-closure support shoes they give everyone on June first. We call it Shoe Year's day."

Jared smiled. "Well, I think I've figured out what to do with the rest of my day. I'm going to take you shopping."

"I get to leave, really, see a real store?" Krista bounced with excitement. She could barely remember shopping with her mother.

"Get dressed and meet me downstairs."

Krista nodded, and the moment he was out of the room she rushed out of her clothes, skipping a shower in her excitement. She ran a brush through her hair, brushed her teeth, and used her deodorant. There were so many things she needed—razors, shaving cream, more deodorant. Picking up a bottle, she realized it was perfume. She paused, grinning, maybe they'd even let her buy one of her choice. She remembered her mother's rose scent. This one was lavender, she was glad they'd provided her with something to make her feel feminine.

She heard the arguing the moment she started down the stairs. She paused to listen.

"What the hell is wrong with you?"

"Security needs twenty-four hours notice if we're taking her out of the compound."

"Where the hell do they even sell women's clothes these days?"

"Oh God, we have to go to the boy-girl store. I do not want to go there!"

"If any men are watching the place, waiting to kidnap her, they'll kill to get her away from us. We're going to look like jackasses by losing her week one."

Krista finished coming down the stairs. "He was just being nice. I don't want anyone to yell at him anymore. Fine. I won't go shopping with him, but I wouldn't mind a few new things to wear and some toiletries. I can just make a list." She hated giving up on leaving. "I could dress like a boy and if only five of you go they won't know it's me," she added hopefully.

"Sorry, the risk is too great," Damon replied without a trace of remorse.

"Why the fuck should we spend any more money? If you don't get pregnant, then we just blew a bundle on nothing," Max stated, looking right into her eyes. She flinched.

"I hope someday I won't be 'nothing' to you. I understand." She turned and started back up the stairs. The book hadn't been too bad and the idea of losing herself in Samuel Johnson's struggle was much more appealing than thinking about how she was an expense expected to get pregnant while pleasuring them all. A hand on her arm stopped her on the second step. She turned to see Brax looking up at her, frowning.

"Don't go upstairs. Max is just being an ass, like usual. Even if he isn't willing to buy you what you need, the rest of us are. You might not get to pick out the clothes in a store, but we have the internet. Make a list of the toiletries you need and I'll send Steve out shopping. We can go online and you can order whatever you like. Is that a suitable compromise?"

She nodded. Deep down she had known she wouldn't be leaving, but Jared had sparked hope. She wouldn't let it happen again. Forgetting what she was to these men would be dangerous to her emotional stability. She was property, and property didn't get to do what it wanted.

"Thanks," she mumbled.

"Come on, we have a computer hooked up to the big screen in the game room. I'm sure we'll all have things we want to see you in."

"I'm cool with naked," Mal replied.

Krista looked over Brax's head to glare at the battered comedian. He looked far worse this morning, and she felt a little twist of guilt that she hadn't checked on him earlier. "I'd hit you, but you don't look like you could take another punch.

How are you feeling?"

"Ha! Love it that our girl is funny. Damn it, woman, we are going to make some fantastically entertaining babies."

She felt the color drain from her face. All this baby talk, as immediately necessary as it was, felt so awkward and strange. She doubted most men were as interested in procreation in the old world.

"You okay? Maybe they'll just be moderately entertaining," Max muttered, scowling.

"Sorry. All the baby talk is freaking me out." She hated the idea of getting pregnant and having no control over what happened to her child. What if they didn't want to keep a child, she wondered. Krista could totally imagine Max and Damon insisting they didn't keep a boy. Girls were the gender that garnered a tax write off. There was no incentive to have a boy, except love, and they didn't seem the affectionate type. Even if she had a girl, the child would be gone on her tenth birthday. She hated the idea of losing her children. Would they wonder if she didn't love them anymore? She'd heard more than one of the younger girls crying and saying that in the protection facility. Did the staff there tell the children they weren't wanted? Too many questions for her taste revolved around procreation in this awful world.

"Sorry, I just—if you get knocked up, I hope it's mine,"

Mal said, grinning.

Oddly, she found his declaration reassuring. If she had his son, maybe he'd let her keep him. Another prang of hope filled her, but she quickly snuffed it out, afraid to give into the idea she could honestly be happy with them. She gave him a small, tight smile. When she looked back at Brax, his darkly furrowed brow turned her smile into a frown.

"I'm sure we'd all like to father your first child, but only one of us can," said Brax.

Krista agreed, but said nothing. She'd really have no choice one way or the other; all of those decisions belonged to the men.

"I'll know if it's mine." DeAnthony laughed, slapping his hands together. They all looked at him, and Krista couldn't help the little bark of hysterical laughter.

"Okay, can we talk about something that doesn't make me feel crazy?" Krista pleaded.

They all grumbled and Brax held out his hand. She took it, conceding not to run and hide. Everyone except Damon went into the game room to surf the web for women's clothing. Krista was surprised to see Max joining the group, but said nothing. Jared turned on the computer and they all piled onto the large "L" shaped sofa in the center of the room.

At first, the guys sat quietly as she picked out a few

conservative dresses and couple of pairs of jeans. She ordered four plain, brightly colored t-shirts. Then they paged to a screen with leopard print items and Mal insisted she order a low-cut dress in the print. After that, it was a free for all. Most of her men had a different type of clothing they wanted to see her wear. She had to keep biting her tongue. Their picks were totally not on her wish list, but she wasn't paying and she'd chosen the items she wanted. If they wanted to buy her more clothing than she'd owned since she was a child, she wasn't going to complain.

Brax hadn't picked anything out yet. Then the screen changed to an assortment of evening gowns. She was going to click the mouse to the next page when Brax leaned over, his hand taking hers, and pushed the mouse to a royal purple dress in the middle of the page. The long, A-line dress was simple and had spaghetti straps to hold it up. The bodice of the dress was dotted with sequins, but the rest of it was simple silk. He clicked *buy*.

"What are you picking that for?" Max asked.

"I like it," replied Braxton.

"It's not like we're going to be taking her to dinner or the prom," Max scoffed.

"Don't care, I like it."

When Brax turned to look her in her face, she held her

breath. She liked him far more than she should allow herself to. In six months, she could find herself with another group of men, or deemed mysteriously infertile and returned back to the protection facility.

"I like it too," she said quietly, replying to his unspoken question. He smiled.

Mal grabbed the mouse from under their hands, breaking the connection she and Brax were privately sharing.

"Now this is what I'm talkin' about." He chuckled and Krista gasped when she looked at the screen. The model on the screen wore a black latex bodysuit and held a whip. There were several outfits on the screen, all of them made of shiny latex.

"Oh, no, no, not a chance," Krista shouted, shaking her head.

"I'm just playing with you...maybe," Mal said. He was leaning between her and Brax. Mal winked and leaned forward, pressing a quick kiss on her mouth. She was shocked by the abrupt display of affection and didn't know how to respond. Brax pushed him back; his grumpy expression told her exactly what he thought of his exuberant friend's actions.

"Do they make a boy's version of that in your size, Mal? You'd look awesome. You could put it on and run around the house. We'd hear all that plastic squeaking everywhere you went and know you were coming. I vote we order one for you," said Krista.

Jared laughed so hard he had to catch himself before he fell off the chair. "We need to show her one of your comedy DVDs, I think you might have met your match!"

Mal glared at his younger friend. Brax joined in the laughter. He put his arm around Krista, and she stiffened a moment before relaxing into his possessive hold.

"How come you get to have your arm around her, man?" DeAnthony questioned. Krista was alarmed to hear real annoyance in his voice. More strife, she didn't want another second of tension, but she doubted it was avoidable given their situation.

"We drew lots. It's my day. Tomorrow is Max's, and the day after is yours. On our day, if Krista accepts, I say she's ours to hold. That means keep your lips to yourself, Mal."

The funny man scowled. "Fine, but I might spend all of Thursday just kissing her if I have to bottle it up."

Krista didn't have any idea how to respond to that. Brax turned to look at her again. "What do you say, Kristannie?"

"If you promise to quit bickering, I say yes."

"You heard the lady—can it, boys. Jared, lighten the mood and put in Mal's new comedy special. I haven't seen it yet."

"I don't think…" Mal started saying.

"Oh, she needs to know how you plan to pay for all these

clothes. I used your credit card number."

"Let's watch the show from last spring. I think she'd enjoy that one more," Mal said quickly.

"What's up?" Jared asked, raising his eyebrow as he looked at his nervous friend.

"Damn it. Okay, don't get mad. I made a couple of jokes about winning the lottery. Remember, my audience is full of guys. Most of them can't even participate in the lottery," Mal replied quietly.

"That bad, huh?" Jared questioned, unhelpfully.

"Just remember, I don't have a trust fund, just a sense of humor and the smarts to know my audience. Are you going to be cool with this, Krista?" Mal looked worried as he asked the question.

"I don't know. How bad is it, really?"

"Bad."

"Oh, now I'm too curious not to watch. Roll the show, boys," Krista demanded. Jared pressed play.

Thunderous applause resounded as Mal confidently walked onto a stage. Many of the men in the audience stood; the clapping didn't even end when Mal motioned for the audience to have a seat. He took a drink of water, paused, motioned again for the men to sit, drank more water, and grabbed the microphone. The men finally calmed down and began to sit.

"Wow, you guys are fantastic. I see my agent went around handing out twenties again. Thanks, Morrie—you rock. Hey guys, tonight I've mixed it up, everything coming out of my mouth is fresh." He put his hand up and huffed out a breath, sniffing as if he were checking his breath. "Yep, the mints are working too. Okay, fresh breath Mal coming at you."

Mal danced around ridiculously on the stage. Krista was already smiling.

"I've been in the lotto a while now and I'm starting to think I'm never going to get laid. Our least favorite uncle, Uncle Sam, likes to keep all the goodies locked up. Most of you haven't even seen the form. Damn that order form surprised me. I didn't see a box that let me chose 'mute', but hell if I'm lucky enough to win, she won't be able to talk with all the cock in her mouth anyway." The audience chortled. "Seriously, I can't believe they keep all those tasty snacks locked up, when all we want is one bite. Am I right?" A couple of the men in the audience hooted loudly. "Oh yeah, brother, shout it out. I don't even care if she's pretty. If they send me an ug-o I've come prepared."

He picked something up he'd left hidden behind the stool where his water sat. Krista realized it was a paper bag.

He opened it and put it over his head. On the front was the

face of a beautiful blond woman with her eyes cut out. Mal
reached up and she realized a slit in the mask's mouth was
open. "Insert cock here," he said in a high, squeaky voice.

The men in the audience roared with laughter. One man in
the audience whistled loudly.

Mal quickly took off the bag. "I'd better take that off
before any of you get ideas. These days, even I'd look sexy in a
dress."

More loud waves of laughter rolled from the spectators.

"Seriously guys, they don't have to make them pretty, just
naked. Am I right?"

The audience clapped and hooted.

"My pal writes that popular Chained and Naked series.
Give it up for my man, Braxton Bray." The audience clapped.
"If you haven't read these books, they're fantastic. I'd love to
have a woman chain me up and rape me any day of the week. I
never understood how they called that punishment in the
books. If there was an alternate reality machine and I took a
ride into one of those novels, it'd be called 'Mal Does Dallas,
and Monique, and Jasmine, and Beth, and...' you get the
picture."

More hooting floated up from the fixated audience.

"I doubt I'd be faithful if the world was populated with
hot, horny women. I'd drop draws and get me a big glowing

arrow and point it south with the words 'free sample' written in neon."

Krista stood up. "I think I've seen enough. I can see why they didn't stock your routines in the movie library." She started to leave the room and then paused. "Ah, screw it." She marched over to him and slugged him hard in the arm. He flinched. "Now you can tell them all you've been hit by a girl when they see your face. Ha!" She stomped out of the room.

"I warned you guys," she heard him say sadly, just before she slammed the door shut.

"Krista, wait up," Max called. She was surprised, but stopped and turned to look at him.

"So guys sit around making jokes about women all day? Super. I'm not trying to be a Grumpy Gus here, but that really irritates me. Does Mal really think all the women left *want* to live locked away in a high security prison? We don't get a say in how 'good-looking' our six are either. I—"

He put his fingers gently on Krista's lips. The contact surprised her so much she stopped ranting.

"I know what it feels like to have things out of your control and have the assholes mock you at the same time. Fuckin' sucks. Just don't be mad at Mal. He made that recording six months ago. He had no idea he'd win the lotto. He also didn't know you. The woman he was joking about wasn't *you*, Krista. Mal was just as pissed as the guys in the audience that the world has become what it is. This is his way, and his audience's way, to feel like they have some kind of choice or power. I didn't know what was on the DVD. He tried to warn us."

"Why do you care if I'm pissed off?" She really had no clue. Since the moment she'd met the man, he'd been nothing but a beast with her.

"I just wanted to return the favor from last night. No one likes to have someone rain on their pissed parade, but I'm raining on yours. You can't let this make you bitter and angry. I know you feel like you're up shit creek without a paddle right now, but give us some time. We have a lot to adjust to. Most of our lives, we've existed without the softness of a woman in the house. It's not the same being around a woman. Don't walk away. Go back in there and keep watching. See if there's something redeeming in Mal's comedy." He blew out a deep huffing breath. "God knows I'm the first one wanting to hit the little fuck, but he's a good guy. Let's get back in there."

"Women are people too, even if we're treated more like pets these days. What do you mean about it not being 'the same' around a woman?"

"The things we think are funny or interesting might not be the same for you. Obsolete feminism aside, admit it, men and women think differently." He spoke quietly.

Her lips compressed into a tight line and she crossed her arms over her chest. She hated to admit that he was partially right. Feminism wasn't obsolete, only put on hold until there were enough women in the world to reclaim it, but men and women did think differently. She glared at him and he glared back. Challenging him on his newfound facing-of-tough-situations, she held out her hand. He looked at it and then back in her eyes. Max took her hand, squeezing it firmly, but not painfully. She let go of the breath she'd been holding, shrugged, and followed him back into the game room.

The routine was still playing. None of the men laughed. They all sat tensely, especially Mal, as she sat back down. She reluctantly released Max's hand, but not before giving it a little squeeze and smiling up at him. He nodded. Even if she was pissed off at Mal, she was happy Max had taken the opportunity to open up a little. Sighing, she watched the DVD with her men. A few moments later, she chuckled as he cracked a joke about the government that had nothing to do with women. A few more jokes had her laughing, snorting even. The men seemed to relax and they began to chuckle or laugh at the appropriate times. By the time Mal was waving goodbye to his audience's standing ovation, Krista felt better. He was funny.

Mal glanced over at her nervously and rubbed his arm.

"Sorry that I hit you, but only a little sorry," she stated, grinning at him.

"Apology accepted. I've learned my lesson about disparaging your people."

She nodded. "I just don't personally want to wind up as part of your comedy routine."

"Don't worry, for security and my own protection, I'm not about to say a word. There are a lot of guys out there who'd kill for one night with you in their bed, literally."

Krista shivered, remembering she'd never be free.

"I'll be steering clear of women jokes, unless I have your permission of course."

"Of course," she agreed.

"I'm glad that's settled," Jared said, slouching back on the couch. "Geesh, I didn't know a little woman could kick big ol' Mal's ass so hard." He grinned at the shorter man when he finished teasing.

"Am I going to live, doctor?" Mal questioned, still rubbing his arm.

"Unfortunately," Jared replied, ducking as a pillow came sailing from Mal's direction. "Violence is not the answer."

Mal rolled his eyes. Krista's mood improved.

They turned off the DVD player. The TV came onto a commercial for fishing equipment. "I haven't watched television since I was little. I remember a few cartoons, oh and the puppet show with the monsters. I liked that one. We were allowed a weekly movie night, but the movies were bland. I'd love to see what kind of shows are popular now."

Mal groaned. "TV will just piss you off again."

"What do you mean?" Krista raised her eyebrow.

"I mean you'll be annoyed. Ninety-nine percent of the viewing audience is male."

He flipped to the guide and she realized what he meant. Everything seemed to be a sporting event or crime drama. Krista took the remote. She flipped it to a kid's channel. A string of commercials for boy's toys played. She turned off the television.

"Don't look so sad. There are lots of books you might like, and movies from before, we'll go online and order those too," DeAnthony suggested helpfully.

"I'm not mad. It's just so— I realize that there is no place in the world for women anymore." Then she remembered the email addresses in the book her guardians had given her. "Can I have an email address? My teachers gave me their email addresses. I'd love to let them know I'm okay."

The men exchanged nervous looks.

"I promise not to tell them anything that might get any of you in any kind of trouble. I'm used to being surrounded by women and womanly things. It's really hard to realize I'm in a world without any of that now."

"I'll set you up with one. Then we'll give you some privacy," Brax told her. She gave him a big happy smile.

"I'll be right back." Krista jumped up and ran upstairs to grab her book. When she returned to the game room they'd already set her up with her own email.

"You are now the proud owner of the email LadyKrista@cityweb.com. Will that work for you?"

"Love it, thanks. Okay, show me what to do. They didn't let us use the internet. I think they were afraid we might learn something about the world."

"What do you have there?" Mal queried.

"This was a going away gift. My guardians were somewhat second mothers to me. I was there longer than many girls were, because my mother was alone and didn't have any family to claim me. I was one of the first girls in our region placed under government protection. The foster care system basically automatically reverted to the protection facilities due to the fact most foster mothers had died and, in the chaos, they didn't want to place girls with non-biological male caregivers." She opened the cover and began showing them pictures.

"This is Cina, she's my best friend. I really miss her. Maybe I can get one of the guardians to give her my email address. If she has a kind six, I hope she'll be able to message me." Krista spoke quickly, excitedly. The idea to have Cina in her life hadn't occurred to her until now.

Brax showed her how to compose, edit, and send a message. He showed her how to read a message she received and how to delete old mail. She felt her first true freedom. Granted, they'd created her address and her password, but Brax showed her how to change the current password.

"You have my promise that you can have some level of privacy here. We have a responsibility to protect you. If you don't do anything foolish, this is at least one small way you can have to reach outside of this house. I don't want you to feel imprisoned, this is your home."

"Thanks, thank you all, I just…this really means a lot to me."

"Let's give Krista some space," Brax suggested.

They nodded and grumbled, leaving the room as a group, and she stared at the blank message, wondering where to begin. She had a feeling every message would be scrutinized by the people who could take her away, so she had to be very careful; there were no guarantees that only her guardians would see the mail.

She sent three messages. They were all very similar. Each assured her friends that she was fine, told them she was doing her best to adjust to a man's world, and pleaded for them to give Cina her email address. After hitting *send* each time, she waited anxiously for a response. Looking at the clock, she realized the recipients would be busy at this time of day. Frowning, she turned off the computer and left the game room.

She wandered into the kitchen. Steve was baking. He looked terrified when she came in. "Hey, Steve. What are you making?"

"You shouldn't be in here with me without a guard or a chaperone. I could be fired."

Her eyes widened. "Uh, sorry." She turned quickly and left, not wanting to get the man in trouble.

He popped his head out the door. "Sorry, it's nothing personal, I just like this job. I washed your laundry. It's folded and lying on your bed. Jared told me you wanted it done."

She smiled at him. "Thanks, I appreciate it." She'd have to talk to her men about making sure she could be in the same room alone with Steve. She'd never cooked in her life, and even if she didn't have to, it was something she wanted to learn. She'd have to have something to do other than read and have sex. Surely her men would understand.

She ran into Jared first. "Hey, can I ask you a question?"

"Anything."

"Steve said he could be fired if I go into the kitchen and

he's alone with me. I'd like to learn to cook, and I doubt any of you want to sit through that. Can we establish some kind of five feet rule or something so he won't get in trouble, but I can still go into the kitchen?"

"I don't have a problem with it, but you can see how my thoughts don't always matter around here." He spoke glibly and chuckled, but there was a sad darkness in the sound.

"You matter to me," she said and winked.

He brightened. "Damn it, I'll never be able to say no to you now."

"Well, I don't want you to be in trouble again. Just have a group meeting and let me and Steve know the rules."

"Hey, my night with you will be on Saturday. I want to do something fun with you and spend the whole day together on Saturday. Is that all right with you?"

"Of course, I'll look forward to it. Thanks for…aw, heck." Krista threw her arms around his neck and hugged him tightly. "Thanks for being so sweet. I really feel like you're a friend."

His face went from happy to sad instantly. "A friend?"

"Don't you want to be my friend?"

"Sure, but—damn it, Krista, I want you to feel more than that for me."

She realized what was upsetting him. "This is all new. Maybe. I'm sure Saturday will be great," she said, backing away. She fled the room, not wanting to see the disappointment on his face. She already knew she'd always like Jared very much, but that was the extent of what would develop. If she were foolish enough to fall in love with any of them, it probably wouldn't be Jared. He was wonderful, but the spark she felt around some of the other men didn't ignite with him.

Chapter 5

Krista went up to her room and grabbed the book she'd started the night before. She sat down on the comfortable, little couch and began reading again. She was engrossed in Samuel Johnson's world. The sex made her cheeks heat, but the story was wonderful. She'd thought Brax hadn't gotten it right, but she was wrong. While the government in the story was far more concerned with actual sex than the real government, Brax touched on the emotions of someone in Samuel's position so well. At one point, she actually cried when Sam's best friend died trying to escape. The fear he felt for authority was so eerily similar to her own, she had to stop reading a few times to take a deep breath.

"So you like the story?"

"Ahhh!" Krista shouted, dropping the book as she jumped. "You scared the heck out of me!"

"Sorry," Brax said, grinning. He had such a beautiful smile, she instantly forgave him.

"I don't like it," she said sharply. Brax's eyes widened and he looked hurt. "I love it so much I can't even put my feelings into words. I'm going to kill you if anything bad happens to Samuel. I feel like he was in the protection facility with me. I don't know how you did it, but I do honestly feel like he is going through the same thing. The sex was a bit over-the-top, but I love it and I'm going to start on the next book the moment I finish this one."

He beamed happily. "That's the best review I've ever had, thanks. I wanted to tell you it's time for supper. Would you join me?" He held out his arm. She stood and took the sight in, feeling as if he'd just stepped out of some cheesy, old movie. "We'll be eating on the patio together. I wanted to spend some time alone with you. Is that okay?"

"Sure. No one was angry?"

"They grumbled a bit, but they know they'll have a night with you too. I'm glad you liked my work. If you aren't busy tomorrow, I have some notes for my latest novel and I'd love to ask you some questions. I want this to be the best one yet, and having someone who really lived the experience will make the book phenomenal."

"I'd be honored to help. My schedule is clear until I die, unfortunately. I'm at your disposal."

"We'll find something for you to do that will give your life purpose, besides doing us. I don't want you to feel like you don't matter, you do."

"Thanks. Did Jared talk to you guys?"

"About Steve?" They walked down the stairs.

"Yes, is there going to be some reciprocity for him and me to be in the same room?"

"We talked with Steve. He's not comfortable being alone with you. He said it's too painful to be around the only woman in town and not be able to touch you. I don't blame him. I'm surprised he didn't quit when we told him we'd won. On his income, there's no way he can even participate in the lottery, and we pay well." Brax opened the patio doors for her.

Knowing Steve had no hope of ever having a family of his own, even if he had to share them, made her sad. The idea that a man would be condemned to loneliness based on income just seemed wrong. This world was so unfair; just because Steve wasn't rich shouldn't mean he was just out of luck. He was so kind. He was a victim of the unjust Giving system too. The more she learned about the how the government selected who was able to participate and who wasn't, the greater her hatred grew toward the politicians who propagated the way the world worked.

Brax pulled out her chair and she sat down. The small bistro table was lovely. A white cloth draped over the black iron she knew was underneath and a candle burned in the center. Square bowls of water with flower buds and floating candles littered the patio area. She could smell lilacs in the distance. The darkening sky set the perfect mood. She picked up her cloth napkin and put it over her lap daintily.

"We did decide to hire a tutor of sorts. There's a service that provides happily gay companions for women. I realize you might want a friend."

"I never thought someone would have to hire a friend for me," she said gruffly.

"It's not as if you can just walk down the street meeting new people. The other benefit is the service provides 'friends' who are trained in martial arts and carry concealed gun permits. You'll be as safe with your companion as with the guards. Tell us what you want to learn and we can hire someone with those specific qualifications. If you don't like him, we'll get another, just try a few out until something genuine clicks."

"That sounds so odd. I've never had to have a friend on 'probationary trial' before."

"It's the best we can do. He'll be a chaperone too, so you won't have to worry about Steve. There's a smaller, second kitchen on the basement level. It'll be your private domain."

She smiled. "Great, now I just have to learn how to use it."

"I'll get you a cookbook and some supplies later in the week. I'll even eat something you make."

"Wow, what a great vote of confidence. Just for that, I'll make sure the others tell me what your least favorite food is, and I'll triple it in my first recipe. But in case I decide not to make you suffer, what's your favorite food?"

"Pecan pie. I love the stuff, but Steve never makes it. The others hate it. They're nuts, because it's fantastic." He paused for a second and she held her breath as his eyes grew dark with desire. "It's a date," he said huskily before clearing his throat. "I'm the only one who works from home, so we'll have a special private lunch when the guys go back to work and Mal leaves for his cross-country tour. I have a few speaking engagements and retreats throughout the year, but for the next six months, all I'm doing is writing my new book."

Steve came out with a tray. He glanced at her nervously before setting a glass of red wine and a plate of cheese, meat, and fruit on the table in front of her. She smiled when she saw the strawberries. He gave her a tiny grin and she knew this was his apology.

"Thank you, Steve."

He nodded and went back inside. She picked up a strawberry and took a bite. Brax smiled at her.

"Delicious. I haven't had strawberries in a long time. Fresh fruit is seldom on the menu at the protection facility."

"Things are improving, but I can imagine it wasn't something Uncle Sam wanted to pay for, fruit is ridiculously expensive these days. There was such a long ban on interstate shipping during the first years of the outbreak while the CDC tried to figure out and contain the spread of the virus, many produce growers just went out of business." He paused and cleared his throat. "Let's not think about anything depressing tonight. It's important to me for you to feel comfortable. You've had a stressful couple of days. I thought we'd have something light now, and later, after…you know, if you'd like—feel hungry, I'll make you something special. I make the world's best grilled cheese."

His awkwardness was adorable. For a man of words, he seemed to be having a difficult time. She shook her head in mock disappointment. "You mean I could be eating the world's best grilled cheese right now? Well, I guess these strawberries will have to do. I believe I would like to try your sandwich, if you promise to show me your secrets for making it the world's best."

"I wouldn't teach just anyone, but you seem like a nice girl. So when we have the house all to ourselves and everyone's asleep, if you aren't too tired, I'm going to rock your world with my culinary skills."

"Wow, author and chef. I'm a lucky woman."

"Yes. Yes, you most certainly are," he teased.

She laughed and began dipping her berries in the pink fruit dip that sat on her plate in a little cup. The cubes of cheese and round slices of meat tasted wonderful with the wine. She'd never had wine before, and it took her a moment to adjust to the almost bitter flavor. After a few sips, she decided she liked it. The warm feeling it gave her didn't hurt either.

"I'd like to rock your world in many ways tonight, Kristannie."

The way he said her name made her shiver. None of the others used it the way he did. He was so handsome. If she had to choose whom she'd be going to bed with tonight, she'd have chosen him. The realization was a surprise. She'd been so sure she wasn't going to like sex. She picked up her napkin and used it to hide the heat she felt on her cheeks. She didn't want him to see her blushing. He'd know.

His observant eyes didn't miss her action or her blush. "What are you thinking about?"

Damn it, can he really know? I have to pull myself together. If I let myself care about him, I'll regret it. "How much I like wine. Can I have a second glass? Jared spilled the beans about your orders on what to feed me, and I'm sure this isn't on the list."

"What those people don't know won't hurt them." He reached out and took her hand. She let him while the napkin fell to her lap. "Goddamn it, woman, you make my cock so fucking hard."

She didn't know what to say. She was obligated to sleep with him, he didn't have to make it anything more than it was. He could legally throw her on the ground and claim his rights to her right here and now. She knew she should be afraid or angry, but she wasn't. Against her better judgment, she wanted him too. Her appetite was gone. She pulled her hand away and finished off her wine without looking at him.

"I want you too," she whispered shyly. Even after the group sex from the first night, she still felt like a virgin. Tonight, it would just be the two of them. Her pussy literally began aching. The idea of his hands on her, his mouth…she wished he were touching her right now. With the others, she didn't feel such a raw, desperate want. The sensation made her feel guilty, but she wasn't strong enough to push the desire away. She was suddenly glad he'd waited. "I'm not really hungry anymore."

"Me either." He growled, throwing his napkin on the table. "I'm taking you to my room tonight."

She nodded, unsure of what to say or do. She could hear her own heartbeat as it pounded painfully in her chest. After her drastic initiation into the world of sexual activity, she marveled that the idea of Brax inside of her could make her so hot. He stood, his eyes never broke contact with hers, his chair slid back, and he moved around the small table with long, purposeful strides.

Brax held out his hand. "Come to my bed, Kristannie, and make me the happiest man in the world tonight."

That has to be the most romantic invitation for sex any girl's ever received. I have to stop letting myself forget I'm just a prize. He doesn't love me. For him, I'm the last woman on Earth.

Her eyes focused on his large, tan hand and she just contemplated it quietly for a moment. She slowly began moving her hand toward his. There was something in his eyes that told her this act meant something more to him, she was conceding something if she took his offering.

"I would have chosen you."

She stilled, looking up into his face. His expression was earnest. A chill ran through her, his words were so eerily close to her thoughts, it spooked her. "You are more than I deserve. Thank you." *He had me at 'chosen' dang it.* She knew there was no way she could keep her heart out of this now.

Having felt a sense of protection from him the night before and reading his book, a story that touched her deeply, her vulnerable heart longed to care about him. Her head was smart, but her heart didn't have a bit of common sense. Having a favorite risked the security of the peaceful home she longed for.

Her hand found his and he gripped it tightly. Seeing something move out of the corner of her eye, she looked up at the sky. Fancifully, she thought she saw a shooting star. "Look." She pointed up.

"I don't need to look at the stars anymore. You're exactly what I've been wishing for. You're mine, Kristannie. Tonight, every inch of you will feel how much you belong to me. I want to make you happy. Someday you'll feel safe with me. You were meant for me, I knew that the moment I looked into your eyes."

The writer in him was really working overtime. She rolled her eyes, tipping her head to the side and feeling duped. He was just ensuring she wouldn't have a "headache" when it was his turn, nothing more. The sappy words made her as hot as they made her angry. She wished she could believe them, but Krista was a realist.

He tilted her chin up and forced her to look into his eyes. "I'm going to prove to you that I do want you, Krista. Tonight will be unlike any night you spend with the others. I'm going to make you mine in a way that will be exclusive to us. Before the night ends, you will tell me you belong to me more."

She shivered. As bossy as the man was, she hated herself for liking his dominance. With so much of her life out of her control, it felt good to feel like he was the one pulling her strings. She liked the illusion that he could keep the government from taking her away and could give her real commitment and a home.

He led her toward the house, their meal mostly untouched. The others had left the dining room and she could hear noise coming from the game room. The kitchen was dark; Steve had called it a night too. She followed Braxton into a part of the house she hadn't been in before.

"This is where my room and office are. Our only guest rooms are here too. My work requires a lot of solitary focus, so when we built the house they put me here." He chuckled.

"Wow, your office is great," she told him. There were shelves full of books and a big, heavy, old-fashioned desk with a sleek and very modern laptop sitting on it. He had a bunch of promotional items hanging on the wall.

"They made the book you're reading into a movie."

"With all that sex…how?"

"Sex in movies is becoming more common. Fantasy is all guys have. They actually found a few real women who were working for a protection facility in California to star in the film. Security was a nightmare. I'm glad I didn't have anything to do with the production. California has a very progressive governor right now. The guardians at the facilities out there don't even have to live on-site. Most still do, the danger is enormous. I heard one of the actresses married one of the actors on a trip to Canada. It's caused a big legal mess, because marriage has been legally abolished. Religious protestors came from all over the country to fight for the right to be married. They'll be voting on the constitutional legitimacy of not allowing marriage. If any state brings it back, I think it will be California. The government is afraid once they return heterosexual marriage rights, they'll be fighting the gay marriage fight again. They're assholes for banning both."

He sighed and rubbed her cheek with his thumb for a minute. His eyes darted back and forth as he looked at her face, and she realized he was looking for her reaction.

"I don't know how much news you were able to watch in there," he continued, "but there was a big push for legalizing gay marriage, since there were no women. I support it completely, but even in these times they're so afraid to allow it. I'm amazed at the level of hierocracy the government perpetrates sometimes."

"I don't see why they don't allow it, especially now. Just think about all the taxes they could suddenly come up with." She grinned.

"Now that's the argument the proponents should use. Gay marriage would be legal in a week." They both laughed.

Krista looked at some photos he had hanging on the wall.

The one with a woman holding a little boy caught her attention.

"I was nine when my mother died, I didn't have siblings. It was hard, but you know that. My father wasn't around much, he traveled for business, but then his company went under due to the state of the economy. He killed himself. I lived with my cousins. I think that's why we're so close, so connected. I really thought we could share. I wish I hadn't fooled myself now, but I'm glad you're here."

Krista turned from where the happy image hung, frozen in time on the wall. Brax's expression was dark. He ran his hand through his hair.

"Can you handle me, Krista?"

The question was very strange and slightly worrisome. "What do you mean? I think I proved I can handle a lot last night," she replied. Brax gave a short bark of laughter, but she didn't hear true humor.

"I've never been good at sharing. I want there to be something different between us."

She frowned, her head tilting to the side.

He turned and stared at her intensely. "If I told you to take off all your clothes and get on your knees, right now, would you do it?" He raised his eyebrow.

"I—yes," she replied. The answer surprised her.

"If one of the others told you to do it, would the request

feel the same for you?" This time his eyes narrowed as he asked the question.

"I don't know."

"Before tonight is over, you will know. Take off your clothing for me, slowly, lay it on the chair, and get on your knees."

She'd expected a lot, but not this. She didn't know why he was asking her to do something so unusual. She hesitated.

"You're mine, Krista. You know it and you want to please me. Take off your clothing."

She began slowly undressing. While she wasn't ready to belong to anyone, more than she already did on paper, she couldn't resist his request. She'd expected to have time to go change into the nightgown he'd given her. He'd been so kind, a bit bossy, but she hadn't felt domination from him until now. He leaned against the wall, his arms crossed over his chest and one of his feet resting up against the beige surface behind him. Her mind briefly flicked over how he'd explain a shoe print in the spot if Steve asked him about it.

"I'm going to take this slow with you. I promise. My desire is to have you all to myself, but that's not possible. Since we can't have that, I want you to submit to me, willingly. Would you do that for me?"

He was risking a lot asking for this. If she decided this

was threatening, all she had to do was press the panic button and they'd all lose her, and he'd lose his friends. She knew in order for him to ask for this, he must want it more than he wanted anything. Something deep inside of her responded to the request, they had chemistry and she was curious to see how it would play out.

"Yes," she whispered as she finished taking off her clothing and laid all of it neatly on the chair. She knelt in front of him, the plush, mauve carpet cushioning her knees. "Please."

He groaned and hurried to free his cock from his jeans. He was fully dressed, except for his cock and balls. They dangled out of his pants and she leaned forward to take him in her mouth.

"I didn't tell you to," he said. She stopped, feeling confused. "With the others, do as you want. Here, when we are alone, you are mine. Do you understand?"

She nodded.

"Tell me," he requested quietly.

"I am yours." She couldn't believe she'd actually said the words. They felt right coming out of her mouth. She'd been terrified of this happening, but now she embraced giving him this willingness.

"Suck me," he ordered.

She leaned forward and took him gently into her mouth.

Brax took a fistful of her hair. He'd scolded Mal for the same thing just the night before. His hands felt different, rougher. She allowed him to set the pace and to dictate how much of him she had inside her mouth. Brax wasn't small, but she was grateful he wasn't as large as DeAnthony.

She let her tongue press into the channel on the bottom of his cock. She drew in as hard as she could on one stroke, while lightly running her teeth over him on the next. He exhaled slowly and she knew he liked it. She knew she wouldn't have been so keen on playing this way with the others, but Brax was different, and her feelings for him were too. She didn't know why, but for him, she'd do this and more. The realization startled her and she pulled away to look up into his face.

His eyes were dark and he frowned. "What is it, Kristannie?"

"I—I want this," she mumbled, a bit awestruck.

"Yes, you do. Tell me."

"I want to be yours."

He groaned and pulled her to her feet, dragging her roughly into a wild kiss. His tongue plunged into her mouth. The sound of his inhalation and his growl were the only noises in the room. She'd never kissed like this before; it was so much more intimate, deep. She let her tongue glide along his. Krista wrapped her arms around his neck and he kissed her until she

Given / Ashlynn Monroe

couldn't breathe. When he pulled away, she sucked in a deep
lungful of air.

"I'm going to make you mine, slowly, one night at a time.
Come with me." He took her hand and began walking out of
the room.

"What if someone sees me?" She'd been naked in front of
all of them, but the idea of streaking down the hall made her
uncomfortable. Worse, if Steve or one of the guards happened
to be in the hall, the mortification would be unbearable.

He turned and scooped her up. She squeaked at the sense
of helpless fear that rose inside of her. If she was too heavy and
he dropped her, it would hurt. Her average height and weight
didn't usually lend to a feeling of being dainty, but in his arms,
she felt his power. The sensation was definitely a turn on.

He walked into the darkened hallway and, to her relief,
they were alone. The guard wasn't making his rounds through
the house yet. He shut the bedroom door behind them as they
entered. Braxton deposited her on his bed. "Lay on your
stomach."

She did as he'd requested, without question. She could
hear him undressing and moving around the room. The
sensation of something cold drizzled on her back and
shoulders, and her body flinched involuntarily. Her butt stung
sharply under Brax's hand. The whack reverberated through

the room, but didn't actually hurt. Krista turned to gape at Braxton in shock.

He grinned. "Hold still." She did.

His hands rubbed musky scented oil into her skin. He worked at the knots between her shoulder blades and wonderful warmth saturated her muscles. The sensation of his large, strong hands on her skin was heavenly. She relaxed, laying her cheek on his mattress. The sheets smelled like him, like his soap and cologne. The heady combination left her feeling light, almost as if she was floating. His hands began working on her ass next and she jerked in surprise. Another quick slap made her gasp. She heard him chuckle. The feeling of intimate violation made it a struggle not to wiggle away from his hands.

"Don't clench. Relax."

She tried to obey, but no one had touched her like this. The group session had been so different. She was amazed at how much it made her want more. Taking a deep breath, she forced herself to relax and enjoy his hands massaging her rear. When she focused on the sensation, instead of how strange it was, she sighed. He was making her good and relaxed.

"Roll over and close your eyes."

She obeyed again. There was something so sexy in his voice when he gave a command. She could hear how much he was enjoying it.

"Spread your legs."

She did, as wide as she could. Her pussy ached for his touch. Her moisture ran over the soft, intimate flesh and it made her squirm. Brax's warm breath swirled around between her legs. She moaned. Then his tongue darted out to flick her clit. Her hips bucked, he didn't reprimand her this time. His quick motions made the sensitive flesh come to life. Every nerve ending burst with pleasure and Krista gripped the sheets, clawing wildly. Her head thrashed from side to side.

Deep whimpers escaped her lips, even though she had them pressed tightly together. "Brax!" Her cry echoed in the room and she arched her back, panting as she came, crying out with little mews of delight. He kept flicking the sensitized little nub until her ass was back on the bed and the whimpers began to subside.

The bed dipped and she looked up. Brax hovered over her, like a vengeful master. His dark handsomeness was easy on her eyes, and she reached up to brush a loose strand of his hair out of his eyes. They just looked at each other for a long, quiet moment. He was beautiful in an all-male way that made her glad to be in his bed. She'd been so afraid she wasn't going to like sex, and here she was, crazy with wanting more of it.

He grabbed both of her wrists and slid her hands up, pinning them above her head. He balanced on his knees and leaned down to take her right nipple in his mouth. His teeth and tongue worked together to give her both pleasure and pain. The combination was amazing. Gasping, she flexed her neck back and closed her eyes, relishing the feeling of his hot mouth on the tender place. The more he toyed with her, the more sensitive it became. The pain grew, as did the pleasure. Her pussy contracted, still having spasms from her earlier orgasm.

He moved to repeat the process on her other breast. The vacated nipple was wet and grew cold, which only served to make her more aware of how it still tingled from his ministrations. She opened her eyes to look at him. The intensity on his face was one of the most wonderful things she'd ever seen. She knew it would be burned into her memory for life. Krista wanted him inside of her.

"Brax. Please."

"Oh, I'm not done yet. I've waited a very long time for tonight."

"Please. I want to touch you," she begged quietly. He released her hands.

She reached out to touch his cock and he blocked her hand with his knee. "Don't. I want to enjoy you, and if you touch me, I'm afraid I won't be able to handle myself. I've waited a lifetime for you, Krista, and I don't plan to disappoint you."

His words touched a place deep inside, a spot she'd

promised herself they wouldn't enter. He was right, she was his, and it hadn't been a lie or a game. This was a dangerous position, giving too much to any of them could upset the entire balance of their "arrangement", and she didn't want to live in a house filled with anger and jealousy.

He placed a tender kiss in the middle of her stomach. Then his hands were under her butt and he pulled her closer. Brax picked up her legs and rested her ankles on his shoulders. Her eyes widened. He grinned. His index finger dipped into her wetness and he began swirling it against her clit, hard. Krista moaned and laid her head back, closing her eyes again. He worked her body with quick hard caresses and she built toward another orgasm. The caresses suffused her with a pleasure that quickly spiked higher.

He thrust forward, his cock sliding inside of her. The angle of his entry intensified the feeling, and she instantly surrendered to the raw need. All the amazing sensations caused her to shudder violently. She wrapped her arms around his chest, crying out with a single gasp.

"Tell me you're mine," he demanded. She cried out; the feeling of pleasure was overwhelming. "Tell me what I need to hear."

"I'm yours," she cried.

Her back arched and the cresting desire hit its zenith,

tumbling her into the mindless ecstasy of intense orgasm. She came so hard that her scream was a raw, low, primal sound reverberating in the room as she bore down on the pleasure, panting with the force of her release. Her pussy gripped him tighter and Brax stopped rubbing her to catch himself, hovering above her.

He closed his eyes and threw his head back, yelling with a triumphant roar. The heat of his release filled her. Krista lay back, feeling him inside of her, their bodies joined as one. It was beautiful. She had to hold her breath, or she was afraid she'd start crying. She'd been afraid of so much, but this man had given her more than she'd ever expected. She hadn't wanted to like any of them, but she found herself feeling something so profound she was afraid to try to give it a name. It was too early to give the emotion the name it deserved.

Brax wrapped his arms tightly around her, rolling to bring her to rest on top of him. She laid her cheek against the rough hair and sweat on his chest. There was something so fully primitive in the moment, she sighed with bliss. For a moment, she let herself pretend it was more than she knew it was. *If only...*

"Do you want me to go now?" she asked.

"God no. This is still my night. I want to wake up with you in my arms. Will you stay with me, Kristannie?"

"Yes." She didn't even have to think about it. She wanted to be with him, more than she knew was prudent.

He turned and she found herself on the mattress, her head cradled on his muscular bicep. Braxton gazed at her with soft eyes as he pushed her hair out of her face. "You're beautiful. Tonight meant something to me, it wasn't just about the release."

"I know," she whispered, feeling drowsy. She'd seen the truth of his words in his actions. There was darkness in him, but she knew what it was to be filled with hopelessness and his own inner pain was appealing. Misery loved company, and she was glad she wasn't alone.

He leaned forward and kissed her forehead. His free hand kept touching her face and shoulders while the one that cradled her rubbed her back. The combination was soothing, and she was having trouble keeping her eyes open.

"As much as I don't want our night to be over, I know you need sleep." He pressed his cheek against the top of her head. She heard him inhale deeply. "Damn, you smell good. Everything about you is good. I'm a lucky man. I can't imagine never feeling someone so soft in my arms again."

She was worried about that too. Even though she hadn't chosen to be there, it could be worse. She didn't want to be taken away and have to go through the awkwardness of it all again with men who might all be like Damon. He was the only one who really didn't seem to care. At least she liked them all, even Max.

"Are you just saying that?" she mumbled, already half-asleep.

"No. I mean it. Even if I could walk into the nearest protection facility right now and pick a girl, I'd pick you. I'd worried about our woman cowering in the corner and laying in bed stiffly. I didn't want to live with some hysterical who thought of me as a rapist. It's nice to feel like we have a shot at a real family, even if it's the new definition of what that means."

That's exactly what she wanted too, a life of peace and happiness. Her mind drifted away with the image of a house full of kids, a big Christmas tree with a roaring fire, and smiling men looking at the family they'd built with pride. If they could only keep the jealousy out of the house...

Krista jerked awake. Something cool touched her neck.

"Shh, it's only me. I'm sorry. You looked so pretty, I couldn't resist a quick kiss." She felt his erection pressing into her leg.

"What time is it?" she mumbled.

"Five o'clock, almost dawn."

She scowled. She'd never been a morning person. Brax's

hands rubbed her back and neck. She snuggled deeper into the warmth of his body. She sat up quickly, pulling the blankets over her breasts.

"Oh my God! Your arm, I slept on it all night!"

"It's okay. I didn't sleep much. I wanted to enjoy my night as long as I could."

"My clothes, are they…"

"I'll get them," he said, grinning.

Brax slid out of bed, and she had a good look at his tight butt in the gray light of early morning. Perfection; she wanted to run her hands over those round cheeks and feel the firmness. He was back in a moment with her pile of clothing, setting it on his dresser. She saw his cock bobbing as he got back into bed.

Braxton kissed the hollow of her throat. His hand slid up her stomach, causing the muscles to clench. When he reached her breast, he pinched her nipple gently. His lips moved to the side of her neck and he sucked her skin, hard. Drowsy, she sighed. Brax's hand slid from her breast and back down her stomach, swirling over her skin in a wavy motion. The movement tickled and she giggled. He smiled against her neck but continued kissing and sucking. The wonderful sensation built inside of her and she turned just a little so that her hand could caress his back.

He reached between her legs, and she parted her thighs for

him. His fingers dipped into the gathering moisture and then he began rubbing her clitoris in small circles. Krista whimpered and closed her eyes. Her legs spread even wider.

The bed dipped and she opened her eyes. In the darkness, she could see him hovering above her, between her legs. His penis entered her quickly and she let go of a low primal moan, unprepared for him. Then the pleasure replaced the feeling of invasion. He slid more easily as her body accepted him and the gratification each stroke of his thick shaft erupted inside of her. Krista relished the gathering excitement as she built toward the wondrous, mindless place where only sensation existed. She wrapped her legs around him, holding him to her.

Brax's penis slid in and out of her slowly, and then his thrusts increased in speed. He slid his hands under her ass, elevating her, and the difference in angle increased her pleasure as his cock rubbed against her g-spot, sending her over the edge.

"Yes. Harder. Braaaxxx!" Krista screamed, not thinking about how loud she was.

"That's it, Kristannie, scream my name," Brax pleaded.

"Braxton!"

"Come for me. God, I can't hold on. Come, Krista!"

She came. "Braxton!" His name sounded like an animalistic growl as she arched her back, meeting his thrust.

Then he released into her. She couldn't see his face in the darkness, but his long, low cry filled her with joy.

He rolled over, pulling her on top of him again. His dick was still hard and inside of her. She kissed his lips. Her hands splayed in his thick hair, and she ground her hips against him. She could feel him growing inside of her again.

"You're amazing," he whispered when she pulled her mouth away.

She sat up and began to shimmy her hips a bit. As his erection elongated, the pleasure inside her returned. She kept the gently rocking motion going. He reached up and played with her breasts. She reached her hands back, grabbing his hips for support as her motion increased to a bounce. Brax groaned.

"Oh Christ. Yes!" Brax cried as she increased the length and speed of her gyrations. His hands were wild on her breasts and he squeezed them while tweaking her nipples with his thumbs.

Growling, Brax moved so suddenly that she only had time to issue a small squeak before he had her pinned to the mattress, fucking her with a raging need that added fuel to the flames inside of her.

"Fuck yes!" he shouted. "Tell me it won't be like this with anyone else," he demanded.

She didn't, instead she cried out, clinging to him as her

body shuddered with the radiating pleasure of her orgasm. He kissed her mouth hard. His head tilted and he pressed his forehead to hers as he growled with release.

Brax collapsed next to her on the bed, and then dragged her into his arms. She lay with her head on his chest. The only sound in the room was their ragged breathing. They lay like that for several minutes.

"Time for a shower," Brax said, sliding out of bed. He held out his hand and she took it, and then followed him from the soft, warm mattress.

She shivered with the chill of the morning air as Brax turned on his large, private shower. He grabbed a washrag and kissed her as he walked backward with her into the shower, closing the glass door behind them. The warm spray hit her and she squeezed her eyes tightly as the water beat against them, splashing their faces. The kiss and the spray made it hard to breath, but she was still in a sort of erotic trance, not caring or concerned about anything besides the man making her feel so alive.

He pulled away and squeezed some liquid body wash into the rag. He began to sensually rub her body with the cloth, and she stood still, unsure as to what to do while he washed her from head to toe. He spent a ridiculous amount of time on her breasts before turning her around and washing her ass cheeks with small circular strokes. Krista moaned, but when he dipped the cloth between those cheeks, she clenched, feeling violated.

"Relax," he instructed.

She did her best, but there was something so much more forbidden in him touching her there, she was having trouble.

"Some men like to fuck their partner's ass. Don't let any of the others have that, Krista. If you ever want to try that, let that be mine. Would you do that for me?"

She shook her head mutely. It was very unlikely she'd be begging for that anytime soon. If giving him this promise made him happy, she didn't see the harm. Her asshole was still slick with soap. He moved the rag and gently rubbed against it with the tip of his finger. She shivered. Then he stopped and began rinsing the suds from her skin.

Strangely, she realized she was disappointed he'd stopped playing with her ass. As wrong as it felt, she'd enjoyed his touch. The idea of something secret and special between them was intriguing. She took a deep breath of the steaming air. Brax was her favorite, she had to admit it to herself even though playing favorites wasn't a good idea.

He put some shampoo in his hands and began working it into her hair. The sensation was wonderful. She sighed. He rinsed her hair and then picked up the fallen washrag. She watched as he began to lather himself.

"Let me," she whispered, taking the washrag from him. Slowly, she began to wash him as he'd done to her. She noticed his flaccid cock was semi-erect. "Aren't men supposed to have a recovery time? I remember learning about that."

"I've been waiting a hell of a long time, my body's been very deprived."

Krista chuckled. Then she rinsed him and tried to wash his hair, but he was too tall. Brax finished the job quickly before pinning her to the wall for another kiss. The heat and steam swirled around them. It seemed like she'd gone to a mythical land of perfect sensation, not just an ordinary shower. When he pulled away, she realized her fingers had wrinkled. It was time to get out of the water.

Brax turned off the spray, and they stepped out onto the large white mat. The chill made her shiver. He quickly enveloped her in a big, fluffy, white towel, rubbing her briskly. Brax took a new towel and began drying his own skin. They went back into the bedroom and picked up her clothing from the night before. She didn't want to walk across the house naked.

"Here, I had this brought down. I like to think ahead." He opened his dresser drawer and handed her the white nightgown and robe.

"Thanks," she said quietly. It wasn't as if Steve didn't

know she was there for sex, but knowing Brax had asked the housekeeper to bring her intimate clothing to him made her a bit uncomfortable. She was glad not to be putting on yesterday's clothing, but it was just weird that he'd so precisely planned for her to stay. Shrugging, she put on the nightgown and robe.

"Lay with me before you go," Brax requested.

"Okay." She crawled into his bed and he wrapped his arms around her. The smell of his shampoo and body wash filled her senses. She felt completely engulfed by him. For a long time, she listened to his heartbeat. They were silent.

"Are you really jealous of the others? Is it just because you're territorial?"

"Territorial?"

She chuckled. "They put you in your own area. I suspect it's because they see what I see, a man who likes his space and *his* things left alone. Am I just one of your things?"

"You don't belong to me, Kristannie, but I wish you did. If this was another world I'd...doesn't matter now." He reached out and touched her. There was so much tenderness in the caress, she closed her eyes and savored the moment.

"I guess not. I'll see you later." She slipped from his arms, but he grabbed her and pulled her back. He kissed her with a hunger that left her panting. If she had a choice, she would stay with him, and only him. She didn't have a choice though.

Krista pulled away, and saw the fleeting look of disappointment in his eyes before she left the room without looking back. She didn't know whom she belonged with today, but she knew it wasn't Brax and the thought hurt. She didn't want to be intimate with the others today, not after spending the morning in Braxton's bed. She felt a connection to him that she didn't with any of the other five. Playing favorites would just hurt them all.

She hurried through the darkness to her own room and shut the door. She wouldn't be getting any more sleep, so she dressed and sat down on the little couch with the book she was reading. Soon she lost herself in Samuel Johnson's struggle.

Chapter 6

A soft knock on the door startled Krista.

Jared walked in. "Are you coming down for breakfast? We're waiting for you."

"Oh sorry, I was reading and didn't look at the clock."

"So you like the book? I'm kind of surprised."

"Why? It's the closest thing to my situation I've seen. There's a lot that's different, but Brax really got the emotion right. I'm already almost done with this one. I can't wait to see what happens to Samuel when his punishment ends. I just want to cry worrying about him, ridiculous I know. I almost feel like I know him, even if he's fictional."

"The man can write. Are you okay? There are bags under your eyes. Did Brax hurt…never mind."

"No, he didn't hurt me. I'm still just adjusting. Is tonight your night?" She hoped so, she liked Jared and if she couldn't sleep with Brax, she had a feeling the sweet, young man would be gentle and it would be over quickly.

"No, Saturday is mine. Last as usual, low man on the totem pole. Do you want me to write the list down so you'll know? We promised to stick by it unless one of us is gone. Then it's your choice or you get the night off. Oh Christ, that sounds so wrong. I didn't mean—you're not working for us or whatever."

Krista bit the inside of her cheek to keep from saying something nasty. His words bothered her; she did feel a little like a prostitute, or worse, a sex slave. Having a patriotic duty to have sex for procreation wasn't the most wonderful future, but it beat placement with new men. The stress was bad here, but she felt a connection of sorts with these men. It would be worse to have to begin all over again with six new men. The idea of never seeing Brax again really bothered her. She hoped they'd get her pregnant soon and then the pressure would be off her shoulders and theirs.

Jared grabbed a piece of paper off the small desk. He scribbled down days and then names before handing her the paper.

"Wow, no wonder you want to be a doctor, your handwriting is awful."

He flushed, but grinned. "Thanks?"

She read the paper. *Brax Monday, Damon Tuesday, Mal Wednesday, Max Thursday, DeAnthony Friday, Jared Saturday, Sunday lady's choice.*

"Thanks for the schedule. I guess I'm Damon's today. I don't think your brother likes me very much."

"He's happy, we all are. He's just not as into the whole

relationship thing. I think he's scared we'll lose you and he doesn't want to get hurt. Sharing isn't easy for any of us."

The explanation made some sense, but Krista wasn't convinced. "Okay, thanks. Let's go eat, I'm starving."

"If you aren't doing anything this afternoon, would you like to play video games?" Jared asked.

"Yeah, that'd be fun." Krista smiled and gave him a quick hug. Being with him almost felt normal—as if they could be friends. She liked the idea of a friend they didn't have to hire for her. She followed him downstairs.

Jared pulled out her chair and she sat down. They were all looking at her expectantly. "Good morning," she said.

"Morning." The men spoke in mumbled unison.

"Have a nice night, beautiful?" DeAnthony asked, making her blush.

"It was wonderful," she replied quietly, before glancing at Brax who was grinning from ear to ear.

So much for not playing favorites. They began eating the mountains of eggs, bacon, and toast. Krista closed her eyes as she took a sip of orange juice. This breakfast must have cost a small fortune. Oranges, even the juice, was precious in the north.

"This is delicious. Thanks, Steve," Krista said as the housekeeper passed her with another platter of toast. Steve nodded, scurrying from the room.

The men ate as if they were starving.

"We're calling the companion service today. Do you have a preference?" Jared asked.

"I'd like to learn how to cook, maybe to paint too, if that's not a problem with you guys."

"I think it's a foolish waste of money. Let's just hire a gay housekeeper and we're fine," Max grumbled.

"Steve has worked for us a long time. He's good, and I don't want to be the asshole. Would you want to be the one who fires Steve?" Brax said, frowning.

"Quiet, he'll hear," Jared whispered.

"Fine, call the service, but don't let them talk you into anything more expensive than the basic services," Max replied.

Krista rolled her eyes. She stuck out her tongue at Max and his eyes widened, and then he chuckled.

"Fine, buy her what she wants. Damn expensive woman," Max grumbled, but he was grinning.

"She's worth every penny," Jared defended. Heat crept up her cheeks.

She put her napkin on her plate. Steve's cooking was wonderful. She'd have to start exercising again or she'd be the size of a house soon.

"Are you done?" Damon asked.

She turned to him. "Yes, it was delicious."

"Great, let's go."

"Where?" She was surprised he'd made plans with her for the day. He hadn't seemed that interested in getting to know her before.

"My room or yours?"

She looked at the men sitting around the table. Jared and Braxton looked angry. Max glanced back and forth between Krista and his friend as if he was trying to decide how to feel.

"You don't plan to keep her chained to your bed all day, do you?" Mal teased, but she could hear the genuine concern in his voice.

"It's my day, stay out of it. Let's go to my room." He held out his hand.

She paused, not in the mood to go have sex with him, especially when they'd just finished breakfast. He shook the hand he held out impatiently. She didn't take it, but she did stand.

Brax also stood, his chair scraping back loudly. "Do you really think this is the best way?"

"I've waited long enough. I want to have sex. She's here to get pregnant, not to be my new best friend. You guys are making me a little sick, acting as if you can all play house with her. She's playing you, don't forget that, Jared." He pinned his brother with a dark look, then looked back at Krista. "You don't love us, Krista, and we don't love you. Love isn't something you can win, but these days sex is. Let's go."

She didn't want to. Her face felt like it was on fire. She was so embarrassed. Steve was standing in the doorway watching too. "I'd like to get to know you. I didn't sign up for this either. I'm sorry you don't like me, but could we wait until a little later? Maybe if we could just talk—"

Damon interrupted her. "No. Let's go."

She looked back at the others, she felt like she might cry. "What if I want to pick someone else today? Jared is stuck with Saturday. I think we should put you on Saturday." She didn't look away this time, but instead forced herself to look into the rude man's eyes.

"Bullshit! Jared, you fucking know what we agreed to. Did you go whining about being the one to get her at her most used?"

Krista flinched at the description. She really didn't like Damon.

"I didn't whine. She saw the list. Who'd want to have to wait? I don't think Saturday makes her used, but I'd take Tuesday."

"Okay, Jared is Tuesday and you're Saturday then," Brax said.

"No. I don't accept that. We made an agreement. Do you think I'll love you by Saturday, 'cause that's stupid shit, woman."

"Watch your language in front of Krista. She's our lady, treat her like it." DeAnthony stood too. His fists clenched.

The situation was spiraling out of control. Krista hated causing turmoil by rejecting the asshole. She hadn't really wanted emotional sex, not after Brax, but she didn't want to be used either. She'd just get him over with and keep on trying to obtain some sort of Zen and harmony. At least she wouldn't have to deal with being in his bed for another seven days.

"Fine. Let's go, I don't want fighting," Krista shouted. She looked back sadly at the remaining men. "I'll get through it." Then she took a step closer to Damon. "Lead the way," she said as sassily as she could.

He didn't look any happier than she felt. She followed him up the stairs. He closed and locked the door behind them and began taking off his clothes. He paused and looked at her. "What are you waiting for?"

She'd hoped he'd change his mind. She wouldn't want to be with an unwilling man. Clearly, her willingness didn't matter to him. She began taking off her clothes. He was being a jerk, and didn't seem to care. His cock was erect, but his eyes were hard, cruel. He didn't look horny, just angry.

"Get on the bed."

She lay down on the bed, still hoping he'd change his mind and let her leave. This was the first time she thought about the panic button. The idea of someone swooping into the house to take her away from him was appealing. She didn't really want to go through the trauma of being placed with a new six though, so she remained still.

"Spread your legs."

She began to panic, but slowly parted her thighs a little. She lay naked and stiff. "We could talk for a while. I'd like to know you, Damon."

"Shut up and relax. You seemed to like it well enough the other night."

She watched him get on the bed. Her body wasn't ready for him and she knew it. He tried to push inside of her, but she was dry and tight. He spit on his hand and rubbed it on the head of his cock. *Oh, gross.* Then he forced it inside of her. She arched her back, crying out in pain. He thrust inside of her. She thought about Brax's tender touch earlier. Her mind tried to detach from what Damon was doing. *How can it be so good with one man and so bad with another?* When he stiffened and cried out, she felt his limp cock slid out of her body and slap against her thigh. She shuddered and sat up quickly, covering her breasts.

"Are we done?" Her voice trembled and it made her angry with herself. The realization that she'd have to endure him once a week was almost overwhelming. That had been the worse experience of her life, and so far, life hadn't been so good.

"If I want to do it again later, the whole day is mine."

"Fuck no, you had your turn. You will get me again next Tuesday. I think I hate you."

"You can't tell me you like any of them better."

"I can and I will. You're the only one who raped me."

He flinched as she said the words. "Just get the hell out of my room."

She didn't need to hear it twice. Her room was close enough that she didn't even bother to put her clothes on, she just streaked down the hall. The moment she was out of his room she let the tears fall. She slammed her door shut and locked it. Krista let her body slide down the door and she sat for a moment crying until she realized his ejaculation was running down her leg.

Tossing her clothes on the bed, she rushed to her shower and turned on the water as hot as it would go. Once she was under the scalding blast, she cried again. After washing herself between her legs three times, she still felt dirty. She stayed in the shower until the hot water turned cold, then she stumbled out and found a towel.

Krista cried until she was out of tears, then dressed and sat back down on her little couch with the book. She couldn't concentrate, but just holding the book made her feel better for some inexplicable reason. Whether it was her connection to the character or the fact that Braxton had written it, she just wanted to stay there alone and having it near her felt comforting.

She'd thought she was out of tears, but before she knew it, she began crying again. There was a soft knock on the door. She didn't get up.

"Krista, are you all right?" Jared yelled.

She got up and unlocked the door then returned to the couch. He didn't come in right away and she wondered if he'd left. Then the knob turned. She held her breath, afraid it might be Damon. When Jared walked in, she let out the breath she'd been holding and bit her lip, afraid she'd start crying when she saw his sympathetic look.

"I just wanted to see if you wanted to play Battlestar Three with me. It's a fun game."

"No, I just want to be alone, sorry."

"Did he hurt you?" She could hear anger in Jared's voice. He reached out to touch her and she flinched. He pulled his hand back quickly.

"I don't want to cause problems, especially not between brothers. That's why I had sex with him, so there wouldn't be fighting. Just—don't let it all be for nothing by fighting with him."

"I'm sorry."

"You didn't do it. You have nothing to apologize for."

"Yeah, well, he's my brother, and I feel like shit that he hurt you. I don't understand why. He always says how great it would be to have a wife and a family. Even if there's no marriage anymore and we have to share you, at least we can sort of have part of the dream. I'm going to talk to him."

She regretted rejecting the comfort Jared had tried to offer her. She felt so used and dirty. Seeing the kindness in his eyes made her own fill with unshed tears.

"No, please don't, just…could you hold me for a while?" Krista whispered.

Jared's presence was so comforting. He really would make a great doctor someday. He hurried over and sat down next to her. His arms wrapped around her tightly and she cried again. Hard sobs wracked her body. When she'd spent her tears, she pulled back and wiped her eyes.

"Sorry," she mumbled.

"Don't apologize to me for crying. I'll have a talk with Damon. Maybe he'll be more careful next week."

"No. I don't want problems. I just want this to be a peaceful place. If this is my home, I don't want it to be full of fighting. Please don't tell the others, this will just be our secret."

Jared wiped a stray tear off her cheek. "Do you want me to examine you, was he rough? I'm not a licensed doctor yet, but I do know ways to help you."

"I wasn't torn, if that's what you're worried about. He was rough, but not violent. Thanks, but all I want to do is keep my pants on."

"We missed lunch. Do you want me to bring you something?"

"No. Thank you for being here for me." She squeezed his hand. "Why don't you go get something to eat? I'm going to read for a while. I want to see how the book ends."

"Are you sure? I'll stay."

"I know, but no thanks. You're a wonderful friend."

He grunted. "Yeah, well, just feel better."

She could tell he didn't like the word "friend" and that only intensified her sad feelings. She'd sleep with Jared because she wanted him to feel the pleasure and joy, but she knew she'd never feel about him as she did Brax, and that was what he wanted. Her desire for a peaceful, happy home seemed impossible.

She forced herself to focus on the book, and it did make her feel better until she read the last page. She wanted to cry.

The book had helped so much, and now it was over. Even if there was another one, it wasn't this book. She didn't want to return it to the shelf, but it wasn't hers. Unable to bring herself to return it, she sat it on the stand next to her bed, knowing she could at least hold on to it for a few more days, even if she grabbed the next one. She doubted anyone would miss it until then.

The clock told her it was time for supper, but she didn't have any appetite. She went downstairs and tried not to make eye contact with the men. Damon looked angry, and she hoped Jared hadn't said anything. Brax jumped up and pulled out her chair for her. She thanked him quietly and sat down. None of them said anything. Even Mal was unusually silent as they began eating. When Steve served her a huge piece of strawberry shortcake, she knew they all knew and it made her feel like hiding under the table. She thanked Steve quietly and he nodded. She hadn't touched much of her meal, but she did manage to polish off half the shortcake, unable to resist the delicious dessert.

"Stop looking at me like that! None of you are any better. She's putting on. I think she liked it," Damon suddenly growled.

When she glanced up, he was giving her the meanest look she'd ever seen. She shrank back, but then her anger built inside and overshadowed her fear. Krista glared at him, but when he gritted his teeth and narrowed his eyes, fear made her focus on her half-eaten dessert again. She was ashamed of being afraid, but she knew if today had been bad, he could make next week even worse.

"I'm going to grab a book and head to bed," she said, getting up.

They all stood and she rushed away. In the game room, she found the next book and headed for her private space. She wished Brax would come to her, just to hold her. After what they shared, she wondered if it'd been a lie. His absence seemed strange after the declaration of protection he'd made. She thought he would at least want to make sure she was all right. Shrugging off the feelings of abandonment, she began reading the next book. Samuel Johnson's day was starting off much as hers had. Reading about his abuse made her cringe even more than she had before, it was personal now.

After a few pages, she thought she might cry again. She wanted to know what happened, but she needed some air. It was late. The men would be in the game room or in bed. She thought about going to Brax's bed, but she didn't want to be seduced and if he hadn't come to check on her, she didn't want to seem needy. What he'd said conflicted with his actions, making a liar out of him.

She went outside to the patio. The crickets chirped loudly, the full moon was high in the sky and very bright tonight. The cool breeze touched her face. Fall was coming. The crisp smell and nip in the air made her regret not spending more time outdoors. Soon, the winter chill would force her to say cooped up indoors. She might even be pregnant by then and her actions would be further restricted. Sighing, she leaned on the railing.

"Can't sleep?"

She squeaked with surprise, turning. The full moon made it easier to see than usual. Max. "No. You?"

"I never sleep well. What happened to you is bothering me. I should've stepped in. Christ, I thought I was going to have to lock Brax up. You didn't want a fight, so I wouldn't let him go up there. I told him stepping in would make it worse for you. Damon's entitled to a turn, and if we piss him off he'll just take it out on you. Now I wish I'd let Brax kick his ass."

Her heart stopped. Brax had wanted to step in. "I'm obligated, and at least I got him out of the way. Even if I'd put him off until Saturday, it wouldn't have made a difference. Damon is punishing me for something I didn't do to him."

Max grunted. "You see things clearly. Not everyone has that gift, or curse. Whatever you see it as, don't lose it. I found if you think about something pleasant, it helps. I never have to go through it again, and it makes me sick that you will."

She glanced over at him. He was staring out into the yard. She liked that he was opening up, but wished it wasn't because they'd both shared a horrible experience.

"I thought Braxton was going to kill Damon. He paced out on the patio most of the morning, but when Damon came down whistling, Brax just stood there with his fists clenched, looking like he was constipated. I never saw that look on his face before. One of us should've stopped it. He could've waited until you were willing, at least until later. There was no reason for him to do it as he did. I won't rape you, Krista. If you tell me no, I'll deal."

She reached over and put her hand on top of his. "I know. I won't tell you no, Max. I'd never like to be with Damon again, but you aren't him. Mal hasn't even had a turn yet. I won't let one spoil it for the rest of you. He's right, I'm not madly in love with the six of you, but I understand the need for me to get pregnant, and if it was yours, I'd be happy. You're not as bad as you try to be."

Max grunted. Then he moved his hand from under hers and put his arm around her. She flinched for a moment, but then relaxed. Knowing the contact was hard for him too, made it all the more special. They stood like that for a silent moment, listening to the night. In the distance, she could hear the lake and a lone coyote yipping.

"Goodnight, Krista. Get some sleep."

"Night, Max. Thank you."

He grunted in response and she heard the patio door close. She remained for a while and then went upstairs to find her bed. Her eyes drooped and she yawned. She stripped off her clothing. Exhaustion won and the moment she lay down, she was asleep.

Chapter 7

Birds' song woke her. Krista sat up and stretched. The terrible memories of yesterday came flooding back. She was positive now that she wanted to get pregnant as soon as possible. The idea of Damon forcing her again was bad, but six new men who might all be like Damon was terrifying. Worse, she was sure some men must insist on the woman having sex with all of them every day. The idea of six men raping her everyday was beyond terrible to contemplate. Things here could be worse.

Today belonged to Malcolm. She went downstairs, and she was the first one at the table. In the kitchen, she could hear noise—Steve making breakfast. She got up and wandered into the game room. Picking up the large, complicated remote, she managed to turn on the television and start channel surfing. A news report made her pause on CNN.

"There are new developments in the Northeastern quadrant controversy. All lottery drawings have ceased as of last month. Today we've learned that they are requiring all males between the ages of eighteen and twenty-three who've passed the lottery genetic testing to donate sperm for a new program. Some critics are calling the decision to only allow artificial insemination of female embryos into the women of this quadrant 'a gross abuse of power'."

The screen flicked to a large group of angry men. They waved large signs while yelling bitterly toward the camera. A man stood next to the reporter, glancing nervously at the angry mob behind him. Police stood along the line separating the reporter and politician from the enraged crowd.

"We've been having mixed results with the old system. Allowing nature to take its course is time consuming, and for the last year, we've seen an increase in male babies. Even with the tax benefits of aborting male fetuses, some men are allowing their Given woman to give birth to those sons. We've decided that it's time for a more effective, faster method. Our women are impregnated on their eighteenth birthdays, we're no longer going by the standard of twenty-one, and after they've given birth, they are allowed a six month recovery time before we impregnate them again. We've begun with a small test group of volunteers at the facility. So far, the results are astonishing. We hope other quadrants will follow our example. If the entire country follows us, in two generations, we may once again see a return of women into society. There is hope, but only if the federal government allows us to operate the way we need to for the betterment of future generations." He paused and glanced at the crowd once again. "I know this does little for the men waiting now, but the old system was just not successful, and the women in our facility say they prefer this method to being handed over to random men. There is so much less risk to our women that I'm confident other quadrants may soon follow our lead."

"Thank you, Jonathan, for that report. Now for the weather..."

Krista turned off the television, shaking.

Jared came in and sat down next to her. "You okay?"

"No. I made the mistake of watching the morning news. The Northeast isn't doing the lotto any more. Instead, they're just implanting female embryos into women. I wonder if it's even those women's eggs. I bet it's total genetic engineering."

Jared shook his head sadly. "I wondered how long that was going to take. The lottery has become so restricted that I'm not surprised at all. It's too bad. There's going to be a lot of social unrest there. Well, the good news is Steve is putting breakfast on the table. Want to join me?"

"Yes."

They assembled at the table, but Brax was absent. "Where's Brax this morning?" Jared asked. Krista was relieved that she didn't have to be the one to vocalize the question.

"He's been in his office all night. I think his writer's block has broken."

"Great, he was getting a bit surly lately. I can't wait to read it, whatever he's writing. The last one ended so badly," Mal said.

"Oh, don't spoil it, I've only begun," Krista cried.

Mal smiled. "I'd like to spend some time with you today. Maybe we could take a walk by the lake?"

"Security has to come with you," Max cautioned.

"I know. Anyway, Krista, would you join me?"

"I'd love to see the lake. I can hear it, but I haven't seen it yet."

Mal smiled. They ate in silence. Damon was the first to leave the table. His angry scowl told her clearly he wasn't pleased about something.

"DeAnthony is going back to work on Monday. Even though he has the time off, his crew isn't doing well without his leadership," Brax said.

"Bastards," DeAnthony muttered. "I hate to leave you so soon. We'll have Friday, and I hope you'll give me Sunday as well. I'll be gone for at least three weeks."

She nodded. "You can have both days."

He grinned widely at her. "You are wonderful." He leaned over and placed a soft kiss on her lips.

Mal cleared his throat. "Today is my day. You get two this week, so keep your lips to yourself."

She felt heat rising up her cheeks. She wanted to feel DeAnthony inside of her again. He was so amazing. It didn't hurt that his body was beautiful to look at too.

After they finished eating, Mal took her hand and led her outside. She noticed a man following them. It was one of the guards whom she knew lurked. He followed at a comfortable distance.

"It feels so weird being followed," she said.

Mal put his arms around her. They were the same height, both five four. She was glad she didn't have to crane her neck to look into his eyes. "Don't worry, sweetie, we can duck him if you want to rape me down by the lake."

She punched him in the arm and he feigned injury.

"Oh, domestic violence is never the solution, my dear," Mal scolded.

She rolled her eyes. "Don't worry, when I get violent, I'll let you know so you can hide."

"Very considerate. I'm going to miss you when I leave for my tour."

"How soon do you have to go?" She didn't like the idea of Mal leaving either; his humor was delightful, most of the time.

"Not this Friday, but the following. I have a show in Little Rock on Saturday night. My staff will get there first and start getting things set up. I just have to show up and be funny. They do all the hard work."

"I doubt it's that simple for you. I imagine there's a lot you need to be worried about."

"I'm extra nervous. I'm sure my lottery success is national news, and I don't know how that'll play into my new material or the reaction I'll get from my fans. I just hope the religious wackos and conspiracy nuts stay away. We did hire some extra security, but I hope I'm just being overly cautious."

"Me too. Will you call me while you're gone and let me know how everything went?"

"You really care, don't you?" He pulled back and she glanced up to see his eyebrows raised and his eyes wide.

"Don't be so surprised. Why wouldn't I care?"

"It's not as if we romanced you into coming to live with us. I guess I expected you to be relieved that some of us were going. I know this rotation isn't natural."

"It is what it is. I'll deal, just like you guys have to deal. I would like to be your friend. Some of you are doing better than the others, but it can't be easy to share."

Mal's face scrunched up. "I'm going to have a talk with Damon about yesterday. All he ever talked about before was how much he wanted a wife and a family. You're the closest any of us will ever get to that dream and here he went and treated you like...I don't know, but I didn't like it."

"Don't talk to him. It'll only make things worse. I think he feels like I'm playing favorites, or I'm having some kind of go at making this into a game. It's not a game. You guys are my only shot at a normal life too. At least as normal as life can be now. I don't want anyone to hurt. I want us to be a family too. I don't want to lose my children, but I don't want to lose whatever stability I can have here either. Life sucks so much right now."

"You're preaching to the choir, sweetheart. I've always wanted a child, but the idea that my future son might have to live a lonely life bothers me, worse if you bring my daughter into this terrible world, she'll be taken away and Given without her consent. When I lost my mom, I realized how much family really was worth. Family has been a dream I never thought I'd have."

"It might be worse than that," she said, looking into Mal's beautiful, green eyes. "I saw there's a quadrant not 'giving' anymore. They're impregnating women with female embryos. If there are no boys born, then the world isn't going to be any better off. These girls are just going to grow up to be bred too. A world without any kind of true family frightens me. What makes us human is what we love. Take that away and there's not much left." Shuddering, she squeezed Mal's hand.

He nodded. "You're so right. The lottery has become

more restrictive in the last ten years, and almost impossible during the last two, but there's still hope in it. Take away hope and you end up with a world more lost than this one. I don't know if I want a child to endure that, but I know I don't want to lose you. Krista, you are hope. You are the most precious thing in the world to me."

He grinned. "Damn it, woman, I'm not good at being serious, so don't look at me like that. I'm trying to explain how I feel to you. I want you to know that I'm not madly in love with you, but my feelings are so much more important. Meeting you, seeing you as a person instead of a mythical creature, it reminds me that life will go on. I was feeling hopeless, as if I didn't want to live. I thought about suicide, a lot actually, but I haven't felt like that since you showed up. Thank you for giving me hope. I'm a funny guy, they pay me to be funny, but on the inside there's a lot of darkness. My mom was the fun in my childhood, when she died, I lost something special. I'd forgotten how nice it is to have a female around the house. I'm not going to let Damon hurt you again. He won't be alone with you, unless you request it. From now on, you chose a second, someone to make sure you're ready for him."

She hadn't thought of that. After the debacle with Max, she hadn't planned to have more than one of them with her at a time, but Mal had a good plan. Damon would have his turn, but she'd have someone there, giving her more than a harsh painful moment of hell. In an ideal world, she'd never have to go to Damon's bed, but nothing about this world was ideal.

"I like the way you think, funny man," Krista said, smiling.

Mal smiled back and the dark mood lifted. They walked, holding hands, the guard a forgotten shadow at their backs. A loon cried and Mal pointed out the bird as he landed on the lake, rippling the clear water.

"He's beautiful!" Krista cried.

"This place has become much more beautiful in the last couple of days." Mal brushed a lock of hair behind Krista's ear. He pulled her closer. The sun reflected off the lake, making his blond hair glow with a golden sheen.

She sighed as his lips descended. She liked his honesty. She wasn't the love of his life, but she was something important to him, and that was good enough for her. He wasn't the love of her life either, but she liked him, and if she could give him some kind of comfort, then it made the insanity of their situation bearable.

His hand stroked the back of her neck and he deepened the kiss, stroking the inside of her mouth with his tongue. His other arm locked tightly around her back, and she placed her hands on his shoulders. There was something so wonderful about feeling the breeze and smelling the freshness of the lake that she let herself become lost in sensation. No thoughts, only feelings ruled her. She felt Mal's erection pressing against her hip.

He suddenly backed away, clearing his throat. "I'm sorry."

"Oh, don't be sorry, Mal," she whispered, moving forward to touch his cheek gently. He grasped her hand and turned his face into her touch, kissing her palm. Then he let go of her hand and stepped away.

"I don't want to just use you, Krista. I don't want to demand that you immediately go to my bed, but I don't know if I can stop at just a kiss, so I need to cool off."

He gave her no warning before he dove into the lake. She cried out in surprise and anxiety.

The guard materialized out of the bushes and hurried to her side. "Are you all right, Miss?"

"Mal jumped in the lake," she replied, feeling like an idiot. When her funny man finally surfaced, she let go of the breath she'd been holding. "You scared ten years off my life, I thought you'd drowned. You were under forever."

Mal laughed. "I needed something cold. Want to join me?"

"No. I can't swim, and I don't think I'd like the cold water. Aren't there snakes in there?"

"Yep, and it's right between my legs. Come on in and I'll show you my pet python."

She couldn't help it. He was funny. Krista laughed, shaking her head. "It would serve you right if a crocodile showed up and bit your python in half!"

"Don't worry, baby, no crocodiles in Minnesota. My python is completely safe."

"Look out, sir!" the guard shouted, drawing his gun. Krista screamed and jumped away from the armed man.

The gun fired, and Mal screamed with pain. Krista's eyes widened as Mal grabbed the snake that had bit him by the tail and flung it away. The guard hadn't fired in time. A water moccasin had bitten Mal's shoulder.

"We have to get him to a hospital!" Krista shouted. The guard pushed her back when she tried to go to the water's edge to help her friend.

"Stay back, Miss, there may be more." The guard helped Mal out of the water. Krista and the guard helped Mal to the house.

"What's your name?" Krista asked the guard.

"Timothy Jordan. I'm sorry I wasn't fast enough, Miss."

"Please call me Krista. This wasn't your fault." She turned

her attention back to Mal and held him tighter. "I'm seeing a pattern of epic failure in your spontaneous antics." He didn't look well, and that made her nervous.

Mal had the nerve to grin. "You laughed, and I didn't manhandle you in the great outdoors. The way I see it, success. Damn, my shoulder hurts."

"Timothy, could you get him to the car? I'll grab him some dry clothes and tell the boys. We have to get him to the hospital."

"You can't go Miss—Krista. It's too dangerous. In the chaos of the emergency room, there is too great a chance you could be attacked or taken."

"I want to make sure he'll be okay." Krista glared at the guard.

"You really care?" Mal sounded awed.

"Yes. Blockhead. I don't want you to be alone at the hospital."

"I really screwed up my night. They better not plan to keep me for observation."

"I don't think you should go raising your heart rate with venom in your blood. Think of something nice and calming."

"Can't, sex is on my brain."

They were close to the house, Krista ran ahead while Timothy took Mal toward the large garage.

"Guys! Mal's been bitten by a snake! We need to get him to the hospital!" Krista screamed as she ran toward Mal's room. She went upstairs and opened his dresser drawer. Pushing aside an ancient *Playboy*, she managed to find him dry socks and underwear. In another drawer, she found pants and a t-shirt.

"What's going on?" DeAnthony asked, concern heavy in his tone.

"Mal jumped in the lake and a water moccasin bit him. We have to get him to the hospital."

"You aren't going anywhere, but I'll ride along." He took the clothes out of her hands. "It'll be okay," he said.

She could see the anxiety in his face as he rushed out of the room and through the patio doors. Krista stood at the large windows and watched him running toward the garage. The adrenaline crashed in her system and she sat down on the floor, her clothes damp on the side she'd used to help Mal to the house; she started crying.

Braxton came into the dining room. "What happened?" He looked worried.

"Mal jumped in the lake, and he was bitten by a snake."

"What kind of snake?"

She cried harder. "Water...moccasin...shoulder."

"That idiot. Where is he now?"

"Timothy and DeAnthony are taking him to the emergency room. He said he'd call."

"Come here," Brax ordered, helping her off the floor. He held her as she cried. When she'd let out her worry, she looked up into Brax's handsome face. His blue eyes were dark. "It wasn't your fault, Kristannie."

"I know. Nothing goes right for him, does it?"

Brax sighed. A small grin curved his sexy, full lips. "Mal is wonderful, but he doesn't tend to learn from his mistakes. He thinks with his heart, seldom his head. The moment he calls, I'll give you the phone." She nodded. "Let's get you into some dry clothes. Something came for you while you were fighting snakes at the lake." She raised her eyebrow. "Your clothing order, or I guess I should call it ours."

She smiled. As worried as she was about Mal, she'd never had a whole box of clothing, not since she'd been a very little girl. Brax carried the extremely large box upstairs. He set it on her bed and took his pocketknife out, slicing the packing tape carefully.

"Here you go, a whole wardrobe."

Krista dove into the box. When she'd unpacked everything, she frowned.

"What's the matter, not what you expected?"

"No, it's wonderful, but…"

"But what?"

"We forgot underwear, bras, and socks."

Brax laughed. "I don't want to see you wearing our underwear. I think we can get some of those things locally. A few stores still carry that type of stuff. You also had a list of toiletries that no one has gotten yet. I'll call DeAnthony on his cell and see if he can pick up a few things on the way home."

She nodded. Brax took his cell out of his pocket. "Hey. You there yet?" Brax said into the sleek, touch screen smart phone. "Ah, mmm, yeah."

These sounds weren't telling her much about Mal's condition. She bit her lip, watching Brax's face for any signs things were bad.

"Okay. Hey, before you come back, could you go get those things on Krista's list?" There was a pause and he frowned. "I'll email it." He stood listening. She watched anxiously, wishing she could hear. "Okay. See you later." Brax slid his thumb across the screen, hanging up and locking the device. "Mal will call you when they get him settled. He's going to be spending the night."

She felt irrational disappointment. She realized she'd wanted to give her funny man a special night.

"Hey, cheer up. Would you stay with me tonight?" Brax asked.

She was surprised. He'd been a bit distant since they'd shared the amazing sex. "I thought you were mad at me."

"Why would I be mad?"

"I don't know. I haven't seen you much since the other night—morning."

"I've been busy on my new novel. You've inspired me."

"Really? Things just feel off between us. Maybe I'm being foolish."

He looked down and frowned. "Okay, I might be a little jealous too. I'm also pissed at myself for letting Damon hurt you. I thought he'd make things right once he had you alone, but he didn't, did he?"

"No, he didn't. Mal had a great idea, bring a second in next week. I don't want to be alone with him again."

"Who will you ask?"

"You."

"Okay." Brax smiled. He typed something into his phone then put it in his pocket.

"What was that, a sex reminder?" Krista giggled.

"No, your underwear request. I emailed that list you made, good thing I put it in my phone. I added socks, bras, and underwear. I took a guess on your sizes, hope he brings a receipt."

She giggled at the idea of one of *her* men walking up to

the returns counter to exchange women's underwear.

Brax helped her put away her new clothes. She chose a plain, purple t-shirt and jeans. Her undergarments were fine, so she kept them on. She changed her clothes and Brax watched her, his eyes darkening. She realized she liked knowing he wanted her. Even if she was the last woman on Earth, at least for these men, she could see his genuine attraction to her. The afternoon sun shining in the window illuminated him. Fancifully, she thought he looked like a dark angel. He was handsome, but there was more to her feelings than just liking the way he looked.

They went downstairs. Max and Jared were watching a movie. She and Brax joined them and filled them in on Mal's losing battle with the snake.

"Well, we need to replace Timothy," Max stated. "The man's clearly a bad shot if he missed the snake."

"He did hit it, just too late to keep it from biting Mal," Krista defended the guard. "I like him, so I hope you change your mind."

Max grunted, dropping the subject of firing the man.

"Speaking of employees," Jared said, "your companion is coming tomorrow. He holds a culinary degree and his resume states he's an accomplished painter. His name is Lee Young."

She nodded, still unsure about the companion thing.

"Cool. It's weird, hiring a friend."

"I'm sure he'll be happy to know you. Give it a try."

"I will. Thanks for doing that, Jared."

"We're all footing the bill," Max added.

"Thanks, Max, to all of you. I'm lucky to be here."

Max grunted. "It's not Thursday yet, maybe you'll change your mind."

She put her hand on his. "I know you won't hurt me."

Max frowned, but placed his hand on top of hers. She felt Brax tense. Jared didn't look too happy either. She and Max pulled away at the same time, realizing they were creating tension. The phone rang, causing her to jump. Her emotions were on high alert after everything that'd just happened. Brax grabbed the house phone from its base. Max pressed *pause* on the DVD player.

"Hello." After a brief pause, Brax frowned, asking, "Are you sure that's best?" Another pause and then he nodded. "All right, if the doctor okays it. Hang on and I'll let you talk to Krista." He handed the phone to her.

"Hello?"

"Hey, gorgeous, I'm going to make it home. Doc said I'll live," Mal said with weariness in his voice.

"Are you sure you shouldn't be in the hospital? I won't make you wait a week, I swear. Don't do anything foolish. I hope you don't plan on any more dangerous antics," Krista scowled.

"The doctor gave me the okay to come home. We've just got to wait for my discharge and then we'll be stopping at the store for you. It might get a little late."

"I'll wait for you in my room if you get back after supper. Just don't do anything counterproductive to the doctor's orders."

"I won't. I'm sorry about the way today turned out. I was hoping to spend time with you, just the two of us."

"Well, next time don't let your python invite friends," she replied, chuckling.

The men in the room gave her a strange look, and she laughed even harder. Brax's scowl pierced her with guilt and she stopped laughing. She realized he was not going to get the night with her he'd been hoping to have. Even if she'd rather be with him, it was Mal's night.

"See you soon," she said to Mal.

"See you tonight, sweetheart. I promise, my python doesn't bite."

Laughing once again, she hung up. "Funny man is coming home," she told the men.

"I think he should remain in the hospital for observation," Jared replied. The young doctor-in-training didn't look happy.

"He's so damn stubborn."

Jared hit the *play* button on the DVD player remote. The movie began again. They watched the World War Two drama in silence. Brax put his arm around her, and both Jared and Max shifted uncomfortably. Max took her hand again. Jared pouted on the other end of the "L" shaped sofa. Krista hated the tension, but after a few moments, everyone seemed to relax again. The movie was almost finished when Damon joined them, sitting next to his brother in silence. He didn't look at Krista or the men who were touching her.

"Supper is ready to be served," Steve said, popping his head into the room.

Krista felt a massive relief to have an excuse to flee the tension. She was the first one up and out of the room. Steve almost ran in his haste to be away from her when she started for the dining room.

"I'll be having one of those paid companions here soon, so you don't have to worry about your job," Krista told the housekeeper.

"Thanks," Steve replied, but he was still rushing away.

She sighed. Nothing was ever easy, not even befriending the only person she knew whom she didn't have to sleep with or wasn't paid to like her. Then she remembered her email. Maybe one of her teachers had replied to her.

The meal was delicious as usual. She and the four
remaining men enjoyed Steve's bounty of roast beef,
vegetables with cream sauce, and cheesy potatoes. He'd baked
a strawberry pie, another of her favorite desserts. Strawberries
were out of season, each meal she ate since arriving had
certainly cost a fortune.

"Jared, could you help me with the internet? I want to
check my email."

"Yeah, no problem. I'm almost done." He eagerly scooped
the last of his pie into his mouth. "Want to go now?" he said
around the mouthful, but she was still able to understand him.

"That'd be awesome."

They went into the game room and he grabbed the
wireless keyboard after turning on the computer sitting next to
the big screen TV. He turned on the screen and she watched the
welcome message pop up. After a moment, he hit the browser
and began typing. When he had her email pulled up, she took
the keyboard.

"Do you want me to leave?"

"It's up to you. I doubt they'd reply back with anything so
personal you can't see it."

He shrugged. "I'll give you some privacy. See you later."

When he left, she clicked on the inbox. She only had one
email. It was from Miss Neal.

Dearest Krista:

I miss you, my dear girl. You've always had such a good head on your shoulders, I'm sure you'll be able to navigate your new home life. Just remember to show them your heart and you'll find a balance. I remember when I was in your shoes, I wish now I hadn't held myself back and expressed the different levels of emotion the experience created. They may have chosen to keep me if I'd given them who I really was instead of being afraid of them seeing the real me.

I have some sad news. Cina has run away. She was never as realistic as you, my dear, and being alone here took a toll on her that we didn't see until it was too late. I hope she is safe, wherever she is. If she returns, I will give her your email address. I can only pray she is unharmed. She doesn't know how dangerous the world really is now. I believe she'll attempt to go to her family, we have watchers keeping an eye on her father and brothers, but she hasn't gone to them as far as we can tell. We

need to get her back into the safety of the
facility. If she contacts you, please help us
convince her to come home. Her Giving Day is
not so far off.

    I wish you the best, and I look forward to
hearing from you again soon. I can't wait to
hear you've become pregnant and found a
secure home. If you have a daughter, know I
will look out for her as if she was my own.

    Your friend,
    Mary Neal

Cina hated the protection facility, but Krista had never believed she'd actually escape. She hoped her friend made it to family. Canada was her most likely destination. There was supposedly an underground network of men who believed women should have a choice and that the US government was using the lack of women to achieve their objective of genetically engineering a smarter, healthier population. She didn't doubt there wasn't some truth to the suspicion, but she knew there was no guarantee of protection in Canada.

    While the country offered any woman asylum upon request, without a network of friends or family who were willing to be on guard for you twenty-four seven, the odds of enduring rape or abduction were frighteningly high. There were "female friendly" communities who guarded against strangers and would shot to kill intruders, but without a support system, running was not the safe choice. At least the lottery gave you a chance to find men who would care. After what Damon had done to her, she hated the idea of another man forcing himself on her, and the thought of that happening to Cina made her want to cry. Cina wasn't as strong as she was; she'd been far more sheltered and pampered. Harsh reality hadn't ever been easy for her friend to accept.

Krista deleted the email and then deleted it from the trash, not wanting any of the men to know her friend escaped, but not really sure why. Taking a deep breath, she began searching the internet. What would happen to Cina now? She needed to know more than she did. She knew how to delete browsing history after a brief tutorial from Jared and she was unusually alone. Reading the numbers of women fleeing to Canada and the number of families who'd left after the government had demanded all ten-year-old girls enter the protection facilities across the country made her realize Cina did have a chance, albeit slim. If she found the right people, people who wanted to make her their agenda of goodwill, she'd be all right. But if the wrong people found her...

Severely disturbing YouTube videos made her cringe. She

closed her eyes. *Private leaked home footage of women who weren't compliant to their six* was one title and showed girls surrounded by military men holding them down as the men received a quick tutorial of government-approved bondage. Horrible images of girls crying and screaming, begging, but no help came, just hard, punishing cocks. The rape was far more brutal than she'd ever imagined. What she saw made Damon look like a saint. There was special equipment, to ensure no injury happened to the girl. It was monstrous. Krista shook. Suddenly, she felt lucky to be here, even if she knew in reality that she wasn't any freer than this brutalized woman was. Tears spilled down her cheeks. Her heart broke for the traumatized woman. By the third man, she'd stopped thrashing and just laid cursing and moaning on the bed. Krista closed the browser. She couldn't watch another moment. She deleted her browsing history. *Do my six know just how far they can actually go?*

For the rest of the afternoon and into the evening she was quiet, worried about her friend. If the men noticed her introspectiveness, they didn't say anything to her about it. She noticed Braxton watching her, but ignored his curious gaze.

Her six talked and joked, but Krista was too sullen to join in.

"We're going to play Xbox. What to play?" Jared asked.

She shook her head. "I think I'm going to bed."

"Don't worry about Mal. He'll be all right."

"Thanks, I'm worried about a lot right now," she replied cryptically. It was better he think she was worried about Mal than he probe deeper for the truth. *Should I have run like Cina? Is this really the life I want? Can six men with their own agenda ever make me happy?* In her heart, she knew she wanted a real family, not this mockery. Cina's escape reminded her that she did have a choice. Danger lurked away from this compound built to disguise her prison as a home. She looked at Jared. "Goodnight."

He gave her a sad smile. "Sleep well."

Nodding, she turned before he could see the tears threatening to spill from her eyes. Her feet had just hit the stairs when a hand gripped her elbow. Krista didn't turn around. The small scent of light, musky cologne told her Brax held her arm. She didn't want him to see her cry.

"I want you to be with me tonight. I haven't been able to stop thinking about my night, or my morning. I think you might be an addiction."

His words sent a thrill through her, but it wasn't enough to dispel the melancholy she'd been feeling. He might just be saying those words to manipulate her. She was an agenda, after all. None of these men loved her. If she allowed herself to love them, then she was deluding herself.

"It's not your night."

"Would you rather be with Mal? Is that why you're upset, Kristannie, you wanted him?"

"What I want doesn't matter anymore."

"That's not true. What's happened since this morning? Last night I thought…never mind."

"I'm going to bed. Goodnight, Braxton."

The hand on her arm tightened. His body shifted and she knew her words had hit him hard. If she looked at his face, her resolve would crumble, so she focused on a single spot of discolored carpet on the stairs. *A woman would've known better than to choose white carpet.*

"Sleep well. I hope you'll feel differently next Monday." His voice sounded strained.

For a moment, she almost allowed herself to turn to him. Losing herself in his arms, in his body, it would be so easy. She needed to be careful not to allow herself to indulge in a fantasy world.

This would be so much easier if Cina hadn't run, if Krista hadn't realized she'd been a coward. She'd taken the easy way out, and now she felt ashamed. She'd let her government use her. Each sexual encounter might just as well have been performed by congress instead of these men. She had to find a balance again. Courage had never been her strong suit, because she hated conflict and the two usual lived together, simultaneously in the moment, one needed to draw on inner strength. Her friend had courage. All she had was a future of servitude. Her body would provide these men release while her womb provided her country with citizens who would grow up in a choice-less world. Bleak. Tears tickled her cheeks.

Braxton let go of her arm, and she went to bed.

Chapter 8

Krista felt a hand on her back. She shrieked, turning so quickly her neck ached. Half sitting, half laying on her stomach, she peered into the darkness. It was Mal. "How are you feeling?" she muttered sleepily.

"Horny."

"The doctors give you anything for it?" She wasn't in the mood for sex and hoped he'd take the hint.

He snorted. "He knew I had a home remedy waiting for me. It's still my night. You okay with me crawling in bed with you?"

She paused. She'd fallen asleep feeling the sting of having told Brax no just because she could. She really wanted to be with Brax, but her body wasn't her own anymore and allowing him an extra night just didn't feel right. She wanted to hold whatever true freedom she could, like a precious thing in need of protection.

Dim hallway light illuminated Mal's face, he looked determined. Her funny man sat on the bed. She liked Mal, but with the new knowledge that her men could abuse her, taught by and endorsed with a government stamp of approval, she just wanted to be alone to think. Yes, she knew these men weren't the worst she could have "won", if she was willing to let herself look at the lottery in reverse, but they were still her "keepers" and at the moment that made them feel like the enemy.

"It's late, I'm tired." She hoped he'd do the gentlemanly thing and let her go back to sleep.

"I'm a little groggy, but I'm not going to miss my turn, baby." *Nope.*

"I think you should rest. It's been an eventful, almost fatal, day."

"All the more reason to have you, life is short." He touched her breast through her thin, silk nightgown. Flinching, she scooted away. He looked upset. "It's my night. You technically have to sleep with me."

She just adored his use of the word "technically" as if he'd call the sex police and they'd hold her down for him. Hell, he could actually do that. She shuddered, remembering the YouTube video.

"Mal, I'm just not feeling it…"

"Bullshit! You've given everyone else their night when it's been their turn. You get sex every day, but we have to wait."

"Oh, and I'm *so* delighted to be *so* in demand. You have no idea how I feel. At first, everything was novel, I sort of thought I could keep you all happy and be able to just let you guys have sex with me every day. Please let me go back to sleep."

She began to roll over. He took her shoulder and turned her to look at him again. "Damn it, Krista, no. I want you. I don't want to wait until Sunday. Please. I need this."

The pain in his voice made her heart ache. She didn't want this, any of it, but she didn't want to go back into the protection facility. She just wanted one man, not six. She wanted romance, not just sex. She doubted she could truly love six men, but she wanted to be their friend. They were all she had. Tears filled her eyes. She wasn't being fair, but she was hurting too, and the worst part was she didn't have anyone she could confide in.

He ran his hand through his hair. "Don't cry," he whispered. His thumb wiped at one of the tears on her face. "Don't." Mal stood and left the room without another word, he didn't look back.

She closed her eyes, her pillow soon felt damp. Sleep took it's time returning.

* * * *

Krista walked slowly down the stairs, late for breakfast as usual. Hearing her name caused her to pause.

"I don't know. Maybe she's on her period. Don't they get

moody around that time?"

"No, according to the information packet they gave us she's not premenstrual," Jared spoke in his most doctor-knows-best voice.

They gave them a packet about my cycle. She wrapped her arms around her chest, feeling another quick burst of violation.

"I thought she was upset because you were hurt, but it's something else," Jared said.

"She was on the computer yesterday. I should've looked at what she was doing, but it just felt wrong to spy," DeAnthony chimed in.

Krista bit her lip, worried she'd just lost a small freedom.

"Well, no more fucking internet for her," Mal said. I'm not the kind of guy who supports forcing a woman..." He coughed. "...Damon. Nevertheless, I don't think we need to let her get so damn elevated in her belief she is in charge. No, when it's your night, it's your night and that's it." He sounded terribly bitter.

Krista cringed. Her fears had been spot on.

"I don't want anyone hurting her. She's not a sex toy or a prostitute. This polygamist situation wasn't her choice any more than it was ours. We need to give her some time. Whatever upset her needs to be resolved. Maybe she's still upset about Damon," Jared said quietly.

"Damn it, I didn't beat her. Stop acting like I'm some sex-crazed monster!"

"Okay, we agree we won't hurt her. It's going to have to come down to her realizing she does have a commitment to us. If she's not pregnant in a few months, they'll take her," Max added.

"I don't want her hurt." Brax growled.

She started back down the stairs, having heard enough.

"Good morning," Krista said quietly. Heat crept up her neck and burned under her cheeks. She knew they could see her embarrassment and didn't try to hide it. "I'm sorry about last night, Mal. You do have Sunday. In my defense, I've never been much of a morning person. I guess it's time to be real here. I thought I could do this, but I guess I didn't realize how *this* included sex every single day. It overwhelmed..." She sighed. "I don't know. I realize now how little control I have over my life here. At least at the protection facility I controlled my body, at least until the end. I know there's no going back to that. I want what every woman since the dawn of time has wanted—love. I know you guys aren't the worst six I could belong to, but it's all so hard. I'm sorry. I don't want drama. I want to try to make some kind of happiness. It all hit me yesterday. I realized I wasn't as brave as I thought. It was a big pill to swallow and left me...not myself. Sorry." She didn't look at them as she finished. Instead, she looked down at the poached egg on toast Steve sat on the table in front of her. She took a quick sip of orange juice.

"Okay. I get it, really I do. Let's agree that from now on you'll save your inner turmoil for Sundays. Just not this Sunday, you know you have to get pregnant. The pressure is on until then. We don't want to lose you, and you don't want to be taken away, do you?" Mal said.

"I don't," she said quickly, looking at the worried and unhappy faces of her assembled six. "I'm sorry Mal bore the blunt of my soul searching. I really thought I could do this without a meltdown, but that's asking a lot. I know a lot of guys would've have just forced themselves on me." She looked pointedly at Damon. "I appreciate you giving me time, Mal. I'm sorry you have to wait."

His grim look told her he was sorry he had to wait too. "Damn, it's just been a dream of mine to be inside a woman. So far, other than oral, I'm still a virgin."

DeAnthony snorted. "Don't tell Rosie Palm that, poor old Rose is usually chaffed from all the lovin'."

Mal scowled at his best friend. A few of the men chuckled, but the ones still on the waiting list didn't look any happier than Mal about the situation.

"I just want to be happy," Krista whispered.

"So do we," Jared said. "We will be. This just needs time. We have to get used to the arrangement, okay?"

Krista gave him a small smile. "Okay."

They finished breakfast. She didn't eat much, but she had a second glass of the delicious orange juice. Krista stood, ready to leave the uncomfortable gathering.

"Today is going to be a busy one for you, Krista," Brax said. "Your social worker is coming to check on your welfare. We also have our first interview for a companion scheduled. Do you want to cancel the companion?"

She sighed. "No, I just want to get it over with."

* * * *

Krista sat at the kitchen table, waiting for the interview with her new "friend" nervously. There was a knock on the door. Steve showed a tall, lanky man into the room. He walked with a flourish of confident grace. This newcomer held out his hand to Brax. A hot look on his face told Krista the companion candidate found her favorite just as appealing as she did.

"Hello. My name is Lee Young. I'm here for the companion position."

"Thank you, Lee, please have a seat." Brax seemed a bit uncomfortable under the man's hungry gaze. Krista immediately gave the man a mental point. She liked seeing Brax squirm.

He walked over to her, looking her in the eyes. "You must be Kristannie."

"Call me Krista."

"The agency tells me you'd like to learn to cook and paint," Lee said, sitting down and folding his hands in his lap with an exuberant flourish.

"Yes, I'd like to very much. I've never had to have a friend 'purchased' before. Please tell me why you chose this line of work?"

"Well, honey, I've had a hard time being me. Not everyone accepts gay men, even now, so this was a job that appealed to me because of my sexual orientation. I can be me."

Two points for Lee. That response is honest enough for me. "Reasonable. Tell me about yourself, Lee."

"My mom survived the plague. I was a lucky kid. She died two years ago, the disease weakened her, and the last five years of her life she was disabled. It wasn't easy. I did all I could to protect her, but she was raped twice. She was my best friend. When she died, I applied for my position as a companion. I worked for a woman in Duluth until six months ago."

"Why did you quit?" Krista was curious. She'd never have been so forthright questioning a real friend, but she was interviewing him for a job.

"I didn't. She died."

"Oh, I'm so sorry to hear that. Was she ill?"

"Suicide," he whispered. His eyes looked haunted.

"I think we've heard enough. Thanks for coming, Lee." Brax spoke gruffly as Lee opened his mouth to elaborate. Brax grabbed the man by his arm, pulling him to his feet.

"I didn't get to show you samples of my art," Lee cried desperately.

"That's fine, we'll be in touch," Brax said, all but pushing the man out the door. He looked over Braxton's shoulder helplessly.

"Wait, I'd like to see them," Krista called as Brax pushed the man out the door.

She heard the lock snick as Brax turned back around. "We'll have them send someone else tomorrow."

"I wanted to hear more. I really think he might be right for the job."

Brax scowled. "I…" He ran his hand through his hair. "Damn it, Krista, no depressing people. I like you happy."

"If you don't bring him back, I won't be happy. I think Lee could really be someone I'd feel friendship with. He's experienced in this, more so than I am."

"Yeah, sounds like he did great with his last position," Brax grumbled.

"Who knows why she did it, but I doubt painting and

cooking drove her to kill herself. I'd like you to hire him. You just don't like him because he looked at you like he did."

"It had nothing to do with that. Just, humor me please. Let's find someone with a more—acceptable backstory."

"Life isn't some novel with backstories. If we're going to do this, let me pick someone I like because they're real. If I have to have a 'fake' friend, at least let them have a 'real' life story." She put her hands on her hips, glaring at him.

His lips compressed into a thin line. "I just want to do what's right for you. I know something is bothering you. I don't want you to be unhappy, Kristannie. No matter what you believe, I do care about you. More than I probably should, considering you belong to all of us. I want your heart, not just your body."

His words thrilled her, even if she knew she shouldn't trust them. He was a man who made his living with words. He could easily just be saying what he knew she wanted to hear.

"Okay, if you want Lee, he'll be your companion," Brax said unhappily.

Krista squealed and bounced off her chair. She threw her arms around Braxton. Steve cleared his throat. They turned. Standing with the housekeeper was a short man with a long face that reminded Krista of a rat. Rat Face carried a briefcase and wore a very nice, tailored suit.

"Hello, I'm Ken Bentley. I'm Kristannie's caseworker."
He spoke quickly, extending his hand.

Braxton shook it and Krista did the same. They all sat
down at the table.

"I'm pleased to see affection," Ken stated as he opened his
case and started pulling out some papers. "Will the others be
joining us?"

"Steve, could you please tell everyone Mr. Bentley is
waiting?" Brax asked politely.

Steve hurried away. Mr. Bentley looked pointedly at Brax.
"Is your housekeeper straight?"

"Yes," Brax replied truthfully. The caseworker frowned.

"I'm getting a companion, a gay companion, will that
resolve the issue?" Krista said nervously. She didn't like Ken
Bentley, but she couldn't put her finger on the reason why.

"I see," the man said vaguely. He looked at some
paperwork he'd pulled from his briefcase. "You'll have to have
the companion here during the hours the straight male
employee is on staff. He lives in a separate building, so as long
as you have cameras monitoring his home at all times and he's
only in the residence when Krista is chaperoned, there won't be
a problem. I've been reviewing the menus that you've sent and
they seem in order, however I noticed she was given wine. You
do realize this is an off-list item. It's counting against you. If

there's another instance of this, she'll be put back into lottery circulation."

Brax's quick intake of breath told Krista he didn't realize how serious the "special" dinner really was. "I'm very sorry. We won't be allowing it again."

Krista's anger rose. The men were talking about her as if she wasn't in the room. "I'd like to stay here, Mr. Bentley. I'm content with my placement."

"That's very nice, Kristannie, however your presence here is a privilege, and no great privilege comes without great responsibility. Do you understand me, Mr. Bray?"

"Yes. It won't happen again," Brax replied before gritting his teeth.

Krista squeezed his leg. The realization of how carefully they'd need to tread during this man's visit made sweat bead on her forehead and her palms began to feel moist.

"I've viewed her records from the protection facility and I see that next Monday is the most fertile day of her cycle. I'll have the forecast emailed to you later this week. Please print off the menstrual cycle tracker." He turned his attention in Krista's direction. "Please keep thorough records of your cycle. This will help you become pregnant by allowing us to track any changes to your fertility pattern and provide invaluable information to our experts in Washington. Will you be responsible for this? It will only help keep you placed here."

Krista nodded, feeling frantic. She'd tell them anything to keep herself from enduring this awkward process of a sexual meet and greet all over again with a new six.

"I'd expect you to allow all six men to have intercourse with you on Monday," the rat-faced man informed her coldly.

She shivered and bit her tongue in time to stop her declaration that Monday was just for Brax. Once he left, what they did with the schedule was their business. As long as she was pregnant quickly, they didn't need to know how many men she took on a night. Sitting with the cold, clearly uncaring social worker left Krista feeling dirty. Brax took her hand under the table.

"I'm pleased to see genuine affection, but emotion only goes so far," the man stated. "We need to see results. Your placement here is about pregnancy, not about romance. I'm sure you know that."

"Yes, I believe that was covered by the wonderfully informative video presentation I watched on my last day in the protection facility. Thanks for that, really helpful stuff." She couldn't stop her natural sarcasm and immediately regretted it as the man began scribbling furiously on his legal notepad. "I know my place, if that's what has you worried. These gentlemen have performed their duties well, and if I'm not already pregnant, I'm sure it'll happen soon."

Mr. Bentley glanced up over his glasses, and then began writing again. She gave Brax an apologetic look, but his quick grin told her he wasn't angry.

"I will be delighted to provide these fine men with many children. We are working at that diligently," she added. Once more, the social worker paused in his writing to look at her. She decided it was time to stop talking.

The others came in and sat down. Twenty tense minutes later, Mr. Bentley shook everyone's hands and left. Krista let go of an audible sigh of relief and slumped in her chair.

"Well, that was uncomfortable." Jared's words were met with nods of agreement.

"Damn, I think he hates us," Max added unhelpfully.

"Hey, dude's gotta do his job," Damon said.

Krista glared at him, and she wasn't the only one.

"Let's just make sure we do what needs doing and that Steve doesn't transmit the food list until we double check that only 'approved' foods appear," Jared suggested.

"So what are we doing about Monday? He wants us all to sleep with Krista. I know it's your day, Brax, but I think we should do our best to maximize her odds of pregnancy," DeAnthony said.

"I'd accept that, if Brax agrees to it. I'd like to spend the night in your arms again Brax, but how will you feel knowing I'm so…used." She looked down at her hands, studying her nails so she wouldn't have to see his face.

"I could never see you as *used*, Kristannie. If you're all right with it, then I can accept it. Take them as you want throughout the day, but I'd like us to have supper alone together in my room, and spend the night with you in my bed."

"I'd like that too."

"Sorry to interrupt the love fest, but tonight is my night. You okay with that?" Max asked. Krista thought his voice sounded a little off, as if he were nervous.

"Yes, Max. I'm okay with it. Where would you like to meet?"

"I'd like you to come to my room, whenever you're ready. I'm not too hungry. I think I might just as well skip supper. I'm going upstairs to watch TV." He left the room quickly and as soon as he was gone Jared snickered. Krista gave him a withering look and he quieted.

Steve started serving them supper. Krista loved the delicious cod, but she didn't overeat. Knowing that Max felt uncomfortable made her sad. He'd gone through something terrible and didn't want to hurt her. It made her want to give him the best she had inside to give. When she excused herself from the table, Brax grabbed her hand and squeezed it.

"Max can be a hard man. Do you want me to come with you?" There was worry in his eyes. She knew he was worried that Max might have another outburst.

"I think I'll be all right. Thanks for worrying about me." She leaned over and placed a kiss on his lips, as soft as a butterfly's flutter. There were a few grumbles from the others, but she ignored them. As much as she wanted harmony, they'd have to understand she needed to be human too. If she wanted to kiss Brax, they'd just have to accept it.

She went to her room and put on the dress Max had picked out for her the day they did the internet shopping. It was slutty, definitely not the kind of thing she'd buy. The sleeveless, black dress barely covered her ass. She brushed her teeth and combed her hair. Max was a hard man, Brax was right, but he'd also shown her a human side. He wasn't impossible to reach. Tonight, she wanted to reach him.

She closed her door and walked quietly down the hall. She heard the TV and saw a light, this was Max's room. Krista knocked softly. The door flew open. She stepped back, surprised.

"Sorry," he mumbled.

"No worries. Hi," Krista said as she walked inside. His room was tidy and very plain. Not a single personal effect sat on the dresser and no art or photos hung on the wall. The room looked empty.

"You don't have to do this, Krista. I'll tell them you did, if you like. I don't want you to feel forced," he said, and she noticed the twitch in his cheek.

"I know. That's why I'm willing. Thank you, Max, I promise this won't be rape."

"Really?" She could see how surprised he was.

"I mean it. I like you, Max."

He gave her a doubtful look.

"We didn't start off on the best foot, but I don't think you're an asshole...anymore."

He grinned. "Make yourself comfortable."

She began unzipping the side of her dress. The zipper was on the left side. Max stopped her hand. "Sit down. I want to relax with you a moment, just talk."

She nodded, feeling relieved. "Sounds good. So what do you want to talk about?"

"For starters, I hate your social worker. What a jerk!"

"Agreed." She giggled. Max smiled.

"His visit did make me think. Do you really want to be here? Would you be just as happy if they put you back on the lottery?"

"No. You guys, with the exception of Damon, have been really good to me. I know you've done more than what's expected. This isn't ideal, but it could be a lot worse. I saw things on the internet—terrible things."

"Damn internet, so that's what had you so riled up?"

"Yes, and if I want to look at it, I feel that I have the right to. That's the thing. You guys are letting me be human. The consequence is that I'm starting to care about you, but also that I'm not blind to what's going on in the world. Those things could happen to me, I need to know so I can be prepared."

He grunted. "I get it. I just don't want you to get upset. If you see something that gets under your skin like that again, just talk to one of us, me even, that way we'll understand. Geez, for all we knew you wanted a new placement."

"That wasn't it at all. I saw some men in military uniforms teaching guys how to restrain a woman without injuring her for sex. Damn it, I just don't get it."

"There's a big push to shut the lottery down. You know they've started it out East. One of these days, they might just throw you all back into custody and just go invitro. Things are getting worse. Those who don't know how to treat a woman—girls who can't accept things like you do—they're fucking it all up for the rest of us."

She made a thoughtful noise. "I didn't see it that way. I'm sure most don't. People tend to have tunnel vision when it comes to major life events."

"You're grounded. I was worried we'd get some drama queen, but so far you seem pretty normal."

"Gee thanks, I feel so special."

"I'm not Braxton. I don't have his ability to seduce you with words. I think I'll do a good job with my dick, but probably not my mouth—words, at least. We all have something to offer you, if you let us. Even Damon, I know he feels like shit. I was going to hit him, but he was beating himself up badly enough for both of us. We're all mad about this. He just really didn't realize how hard it was to share. I think he's jealous, and he's also not one who's going to be able to say the right words."

"You seem to be doing okay. I don't want lies or poetry. I want something real. I want a family, and even if this isn't exactly a fairytale, I want whatever joy we can have."

"Do you mean that?" Max's eyes grew wide. She could see the hope in his expression.

"I do. I want to be loved, and I know I can love you all, even if it's not all equal or perfect."

"I'll take what you can give me."

She reached out for him and he flinched. She dropped her arm, feeling hurt. After everything he'd said, his immediate rejection was shocking.

"I don't like to be touched," he mumbled.

"Sorry." She didn't know what else to say.

"Stand up," he ordered huskily. She did.

Max took hold of her zipper, and slowly began sliding it down. She stood still, listening to the sound of the teeth releasing. The fabric slipped to the floor with a whisper, pooling around her feet. She stepped out, naked. She hadn't worn a bra or panties. Max's quick intake of breath and tenting fabric at his crotch told her he liked her nudity.

"You're beautiful," he breathed.

She believed he thought she was. There was nothing but awe and honesty in his voice. "Thank you," she whispered.

"This matters to me. You matter. I appreciate what you're giving me. Can I leave the light on? I want to see you, all of you."

She'd rather have it dark—even after all the sex, she was still shy about her body—but it was a small thing to do for him. She nodded.

He was still dressed. Standing before him, she felt so strange to be the only naked person in the room. He ran his fingers gently down her arms. The sensation left her shivering.

"Are you cold?" he whispered.

"No," she replied quietly.

The only sound in the room was their heavy breathing. His fingers fell away from her arms when he reached her wrists and he lightly ran them over her collarbone. They moved lower, just above her breasts, and finally he touched the rise of them. His fingers were as soft as the merest whisper of butterfly wings over her skin. She sighed. She saw him visibly relax.

"I won't hurt you," he assured her.

"I know. Thank you, Max," she replied gently.

His eyes widened. She could see his surprise. His expression was priceless and put the smallest ghost of a smile on her face.

"Thank you," she said again.

"For what?" He scowled. Those big brown eyes went from saucers to narrow slits.

"I know it hasn't been easy, this situation. I've noticed how hard you've been trying to keep your temper in check. I was afraid of you at first, but I'm not anymore."

He lunged, pushing her roughly against the wall to her back. His hands imprisoned her wrists above her head and his mouth plundered hers with a passion that left her breathless. When he pulled back, just enough to speak, she saw the darkness in him. It stirred something wild inside of her she hadn't known was there.

"Don't decide you've tamed me just because I choose not to bite." He ground the words out, as if they hurt him.

"I didn't ask you to be tamed. I know you won't hurt me."

Disbelief filled his face. "I'm fucking holding you to the wall, woman."

"I know."

"You should be terrified."

A wickedness deep inside that she hadn't felt before gave her the urge to speak. She didn't let herself think about the words that tumbled out. "I don't want you to be gentle. I want to feel the real you, Max."

He gently pressed his forehead to hers. "You don't want that," he mumbled.

"I want to feel you, as you are. Don't hide from me, Max."

When he looked up at her, there was a tenderness in his expression she hadn't seen from him before. "Damn it, do you have to be like this…damn you."

She didn't think his words were a compliment and frowned.

He kissed her down turned lips gently, and chuckled. "I'm an animal."

"I don't care."

The humor slipped from his face. "Be careful what you wish for, Krista, I'm more than you can handle."

The words were a challenge. Whether intentional or not, he'd given her something she couldn't back down from. "Try me."

She found herself pulled from the wall and thrown to the bed. Max ripped his clothing off, literally. Buttons flew everywhere. One landed on her stomach and she looked at it, caught in a surreal disbelief. He was on top of her. The predatory expression on his face made her stomach do a summersault. He smiled, but the only thing she saw was the dark promise that he was right, she wasn't ready for the real him.

It was too late. His lips caught hers. He nipped her lower lip, and when she cried out with the strange pain and pleasure combination, his tongue thrust inside her mouth. Krista's whole body lay helpless under him. To her extreme self-loathing, she liked it. He stirred up something suppressed inside of her and she wrapped her arms around his neck, moaning into his mouth.

He stilled, just for a moment, and then his fingers began grasping desperately at her breasts, pulling and twisting her nipples until she cried out, arching her back. He kissed her neck, sucking the skin with punishing force. Her pussy creamed, desperate for more. All her own anger over the helplessness in her life seemed to mix with the hot need he was causing in her, making her wild to have him inside her, and make her forget everything except pleasure.

"Oh God, Max. Fuck me!"

He growled. "Not yet." He panted.

Her legs were jerked open violently, and she glanced down to see his dark head dip between her thighs. The first lick made her jump, the second tore a long, low moan from her. Her body was hypersensitive with her raging desire. He lapped at her in long hard stokes, and then stuck his tongue deep inside her pussy. She screamed, bucking her hips against his mouth.

A moment of disloyalty filled her. She knew Brax would hate to see how much she was enjoying Max. The devil on her shoulder shouted *fuck it* in her ear and she thrashed her head from side to side, whimpering.

"Please," she sobbed, tears filling her eyes. The sensation and emotions battered her, and the demon he'd awoken demanded satisfaction. He gathered her in his arms, straddling her hips, and his dick was inside of her with one powerful thrust. She moaned as the sensation of fullness gave way to the first stirrings of release. He moved inside of her, while simultaneously cradling her against his chest. She felt a deep sigh, almost a sob, shake his torso.

"Damn it, don't fucking cry. I... son-of-a-bitch, you feel good. Fuck yes!" He thrust harder and faster.

She tumbled blindly into the abyss of pleasure as sparks exploded behind her eyelids. His cock rubbed against her clit with each thrust at the awkward, but absolutely perfect, angle.

Her pleasure was greater than anything she'd ever experienced, and somehow she knew this was a onetime only deal between them. Two broken souls clawing for something beautiful in their dark world. Krista screamed, clutching him desperately, bucking against his hips. She sobbed, pressing her wet face against his shoulder as she came hard and well.

He stilled, then released inside of her. Max groaned, shuddering. He threw his head back and roared with his release. The intensity made her jump. Startled, she hung limply in his arms, and watched his face. Max had the most erotic sex-face she'd seen so far. There was absolute, artistic beauty in his orgasm and she relished the idea she'd put that expression there.

He collapsed beside her on the bed, but still cradled her tightly against him. His breathing slowly returned to normal and the smell of sex permeated the room. For a moment she let her muscles relax, floating in the afterglow of the best orgasm she'd ever enjoyed.

"Did I hurt you?" He sounded worried.

"No."

"You cried," he interrogated.

"Yes."

"Damn it, Krista, tell me what the fuck I did wrong."

"Nothing. It was—awesome," she muttered, feeling lame

at her pathetic description of a life-altering moment.

"You cried, don't lie to me. I don't want you to spare my feelings. Do you want a doctor? Should I at least have Jared come look at you?"

"Good Lord no, I'm fine." She took his face between her hands, forcing him to look at her, and felt guilty because she knew he didn't want this kind of connection. "Max. It was beautiful, perfect. Don't tell the others. This was frankly the best. It was something we'd never be able to duplicate. Everything just built up in me, like a volcanic eruption or something. I feel wonderful."

He grunted. She let go of his face and scooted back, knowing he'd said he didn't want to be touched. His hand reached for her, stopping her from going too far away. He lay his head down across from her on the mattress and began rubbing delightful lazy circles on her back. She sighed and they just looked at each other for a long time.

She reached out to move hair away from his eyes. He flinched and she pulled her hand back, averting her eyes.

"I've never felt so good," he muttered.

"Me either, I think we both just needed to let something out, and it choose sex to escape us. Thank you."

"Don't thank me. No wonder men used to kill for their women. Christ, I'd face an army for you right now." He made an unhappy noise before rolling onto his back to stare at the ceiling. His arm flopped across his chest. "Damn. No wonder so many of the old guys went nuts." He moved to his side, looking at her seriously. "You have to get pregnant. We can't lose you."

"I don't want to go either."

"If it's mine, would that bother you?" She sensed he was afraid of her answer.

"I'd be happy if you're the one who does the deed and knocks me up. My turn. If I have a son, will you protest me keeping him?"

"Christ no, as long as we all get our night, I don't see any problem with it, mine or someone else's, don't matter. I won't try and stop you."

She leaned forward and placed a gentle kiss on his mouth. He didn't stop her.

"Thank you. Goodnight, Max, that was wonderful." She stood and picked up her dress, slipping it over her head. He didn't stop her, or ask her to come back, but when she glanced back to give him a friendly, small smile, he looked sad. "Did you want me to stay?"

"No. Goodnight, Krista."

She nodded and shut his door quietly.

Chapter 9

Lee came into the house with his grand flourish. Krista
smiled. "Welcome. Thank you for accepting the job."

"Girl, I was shocked when I got the call. Never thought
you folks would be calling. I thought that dreamboat didn't like
me."

"He was just being Brax. No worries, come in and sit
down. Steve made coffee."

"Oh, it's been too long since I've had a cup of that wonder
brew. Coffee is really getting scarce." He took a long drink of
coffee. His eyes fluttered closed. "Mmm—delicious. I like
coming to your house."

"Steve's is wonderful. I'm not supposed to drink it, but
after I fell in love with my first cup, he promised to sneak it to
me and keep it off my food list. It's my dirty little secret."

Lee chuckled. "Steve is yummy. Is he gay?" She heard the
hope in her companion's voice.

"Nope, sorry. It's been awkward, but I think he's decided
he likes me well enough to accept my presence without
freaking out anymore. It feels like I've been here weeks instead
of days. These boys are keeping me busy."

"I bet," Lee said, winking.

"I like it here, it could be worse."

A shadow passed over the man's face. "It could," he said quietly and carefully.

She sensed he had some interesting stories about his first companion, and a few words of caution. *Don't pry. Don't pry...* "What happened to your first companion to make her commit suicide?" Krista couldn't resist querying. *Damn it!* She knew pushing her new "friend" was a bad idea, but she was so curious.

Lee sighed. "She had a baby. They didn't keep it. Things weren't as they seem to be here. Now tell me about Krista. I want to know everything. What do you do for fun?" Lee brightened, the darkness left his face. She knew that was all he had to say on the subject of his tragic first companion. Krista wondered just how bad the poor woman's placement had been.

She told Lee what little there was of her story. He visibly teared up when she explained her goodbye at the protection facility and how much she'd meant to her teachers there without ever knowing. She told him about Cina, but omitted the fact she'd run away. This man was her "friend", but her six employed him. She knew she'd have to be very careful with what she told him. For all she knew, the coffee had doomed her; he might be reporting everything to her rat-faced social worker. She was learning not to trust anyone. There was just too much danger of losing what little security she had there.

"Well, let's go check out that kitchen you were telling me about," Lee said after she finished her life story.

"Great," she replied, standing. Lee followed her down to the lower level of the house. Everything looked new, unused. Lee took a pad of paper and started making a list.

"Here's everything we'll need to teach you to make strawberry shortcake. You said it's your favorite, right?"

"Right." She nodded happily. "Wait, could we make pecan pie?"

Lee smiled knowingly. "So which one of them likes pecan? The tall, dark, and broody one or the young doctor?"

"Brax, the writer you had *your* eye on," she whispered shyly.

Lee winked. "Mmm, dreamy, we can make lover-boy pecan."

Krista clapped her hands and chuckled. "I'm glad you're here, Lee. This has been fun. I feel like we might become genuine friends."

"What the hell is this *might* about, girl? We are already on the way to genuine friends. You're a trip, sweet and spicy. You'll have these boys wrapped around your finger in no time."

"I don't want anyone wrapped around my finger. I just

want us to be a family, do you know what I mean?"

Lee's face softened into a wistful expression. "I know exactly what you mean. If anyone can do it, I bet you can." Lee crossed out some items on the list and wrote more. "Before I leave, we'll give this to Steve. He can pick them up so you can surprise your men—or should I say man?"

She looked away and bit her lip.

Lee laughed loudly. "This is going to be the best pie ever, I promise."

They were both giggling as they went up the stairs. Brax was walking down the hall and when they saw him, the giggles turned into a fit of laughter. He gave them a curious look, and then the expression turned into a deep frown, which didn't help them control their giggles as he walked passed them.

They watched a movie, and both sighed when the hero and heroine found their way to a happily ever after. She didn't want the visit to end. It was so nice having someone there who didn't want to have sex with her. She could be herself with Lee.

"I'm going to look forward to next Tuesday. See you soon, Kris."

No one had called her that before and it made her giggle. "See you Tuesday," she said as she shut the door.

"So you enjoyed your companion?" Mal asked.

She jumped. She didn't know he was behind her. "I did.

Thank you for hiring him."

Mal grinned. "I'm glad to see a smile on your face again."

"I'm sorry about the other night, Mal. This is just so—crazy."

"I know what you mean. I could be worse, you know."

"I know. Thanks for being understanding."

He shrugged. "Not much choice. I'm not a jackass. I won't force myself on you."

"I know. I'm looking forward to Sunday."

He did a double take. "Really?"

"Yep. Now let's go see what Steve cooked for us. I'm starving."

Mal held out his arm. She looped hers around it and they skipped in an almost choreographed display of silliness into the dining room. The others looked at them with disbelief. She noticed Max scowling, jealousy on his face, and it cut into her fun. Mal must have felt strange, because he dropped her arm as if it were on fire. They sat down together.

DeAnthony pulled his chair up close to hers and put his arm around her. Max slid back from the table so quickly his chair toppled with a loud crash that left her cringing.

"I'm not feeling well," he mumbled, leaving the room.

She began to stand, ready to go after him, but DeAnthony held her in place. He kissed her neck. "Don't worry about ol' grumpy," he whispered in her ear.

She shivered. With all the emotion and testosterone, she knew she was treading in dangerous waters.

"You know what would be hot?" he asked in her ear.

"No," she whispered back. Her mouth felt dry. His sexy voice was causing her panties to feel damp.

"If you went upstairs, put on that cute little skirt I picked out for you, and you came back without panties, straddled my lap, and fucked me at the dinner table. Should we ask the others if they want a show with their dinner? I don't mind sharing you at all, sexy girl."

"I'd love to see that," Mal said loudly, clearly eavesdropping. "If you're up for it, I'd take my turn tonight and give you Sunday back."

She felt the heat of their words and her breath came out in little pants. She looked over at Brax. His eyes were dark, and she saw jealousy there. Jared looked uncomfortable. Damon reached down, and she noticed him adjusting his cock.

"I don't want any hard feelings. I'm willing to be shared, if you promise me it won't be like before."

"The only thing hard around here is our pricks. Anyone have a problem sharing my night?" No one spoke up. "Good. Now someone give Steve the night off. I want to take her right here."

"But the patio door, someone might see," Krista protested.

"No one is going to see. The guards are away from the doors and no one is getting into our little fortress. Now go upstairs and change for me, baby girl."

Krista's stomach churned. She'd learned to like sex, far more than she'd expected to. She wanted this as much as her men did, but she hoped Max and Brax wouldn't feel upset.

The idea of them all loving her left her legs wobbly, but she managed to make it up the stairs without falling and breaking her neck. She dressed in the short skirt DeAnthony had requested. In a moment of boldness, she took off her shirt and her bra. Taking a few deep breaths, she waited, giving Steve time to leave.

She applied some fresh makeup and combed her long brown hair, noticing how the sun played with the red highlights. She hoped the men noticed too. Looking in the mirror, she smiled. *Perfect.* She knew she had nice breasts. They weren't too big or too small. The nipples hardened in the cool air as she gazed at herself in the mirror. Her face glowed with a deep flush. She looked into her eyes and didn't recognize herself. She'd changed, become bolder. *Now if I could just be brave enough to choose freedom.* She shook off the stray thought, knowing it was too late. There was no going back. She was here now. She walked quietly down the stairs, once again glad for the home's newness and the lack of squeaking.

"What the fuck is your problem, Braxton?"

"I don't like this. She's not a sex toy. If they decide we aren't treating her right, she's gone!"

"Yeah, you don't need to remind me. I know that, but she's willing to do this. It's not as if we're beating her or hurting her. She wants this and you know it," DeAnthony protested.

"She's sweet and wants to keep us happy. Maybe she doesn't really want this," Brax countered.

"If you want to go to your room, do it. If she'll let us share, we share. The goal is to get her pregnant. They won't care how we do it, as long as we do. Don't be an ass," Mal sounded off angrily.

"Well, I don't want her hurt."

"She won't be," Jared's voice was soft. Krista could hear the strain and assumed desire put it there.

Krista continued down the stairs. She bit her lip, not sure how to assure Brax she was okay. He was her favorite, but that didn't mean she could be his exclusively. They both knew she belonged to them all. If she could choose, it would be Brax every night, but she didn't have that luxury. At least this way he'd be there too.

When she reached the bottom of the stairs, Mal stood. Brax turned and she saw his nostrils flair. He scowled. She smiled at him. He turned away. Her heart squeezed painfully in her chest. A small flame of anger flared. He didn't have the right to be angry any more than she had the right to say no to DeAnthony.

She saw DeAnthony unzip his pants and pull out his erection. Giving Brax a final look, she went over to the handsome African-American and straddled his lap. He smiled up at her before taking one of her nipples in his mouth and pulling her down on his cock. Without preamble, he impaled her. She was already wet, just from the exoticness of being half-naked in the public area of the house.

Filled with the orange glow of sunset, the room was shaded romantically in soft light. Krista closed her eyes and let him direct her. She continued bouncing on him as he sucked on her nipples hard. She was so close to coming, but then he released and he cried out against her breasts.

She stood and noticed Mal had unzipped himself too. She straddled him and his shaft filled her. This time she bounced faster, feeling the disappointment of DeAnthony's quick finish. Mal groaned. He clutched at her breasts and she cried out, arching her back. The clawing need for release was relentless.

Mal clung to her. "Jesus yes!" He screamed as he came.

Once again, she hadn't come. So far, this wasn't going as she'd hoped. Standing, she walked around to the other side of the table where Jared fumbled awkwardly with his zipper.

She glanced at Brax, and he looked disappointed, she looked away. Seeing his unhappiness wasn't helping with her unease.

Jared managed to free his skinny dick and he was shaking as he helped her to straddle him. Before she could lower herself, he pulled her lips to his. The tender kiss he gave her warmed her heart. She tangled her fingers in his hair. Jared rubbed her back slowly. The soft kiss became more passionate. Jared's hands held her hips. She ground her pussy against his cock. He gasped against her lips. Her clit rubbed wonderfully against his shaft.

Krista threw her head back, groaning. This was so damn good. She was getting so close. Panting, she pushed against him with more force. Krista buried her face in his neck. He grabbed her hair and pulled her head back to kiss her neck. She erupted against him, whimpering as she came, her body shaking.

He let go of her hair and pulled her up, ramming his cock straight to her core. She screamed with joy as his cock rubbed the sweet spot inside of her and her orgasm strengthened. A moment later, Jared cried out, making a ridiculous face. He poured into her.

"Krista!" He groaned. He wrapped his hands around her waist, keeping them connected while he nuzzled her neck. "Damn, woman, that was amazing!"

She couldn't agree more, but all she could do was sigh softly. When his hands fell away she stood, wobbly, and stumbled away from him. Damon grabbed her and threw her over a chair.

"What the fuck!" Brax yelled.

Damon slammed into her from behind and her breasts rubbed against the chair cushion, adding to the erotic sensation of his cock's furious motion. He fucked her hard, with no apology. She made little noises, primal sounds. The feeling built until she whined like an animal. Relishing the friction inside her very sensitive pussy, she came again loudly.

"Don't stop, please," Krista begged her nemesis. She was so wet with her own lubrication and the men's release that his rough treatment didn't hurt at all. In fact, it added to her wild, wanton hunger for more.

When Damon stilled, he didn't pull out right away. Instead, he began massaging her back. His touch was unexpectedly tender. He pulled out and helped her stand. Finally, she turned to Brax. His face was unreadable. Her pussy was starting to feel sore, but she wanted him—the most.

She took a step toward him. He didn't move, just lounged back in his chair watching her. Krista went to her knees and unzipped his pants. He still didn't respond. She freed his beautiful maleness. Tenderly, she took him in her mouth, careful to cover her teeth with her lips. Working him for all she was worth, she relished the act of pleasuring him. Her desire for this man was unlike the crazed sexcapades in which she'd just participated. There was something special inside of her that only blossomed for Braxton.

She'd been with them such a short time, and yet it seemed like forever. She wanted Brax's sweet words to be true, but distrusted them, especially while he sat immobile as she desperately tried to draw a response out of him.

He moaned. A happy little bubble floated up, followed by another as he ran his fingers in her tangled hair and tugged, just a bit. "Why do you have to be so perfect for us?" he muttered.

She didn't respond, only increased her suction, drawing a low moan from him. His fingers left her hair and slipped under her to toy with her nipples. They were hypersensitive. Wetness trickled down her thighs. The realization that she remained covered in the other's ejaculation, gave her a moment pause. She needed a shower before Brax came inside of her, offering herself to him in this condition felt wrong. The emotion she refused to name that lived between them deserved better.

She pulled away from his cock. "I'm sorry. I need to go clean up. Will you stay with me tonight, if it's okay with DeAnthony? It's still his night."

"I'm good," DeAnthony said. "I'm damn tired now. That was great, baby girl."

Braxton's expression was blank. He moved, picking her up in his arms. She yelped with helpless shock. Without a word to the others, he carried her toward his room. She glanced over his shoulder to see the others looking as surprised as she felt.

He kicked open his bedroom door and carried her to the private bathroom. Brax set her on her feet and moved wordlessly to his large tub. This one was even larger than the one in her room. She knew it could seat all six of them if they were of a mind to jump in together. He turned on the faucet and put the plug into the drain. She watched him gathering soap, shampoo, and towels. He still hadn't said a word.

"Are you mad at me?" she whispered, afraid to hear his response.

"Never," he replied, but she noticed a tick in his jaw that declared his words a lie.

"I'm sorry. I know I'd said no more group…games. I just wanted… I wasn't bad."

"I know," he replied, still not looking at her.

When he turned, she saw it then, his grief. Her heart

ached, she'd put that terrible look on his face. She fought the urge to be angry. She hadn't asked for this polygamy.

"I…" She didn't know what to say.

"I'm falling for you, Krista. It's not just because you're the only woman on Earth for me. It's you. You're fascinating. When I saw you with the others, I was so pissed, but you were so beautiful. I've never been so turned on in my life." He took her hand and led her to the tub, helping her step over the edge. "You were different with me. I saw it. Why?" Brax questioned softly.

"I don't know," she replied honestly. "I feel something so—it's almost special. I don't know. I think you're my favorite."

He grinned and lathered up the washcloth. He started with her back and neck. She sighed. The sensation of his touch gave her comfort, but also made her lust renew. Krista marveled at her reaction. After all that sex, she could still hunger for this one man. The idea of having him touch her, come inside of her body… Brax excited her more than all the sexual excess she'd just experienced. Krista bit her lip and looked at her bare knees sticking out of the water.

"What is it? Have you changed your mind about being with me tonight?"

"No," she cried, then clamped her mouth shut. She didn't

know how to articulate the bizarre way she felt. "I—you twist me up inside," she finally uttered.

Brax grinned. "Now you know how I feel. There's something developing between us, right? Don't lie."

She nodded, afraid of speaking and giving away just how deeply she was falling for him. She knew she could love Brax if she allowed herself to be that foolish.

"I'm going to make you feel something better than twisted, Kristannie." His hand dipped between her intimate lips. The water in the tub splashed. He began to rub her already sensitive clit.

Her pussy clenched hungrily as a little orgasm over took her. She closed her eyes. The mewling gasp came from deep inside. Her hips bucked, and water sloshed over the side of the tub. Brax replaced his hand with the soapy washcloth. He washed her pussy and inner thighs. She opened her eyes and watched him attending to her. A ghost of a smile tilted her lips upward.

When he looked at her, he smiled back. "What are you thinking about?"

"How I like it when you look so serious. Do you have any idea how handsome you are?"

He grunted. "Handsome doesn't do much good these days, unless you're into guys. Sucks to be straight. Well, it did until you arrived."

"I can't imagine if things were reversed, sharing you like you share me."

He scowled. "As hot as that was to watch, I wanted to bash heads together when I saw you with them, especial Jared. You like him, don't you?"

His question took her by surprise. "I like him, sure. You're my favorite, Braxton." She looked down shyly. Why she felt nervous admitting what he should've guessed was a mystery.

He seemed moderately pacified by her admission. "I just want to fuck you until my name is the only one on your lips, woman," he complained.

She screamed as he pulled her out of the tub so quickly she didn't have time to prepare. He pressed her back up against the bathroom wall, her slick body slid, squeaking against the surface. He wrapped one of her legs around his hip and supported her with his hands on her ass as his cock slid inside of her easily. She wrapped her arms around his neck, burying her face in his neck. He fucked the same way he did everything—epically. Brax was the kind of man who would have had women lined up around the block, but he was all hers. Her inner woman purred, knowing she was the most exciting thing in his life.

Pleasure quickly surged and then crested. She shuddered violently as she came, her back arched. Her pussy tightened around him as it convulsed with the joyous release he gave her. Krista screamed his name. The sound echoed off the bathroom walls. She never wanted to let him go. He cried out, his breath tickling her ear as her half-wet, half-dry hair fluttered against her skin. He came, but unlike the others, she didn't want to wash him away. Krista relished the proof she'd given him her body, because she reluctantly admitted she'd already given him her heart.

Krista rested her forehead on his shoulder and he huffed with exertion. "I think I'm falling in love with you," she whispered.

His muscles tightened and his body went stiff. She was afraid to look at his face. When he tried to tilt her face up, she resisted. He prodded her chin insistently and she finally found the inner strength to meet his eyes. Those beautiful, blue eyes were so bright.

"Good, because I'm fucking crazy about you, Kristannie. I'd call what I feel a whole lot more than lust, I'd call it adoration, respect, awe, and yes, love." He reached back and grasped a towel, wrapping it around her. "Now I'm going to take you to *my* bed and remind you that you're *mine*."

The promise on his face made her sigh. She hated how

much she cared about this man. He had the power to make her want so much more than a peaceful life. When she looked into Brax's eyes, she dreamed of having the fairytale. Real love was lost for her generation, but that didn't stop the non-rational part of her brain from demanding she give into her feelings for him.

Chapter 10

Seven Months Later

Krista put her hand on her distended abdomen. She was due in a few months. Life had become so strange. The live-in doctor and Jared constantly seemed to be disagreeing, and her relationship with Brax had become strained. She'd spent so many wonderful afternoons making love with him after life had found a routine and the others had gone back to work. Everything had almost felt…wonderful. Then she'd announced she was pregnant, and her doctor had almost immediately ordered an amniocentesis. It was done at only fourteen weeks. The child was healthy and Braxton's. Instead of the news making him happy, he seemed sullen.

Max was standing alone on the patio, smoking a cigar. Krista went outside quietly. A winter chill filled the air and she could see her breath. Snow blanketed the world beyond the patio. She had the irrational urge to run out into the pristine yard and make an angel, just to see Max's reaction. The outdoor heater hummed and Krista moved toward the slightly warmer air around it.

He glanced over to her, surprised. "Shouldn't you be inside, away from my smoke? You don't want to get sick, not when you have to be healthy for two."

She grinned at him. Once upon a time, she'd thought he was a jerk, but they'd developed a very unlikely friendship. "I just wanted to say hi," she told him quietly.

"What's up? You've been so sad lately. I've noticed you aren't eating, and I don't like it," he replied gruffly.

"I'm fine. Don't yell at me or I'll go back inside." She stuck out her tongue at him.

He scowled, but then chuckled. "This is about Brax, isn't it?" There was an odd tone in his question.

"Yes," she replied truthfully.

"Do you want me to talk to him?"

"God no!" She responded so quickly, he started chuckling again.

"Love. Fuckin' sucks," he muttered, gazing out at the lake.

He could say that again. As un-poetic as his words were, he'd gotten it right. Then she paused, pondering when he'd ever fallen in love.

"How would you know?" she retorted, annoyed.

His head whipped around in her direction so quickly, she marveled that he didn't have whiplash. "That's my point," he replied. "I know."

Realization dawned on her and she felt small and stupid.

"I'm sorry," she said evenly, not sure how else to respond.

"I never thought it would happen, but right from the beginning you were everything I needed without knowing it. Brax is a fucking idiot. I was really hoping that baby would be mine, something more to connect us. I'd never have gotten cold like he has. I don't care if it's his. I'll love your child, Krista, because I love you."

She rushed over to him, tears filling her eyes. He tossed his cigar into the snow and wrapped his arms around her.

"Christ! You're freezing. Let's go inside. You shouldn't have come out in just a sweater." His arms tighten around her as he led her back inside the house.

There was a fire going in the living room fireplace, and Max kicked off his boots as he ushered her inside. His grip didn't slacken, and she relished the comforting warmth. The realization that he loved her made her ache. Nothing about life was fair, but she hated hurting him. She'd set her heart on Brax from the start.

Max sat her on the ottoman he kicked close to the fireplace and turned the blower on high. Warmth poured over them. "Don't let yourself get sick. I doubt that quack of a doctor would give you as much as Tylenol for a cold."

Max rushed away, but when he returned he held a cup of hot Jasmine tea, her favorite. The fragrant smell gave it away as she took the cup. "Thank you," she said, giving him a small smile.

The worried look left his face and he appeared satisfied. Max crouched down beside her, his hand was cold when he caressed her cheek. "I'll talk to the bastard. He shouldn't be messing with your head, especially now."

"I'm fine, really. Please don't talk to him. Things are weird enough, I don't want them to get worse."

He frowned, his lips thinned to a fine line. "Okay, but just don't feel alone in this. I want to be there for you. I don't care who the father of your child is, I'd be proud to call it mine."

Affection for Max filled her deeply, and she began to cry. She'd been doing a lot of that lately.

"Don't," he mumbled.

"Sorry," she whispered.

Max tilted her face up so she had to look at him. His kissed her tears and rested his forehead against hers. "Don't apologize. You have nothing to be sorry for."

She felt him stroking her ponytail. This was the most physically affectionate he'd ever been with her outside of the bedroom. Knowing how hard it was for him made the gestures all the more meaningful.

Brax walked into the room, his foot hovered in the air, and he froze. It would've been comical if his face hadn't twisted with so much rage. He seemed to recover, then stomped away in the direction he'd just come from, slamming the door. Max stood, and Krista saw the darkness on his face. She grabbed his hand quickly.

"Don't go there, Max, please. The doctor will report any fighting. They're watching us so much more closely. Only another month and a half before the jackass leaves and we can get back to normal, our normal."

Her words seemed to pacify him slightly. "Don't worry. I won't kill him, even if I'd like to. Just get warm."

Max stalked away in the direction Brax had gone. A moment later, Krista heard arguing. She prayed it didn't get any louder. The last thing she wanted was to be taken away during her pregnancy. She'd surely find herself back in the protection facility. The moment her baby was born, she'd be re-given and her baby stolen. Shivering, she stood. Her legs trembled and she fell. She reached out to grab hold of the side table, but all she managed to do was knock over a vase.

The loud crash was followed by the sound of rushing feet. Jared came running in. "Are you all right?"

"Yes," she lied.

Doctor Jackson was right behind Jared. He grabbed her wrist and looked at his watch. Then he glanced at Jared and the men seemed to be having some silent conversation, which annoyed her greatly. "I'll get her upstairs," Jared said gravely as he picked her up.

Max and Braxton's argument escalated in the other room. "What's going on?" the doctor demanded to know. "Did one of those men hurt you?"

"No, nothing like that. I went outside in the cold, my mistake. They're arguing about something not connected to me," she lied quickly."Just ignore them."

The doctor's eyebrow rose, and Krista knew he didn't believe her by the skeptical look on his face. She bit her lip.

Jared was running with her. He rushed past his brother. "Go tell those jackasses to stop fighting and that Krista is bleeding."

His words startled her. She looked down. She hadn't noticed, but she was bleeding. Her jeans had a dark splotch on the crotch. Whimpering, she looked into Jared's eyes.

"It'll be all right," he told her reassuringly. She nodded, but worried he was lying for her benefit. It was too soon for her baby to be born.

Jared laid her on the portable exam table the doctor had in his room. He hooked a stress monitor around her abdomen, and Jared started to turn on the equipment. Krista watched the men preparing. Their tenseness wasn't comforting her.

The doctor began checking readings. "I need to speak with

you," he told Jared.

When they left the room, she laid her head on the table and cried, sobbing hard. She wanted this baby, even if Brax didn't. This was her family and she'd never felt any connection close to what she felt for the little, unborn child in her womb. She wanted to give her child all the love that her government had denied her. For the first time in her life, she had something precious that really and truly mattered. Even powerless, she'd find a way to protect her son or daughter from what awaited it.

The doctor knew if it was a boy or a girl, but she'd asked him not to tell her. She didn't want to worry about her child's fate before she had to. Now her unborn child's very life was in danger. She closed her eyes, hating herself. She'd let her stupid emotions for Brax cloud her judgment about what was best for her child. Not taking care of herself had been the equivalent of not caring for her baby. The guilt she experienced was poignant.

Jared returned, without the doctor. *Not a good sign.* She tried to calm down and stop sobbing.

He pulled up a chair and sat down, then took her hand. "Krista, we need to transport you to the hospital. The doctor feels you would benefit from more advanced diagnostic equipment. Don't panic, we don't know what's wrong yet. Everything will be fine, as long as you stay calm. Stressing out won't help your child." He wiped a tear from her cheek. "I'm sorry, I should've insisted you eat and take better care of yourself instead of letting my anger with your doctor keep me silent. He wasn't doing a very good job and I should've stepped in."

"It's okay. I'm to blame, not you. I shouldn't have let myself get so wound up."

"We'll get you to the hospital, and then everything will be all right."

"Will it?" she whispered.

"I hope so," he replied. The honesty in his eyes made her want to start crying all over again.

"Okay," she replied, willing to do whatever it took to save her child. She just hoped she hadn't come to her senses too late.

The ambulance came. It was freezing outside. The temperature had dropped at least another ten degrees. Mal threw her coat over her torso. She lay strapped helplessly onto the gurney. He handed her overnight bag to one of the paramedics. She nodded to him and the stricken look on his face stopped her heart.

Brax pushed Jared out of the way and got in with her. Jared grabbed his arm. Brax shrugged off his friend's hold. "I'm going with her," he said with finality.

The doors closed. They didn't turn on the siren, and that made her feel a little better. She knew if they'd turned on the siren, things would be much worse. She'd seen security waiting in their cars. Knowing they'd be going to the hospital to guard her was strangely comforting. For the doctor and her six to allow the risk of her leaving the compound, she knew it was serious.

Brax took her hand, and she looked into his face. He didn't look cold, an appearance she'd recently grown accustomed to, instead she saw torment in his expression. His brow creased, and fine lines radiated from his eyes that she hadn't noticed before. His neatly trimmed goatee, a new addition to his face since the cold weather hit, had a few gray hairs. He suddenly looked ridiculously aged and seeing it made her feel even worse.

"I'm sorry, Kristannie. This is my fault," he mumbled.

The paramedic took her blood pressure. "Sir, try to keep her calm," he scolded Brax gruffly.

"Sorry," Brax grumbled at the man, but he never took his eyes off Krista's face. "I'm so sorry," he repeated.

"Don't be sorry. This is my fault, not yours."

"I know I've been…distant." As he said the last word he looked away, guiltily. She said nothing. He still wasn't looking at her. "I've just been so conflicted. I'm happy it's mine, but

I'm also upset."

"What do you mean?" she questioned, anger in her voice.

"Sir, we need you to stop talking now. You're upsetting her. You don't want to make the situation worse, do you?"

"No." He sat back, saying nothing, but still gripping her hand.

"Butt out," she growled at the paramedic. His eyes flew open in surprise. She squeezed Brax's hand. "Tell me, now!" she ordered.

He grinned a little. "Fire. That's what I love about you. I love you, Kristannie. So much that it kills me to know I gave you this child. If this is a girl, it'll destroy us both. I've been so worried that we'll lose the child when it's older. I didn't even worry about what might happen now. You made the doctor swear not to tell us the gender for fear we'd tell you. It's been eating me alive every night. I have terrible nightmares about my daughter being snatched away and thrown into a crowd of crazed men. I couldn't do it, couldn't allow them to take her away."

"I know just how you feel," Krista whimpered, fighting her tears. "That's why I wouldn't let the doctor tell me. I didn't want to lose my hope for a boy."

The radio crackled loudly. "You need to bring her to door ten. We have to save this baby girl. The mother is arriving under a code red, so treat this as an emergency," ordered the disembodied, static-filled voice over the radio as it spoke to the driver. The radio was so loud they heard the words clearly. The siren blared and the ambulance lurched forward as it picked up speed. Krista's eyes filled with tears. She noticed Braxton's lip tremble.

"Denyse, for my mother." He spoke so quietly she wasn't sure she heard him correctly.

"All right, and Alicia for mine, Alicia Denyse," she replied.

He grinned, but there was sadness in his expression. "Why does your mother get top billing?"

"Because I'm the one strapped to the gurney," she retorted.

"Touché, my lady. Okay, you win. Now I have to learn to deal with the fact she belongs to the state."

"I've been dealing with that for a lot longer than you, it doesn't get easier. I've known since my teens that if I have a daughter she'll be taken away."

"I never thought about it before the paternity test told us I was the father." He spoke quietly, and she could hear the apology in his voice.

Krista reached up and touched his cheek. "We'll get through this. We have ten years to love her."

"Ten years won't be enough."

"We'll have to make it enough."

The ambulance came to a stop. Fervor erupted as the commotion began. She couldn't see Brax as he was pushed aside for the rushing paramedics and doctors. They ran with her through one white, sterile hall after another. Hospital security flanked the gurney, and she heard her own private guards shouting as they caught up with the rushing medical workers. The elevator doors remained open and the moment they all crammed inside, she looked around frantically for Braxton.

"Where's Braxton Bray?" she questioned the paramedic she recognized.

"He'll have to wait until we have you stabilized and roomed. He's been detained to fill out paperwork."

"I want him with me, please." She hated begging, but her panic and terror grew to overwhelming proportions.

One of her guards, a man she knew from the compound, stepped closer to the gurney. "I won't let anything happen to you, Miss."

His words brought her only slight relief. "Then get Brax here as quickly as you can."

He looked at the other guard and nodded. "We'll do our utmost."

She sighed. She'd take what she could get. She'd spent so

much time secluded and under guard, the sensation of being in the hospital was disturbing. She'd come to think of her six's home as her home, and right now she just wanted to return there.

The expediency didn't end after they had her transferred to a hospital bed. She was in a private room, and each time her door opened, she saw her guards silently keeping watch outside the room. There was a twisted comfort in knowing they were there. She waited, still no Brax. A nurse came in and took her vitals.

"I'm your nurse this evening. My name is Brad. I'll be with you until five AM, and then Richard will take over."

"Where's the man who rode here with me?" Krista asked. She didn't bother to introduce herself to Brad.

He gave her a nervous and surprised look. "You'll have to speak to the doctor about visitors."

Krista's heart pounded in her chest. "So I assume that means he's not allowed to come in here?"

"You need to stay calm. I'll see about having the doctor come and speak with you."

Krista nodded, feeling ill. What would she do if she never saw him—them—again? She hadn't considered they'd pull her from her six so abruptly. "Please have him come soon. I really would relax if I'm allowed to see Braxton." Brad put an IV

needle in her arm. "Is that really necessary?" she questioned
with irritation.

"Yes, if we run into an emergency we need to know
you're prepped. This is just going to be sterile water to keep the
vein open." He walked around to her other arm and put an
automated blood pressure cuff on her arm. Another nurse came
in and handed him a tray. "This will only hurt for a moment,"
Brad said as he uncapped the needle and flicked out the air
bubbles.

"What's that for?" Krista asked with worry.

"Steroids, for the baby's lungs, just in case," he replied.

Just in case... She began to panic. *Do they think I'll go
into labor early?* Krista wanted to ask, but was afraid of the
answer, so she remained silent. She looked at the bandage on
her arm. They'd removed her tracker as a precaution as soon as
she was settled in her room. If they defibrillated her for any
reason the tracker could short circuit, interfering with
lifesaving procedures. Her heart ached. She didn't want to lose
Braxton's baby. She'd love any child that was hers, but
knowing the daughter she carried belonged to Brax made her
love for the baby even more intense.

The nurse gave her hand a comforting squeeze. "I'll do
my best for you."

The way he said the words didn't fill her with hope. She

shivered. He mistook the gesture and added another warmed blanket to her bed. It didn't dispel the chill in her soul. Were they trying to find an excuse to take her child away and relocate her? She'd seen enough government finagling to believe the worst.

The doctor didn't come. Darkness fell outside and Krista sat staring at the window, afraid and alone. Deep down, she worried about the drastic change her life had taken. She'd been helpless to stop the terrible turn of events from unfolding.

Sleep was a long time in coming. When she finally fell asleep, her hand on the swell where her child lay, she dreamed of men in white coats ripping her baby from her womb and leaving her for dead. A clattering noise woke her. Krista cried out as she opened her eyes.

"I'm sorry I woke you," said a different nurse quietly. He was a bit older than her night nurse had been, but his eyes were kind.

"When do I get to talk to the doctor?" she asked, ignoring basic social pleasantries entirely.

"He should be here to see you this afternoon."

Krista remembered his name was Richard. "Please, Richard, I really need to talk to him about my visitor situation. Could you at least let him know I'd like to see the father? Please."

Richard looked sad. "I'll talk to him. Here's your breakfast. You're on a special diet, so you won't be offered the menu, but if there's anything special you'd like, I'll see if I can get an approval."

She nodded, but said nothing else. Richard changed her IV bag and left without another word. Krista looked at the tray. Yellow, overcooked eggs and apple juice was all she'd been given. She drank the juice and ignored the eggs. Steve's cooking had spoiled her. She'd become accustomed to her new life, and if she had to be Given, she wanted to return to her men.

There was no TV in the room, the only sound was the dripping IV and the low hum of the monitors. Krista lay looking up at the ceiling, feeling hopeless.

A man entered the room with a mop and bucket. He wore a white t-shirt and jeans. She noticed the blue sanitary booties on his feet and a badge around his neck. Krista went back to staring hopelessly out the window. She didn't pay the custodian much attention until the hair on the back of her neck stood up. When she glanced over at him, he was gazing at her in a way that made her entirely uncomfortable. Fear made her put her hand lightly on the call button, just in case.

"Are you here to mop or stare?" she questioned sassily.

"I'm sorry," he replied, still gazing at her. "I've waited a very long time to see you again."

She'd almost pressed the button when the word "again" caught her attention. "What do you mean 'again'?" Krista knew she should just press the call button, but curiosity stopped her.

"I'm here to help you, Kristannie. I'm your father."

Her mouth fell open and she fought the bubble of hysterical laughter that almost erupted. "I don't have a father," she replied, glaring at the interloper.

"You did, when you were little. I'm so sorry I wasn't there when you needed me, muffin," the stranger said. There was true sorrow in his voice.

Her mouth gaped open at his admission. She wasn't sure how to respond to him or his foodie nickname. No one had ever called her muffin. The slightest ghost of a memory tingled in her mind, but she blew it away, like a wisp of smoke.

"I'll call security. Two highly trained guards are right outside, all I have to do is scream once and they'll be in here."

"I know." He spoke calmly, but she could see the fear in his eyes. "I'm risking a lot for you, but I've been waiting months for a chance like this."

"I don't remember ever having a father. I don't know why you'd make such a cruel claim, but I'm not an idiot."

"I know you aren't, muffin. You were a smart kid. Let me

show you some proof." He took a step closer and she held the call button up, showing him her finger was hovering above it, ready to notify the nurse's station she needed help. He held up his hands. "I'm just going to get my wallet out of my back pocket and show you a picture. Okay?"

She didn't respond. He slowly moved his right hand back, keeping the left where she could see it. He brought a worn leather wallet out, taking a few steps in her direction, while holding the old leather out toward her.

"Take it, look at my information. There's a picture in there, just one. Take it out of the plastic and give it a good look."

She didn't move. He shook his arm and she glared at him, but again, her natural inquisitiveness won and she snatched the billfold out of the man's hand. His ID claimed his name was Todd Damiani and he was a forty-five year old Canadian resident. She flipped it and there was a picture, one that made her heart pound, the monitor attached to her made a bleep. He glanced nervously at the door.

"I'll be back later. Calm down. If you can't make your body cooperate, there's no way we can pull off an escape. Keep the wallet for now. I hope you'll believe me, and if you don't, everything I've worked for has been for nothing. I failed you once. I won't do it again."

He hurried out of the room, keeping his head down. A nurse came rushing in a moment later. Krista tucked the wallet under the blanket quickly. *Escape…is it even possible in my condition?* "Are you all right?" the nurse asked as he rushed over to the machines and began checking settings while making adjustments.

"I'm fine. I'm just worried about seeing Braxton Bray. Please talk to the doctor for me. Make sure he knows this is counter-productive to my recuperation."

The man nodded and left. Krista took a deep breath and pulled the soft leather from its hiding place. A father—she'd never imagined she had one who cared.

Just because he showed her an ID claiming they shared the same last name didn't make him her father, she reminded herself. Flipping back to the picture, she took a few calming deep breaths, forcing herself not to react.

Her mother's face, she was sure this was her mother. The woman held a little girl in her arms. It was a picture of her and her mother; she couldn't have been older than two. She pulled the picture out of the plastic. There was more to it; it was folded to fit in the plastic rectangle. She flipped the hidden flap and a younger version of her visitor smiled back at her. She dropped the wallet and the machine went crazy. Krista scrambled to grab the wallet and picture, sliding it all under her leg. She lay back, breathing as deeply as she could.

A man in a white coat rushed in. "I'm Doctor Barnes," he said as he moved to the monitor and began punching in codes. He turned to the nurse who'd trailed in after him. It wasn't Richard. "Have the requested information printed out. I want to compare the last hour with last night's readings."

"Yes, doctor," the man mumbled.

"I'm fine. I'm just panicked because you won't let Braxton visit me," she lied. Maybe her shock would serve her in getting her visitation with the man she loved.

"That's not advisable at this time, Miss Damiani."

The doctor left without another word. Krista's heart sank. She knew she couldn't risk looking at the picture again until she'd had some time to think about the revelation; she did indeed have a father, and he cared about her enough to carry a picture of their little family around in his wallet all these years. The picture was very faded and creased. She could tell it wasn't a recent addition to his wallet. She slipped the picture out of its hiding place. Flipping it over, she read the feminine handwriting. Her heart skipped a beat, she was looking at her mother's delicate cursive. Although she hadn't been able to read it as a very young child, she'd loved watching her mother write, seeing the artful loops and lovely tilts as each letter magically came from her pen. It simply read *Our First Family*

Portrait, October 2017.

That was just six months before the plague. She'd been just over two and a half years old. *Why can't I remember having a father?* Her mind raced as she asked herself the fundamental question. *Who am I?* She began doubting her own memories. *Muffin.* The nickname sparked something, a feeling of love and security. She remembered her blanket, it had pictures of muffins and she'd taken it everywhere with her until the day they'd come and taken her away without a single possession, including her blanket, due to the fear of germs. It had been early, before the disease had done the worst of its damage.

Krista knew in her heart, no DNA test required, that she'd met her long-lost father. Now she just had to figure out what he wanted to do. In her condition, she couldn't exactly jump up and run out of the hospital. Her baby meant too much to her. Even if they took her child away, at least she would be alive if Krista stayed.

Hours passed. Her nurse came in and she asked to use the phone, she'd memorized all the men's cellphone numbers, starting with Brax's, just in case. The nurse shook his head sadly. "I'm sorry, you're not allowed to use the phone for security reasons."

I call bullshit! Her mind screamed, but her mouth

remained silent. She had a feeling things were going to get worse before they improved. She was under medical arrest, and her odds of ever again having back what she'd called her life since leaving the protection facility felt slim. She realized her child was better off dead than living the life she had. Her heart blossomed with love for her daughter.

She watched the male nurse working, resentfully. He was as much a jailer as the guards at the protection facility had been. The nurse left. A few minutes later, she heard the door. When she looked up it was her father, still dressed as a janitor.

"Do you believe me?" He went right to the point.

"Yes," she whispered.

"Do you want to stay, Kristannie?"

"Hell no, I don't want to lose my baby," she told him angrily.

What they were doing made her want to scream and rail against the doctors, the politicians, men in general, even Braxton. He should've found a way to come to her. She had a feeling they'd be placing her with a new six and stealing her baby if she stayed. Too many red flags were in the air for her to accept that the authorities truly had *her* best interest at heart.

"I'm coming back at midnight. That's when there's the largest shift change, including your guards. I know you're worried about your baby, but we'll get you to a hospital in

Winnipeg, and you'll be safe there. The women's free immigration law provides you automatic citizenship and protection the moment you pass into Canada. I've spent years working with the survivors' network, helping families flee to protect their daughters, and assisting women trying to escape The Giving."

"I don't understand. If you knew I was alive, why didn't you save me? Why did you leave my mother?"

"We don't have time for this now," he said, glancing nervously at the door. She crossed her arms over her chest. "I didn't leave your mother. I was incarcerated. I know what you're going through and how it feels to be in jail, muffin. I'm sorry I couldn't save you, but my connection in your protection facility feared approaching you because you were so quick to obey the rules. She feared you'd report her as a snitch and then all the good she could do for so many other girls would be lost. Believe me, we had some heated words, but in the end she'd made up her mind. I'm sorry, Kristannie."

"Krista, you can call me Krista," she told him, feeling a bit pathetic. This man was her father, and yet she felt the need for such a basic introduction. Her anger spent, she just looked at the tall, dark-haired man. There was silver at his temples, and she noticed deep worry lines etched in his brow. *Did fear for me, a daughter he barely knows, put the lines there?* He hadn't abandoned her, but instead had been away by force, not choice. Somehow, it wasn't as comforting as it should be, and she felt sort of deflated. So much had been taken from her by the cruelness of fate.

A sad looked filled his face. "I suppose the days of 'muffin' are long gone. We've lost a lot of time, but I promise you I won't let you down. I've been keeping families together for over a decade. I won't see mine destroyed again. I loved your mother and I was happy for the brief time we had together, the three of us. Be prepared for midnight. Don't worry, I've helped people out of tighter spots than this one."

She nodded and he left. She ate the terrible soup and dry toast they brought her, to distract herself from worry by injuring her taste buds. She certainly wouldn't miss the food or the constant boredom. She wished there was a way to contact Brax. *Would he leave everything to run away with me? Does he love me enough to do that?*

She knew there was no way to get a message to him. If by some miracle they let her use the phone, it would certainly be a conversation someone other than she and Brax were privy to. Unless he snuck in her room right now, she had no way of telling him what was happening. Deep down, she worried the news that her child was a girl had made him give up, and he was already trying to accept their doom.

Even if she was guaranteed she could stay with Brax, she'd eventually lose her child. For the baby's sake, she knew she had to go with her father and flee to Canada. She was still unsure about his story. It seemed strangely convenient he'd show up after all this time, but her options were to trust him or trust her government, which had already wronged her at every turn. She picked daddy dearest. Father. Dad. Daddy. She wasn't even sure what to call the man, so she settled for Todd. Mr. Damiani seemed too formal and Dad didn't feel right yet.

She'd lost so much. Thinking about her unnecessarily sad childhood while dealing with pregnancy hormones brought tears quickly to her eyes. She grabbed a tissue and wiped her face quickly. Krista lay back, closing her eyes. If she slept now, she'd be alert during her upcoming adventures in prison break. Sleep sucked her down without much trouble as her tumultuous emotions begged for respite.

The clatter of metal against metal caused her to gasp; she sat up and blinked at the nurse who set her dinner down. She knew she'd slept at least four hours and felt satisfied she'd be her best for later. She didn't look under the cover, whatever it was smelled so bad she gagged.

"Could I have a book?" she asked the nurse.

"I'll check with your doctor," he replied.

"For a book?" She laughed darkly. "What do you think

I'm going to do, paper cut myself to death?"

"I'll check. I doubt there'll be a problem. If the doctor approves, I'll bring the library cart in."

He left the room. A minute stretched into an hour, no book. Krista blew the bangs out of her face in disgust. They'd confiscated her overnight bag, and now they wouldn't give her a book. This place was worse than maximum-security prison; at least there they allowed you to read.

She laid her head back and gazed up at the clock. Six more hours and she'd have a chance to be free, really free. She didn't know exactly what it would be like living in Canada, but she'd seen it touted on the internet as the closest thing to life before plague times. She tried to imagine living each day as she wanted. She rubbed her large belly. What would it be like for her child to live in a world where she could dream? A small smile touched her lips. For the first time, she let herself imagine her daughter as a woman. Would she appreciate her choice, or long for the father she'd never know? Guilt pierced Krista. She was taking one choice away from both the baby and Brax, but the odds that the authorities wouldn't ultimately take it anyway outweighed the odds that they'd be a family. She just hoped he'd understand, if not now, then someday. Her heart broke. She already missed him.

Whatever happened, she was getting away. Trusting the

stranger who claimed to be her long-lost father was dangerous, but she was out of options. Deep down, she knew staying would be worse than leaving. Taking a deep breath, she watched the seconds ticking away on the large, plain wall clock. There was no color in the room, no art, nothing but that damn clock. She felt as if time was taunting her. Krista let herself cry, sobbing until there was nothing left inside of her but determination.

She might have dozed. The sound of the door startled her. The dim light behind the bed illuminated a large laundry cart and the form of a tall man. "It's just me," whispered her father. Krista let go of the breath she'd been holding unconsciously. "I turned off your room's alerts at the nurse's station. Do you want me to take the IV out for you?" he asked.

"No, I've got it," Krista mumbled, still groggy, but now filled with adrenaline. She peeled the tape painfully off her sore arm and slowly pulled the needle out. Grabbing a few tissues, she pressed them against her bleeding arm.

"Ready?"

"Definitely," she replied. He helped her get into the large bin of towels; she refused to think about how they might've been used.

"Don't worry, they're clean," he whispered.

She chuckled, even with everything that could go wrong

and destroy her only chance of escape, she gave into the stress-induced, inappropriate amusement. Krista gave her father one last look before sinking down lower. The suffocating, buried alive feeling was uncomfortable, but she'd suffer through anything to know her daughter wouldn't grow up to be "Given" or worse, used in some sort of freaky breeding program. She had a feeling the other quads would follow the example the Northeast was setting. Shivering, even in the stifling embrace of the freshly laundered towels, she tried not to imagine what would happen if they didn't make it.

The cart moved at a steady pace. She felt relieved until it paused. She heard her father and another man talking, but the words sounded muffled due to all the cotton over her head. She held her breath and closed her eyes. When the cart began moving again, she sighed with relief. It stopped again. She wanted to peek so badly, the nagging curiosity was almost overwhelming. Then she heard the distinctive *ding* of an elevator and the cart moved a few feet before stopping again. She felt the elevator moving. The sensation was odd, as she was lying on her back. The weight of the baby on her bladder made her feel as if she needed to pee, which was certainly not helping the general discomfort of her awkward position. She'd happily accept all the discomfort in the world if she knew they'd make it out of the country safely.

The cart rolled again. Wherever they were, it was very noisy. She tried to stay as still as possible, to the point she refused to scratch her nose when a fray from one of the towels tickled her. She realized a cough or movement could ruin everything. Krista squeezed her eyes closed and focused on taking even, shallow breaths. Then she heard the *swish* of electric doors. The heat ebbed and she realized they were outside in the winter air. Elation spiked inside of her, they'd made it. She heard a door slam and then her father reached in to help her out of the bin. Someone pulled her into the side door of a large, white van. She heard sirens.

A woman who'd helped her into the van smiled kindly at her. "It'll be all right," she said, but Krista didn't feel reassured. "Lay down," the woman requested.

Krista lay down in the seat and the woman covered her with her own body. "Why are you helping me?" Krista mumbled, her words muffled into the seat.

"It's what I do," replied the woman. "My name is Mara, by the way. I want to see you have a chance to be free, Krista. My half-sister was Given, and the men used her so brutally, she died. They might claim they look out for the girls, but they don't. I've been doing this ever since. I'm just glad my mother left my father and moved to Canada when I was small. I loved my sister very much and we saw each other every summer. It's not right what they're doing. Your father is a good man. He's helped a lot of girls in your situation. I couldn't turn down the chance to help him save his own daughter."

Even with the woman's weight on top of her, Krista slid around on the seat as the van made wide turns before suddenly coming to a complete stop. The sirens grew louder and then they seemed to fade away. She felt the woman let go of the breath she was holding.

"I thought you were crazy when you told us what you'd planned, Todd. I can't believe this worked!" Mara said, sitting up.

The van opened and they all got out. There was a black SUV waiting. A short man opened the back hatch and lifted a trap door in the floor. "Sorry for the accommodations," he said, motioning at the space as if he were a game show host showing off a prize. She didn't like the look of what was behind door number one.

Her father squeezed her shoulder and she looked up at him. "Sorry, muffin, but if anyone sees you, we're done. Mara can wear a disguise, but your pregnancy will give you away immediately if anyone happens to look into the car windows."

Krista nodded, understanding,

"Hey, hurry up," hissed another man she hadn't noticed before. He looked frantically up and down the alley. Snow crunched under his feet. "Rescues in winter suck. It's too easy to be tracked. Damn it, hurry."

Todd helped Krista into the back of the car, and he tucked pillows around her. Then he piled blankets over her.

"We don't have time for this, man," Nervous Guy whispered loudly.

She peeked out of her hiding place to see him pacing like a caged animal.

"We'll make time," her father replied without looking at his cohort.

"You'll only be in there until we hit a more remote area. How are you feeling?" he asked as he readied the cover.

"Scared, unsure, worried about my baby, and a bunch of other trippy emotions," she replied, shivering from the cold.

He grinned. "I'm glad I have you back, muffin. Don't worry. This will all be a bad memory soon. There's a nice female-friendly community in Winnipeg. You and the baby will like it there. I promise."

She nodded, ducking down as he shut her into the suffocating space. She was chilled. Her hospital gown wasn't made for the Minnesota winter. Christmas was in three weeks and her baby was due soon after. She'd planned to spend the holiday with her six, but now she had a completely different man in her life. She'd never expected to spend her first free

Christmas with her father.

The car bounced her uncomfortably in the tight space. She still had to pee. This was the most discomfort she'd ever felt, but if they made it to this community her father told her about, every second would be worth it.

When the SUV finally came to a stop, it seemed as if an eternity had passed. She froze, terrified that the police might have caught up to them. When her father opened the trap door, she let go of the breath she'd been holding.

"Let's get you some warmer clothing," he said.

Unfolding her stiff limbs, she let him help her out of the concealed place. He picked her up and set her on her feet. She stumbled and felt ridiculous as he helped her walk to the door of a small, rural farmhouse. An elderly woman opened the door, much to Krista's surprise. She smiled at Krista and reached up to hug Todd.

"Come in out of the cold, dear boy. So you have her." Martha turned toward Krista. "You are Kristannie?"

"Krista, this is Martha. Martha, my baby girl is going to have a baby girl. Do you have anything warm she can wear? We didn't have time for a change of clothing before I took her on this little road trip."

Martha chuckled.

"I really need to pee," Krista said shyly.

Her father put her on her feet, but had to hold her to keep her steady. Martha pointed to a closed door and Krista wobbled quickly toward the bathroom. When she returned, feeling much better, Martha and her father were whispering quietly. They stopped talking the moment she entered the room.

"What's going on?"

Todd looked as if he didn't want to reply, but then turned on the television. Her picture, the official one for the protection facility file, was splashed on the news and then it cut to Brax and her other men standing outside of the hospital. She saw the deep lines on Brax's face and the bags under his eyes. Her stomach clenched.

"Please, we'll pay any amount you demand, but return Krista to us unharmed. She and the baby need medical treatment. If you turn her over to the authorities, you will receive amnesty for your crime if she's unharmed."

The image changed to the studio reporter. The man ran down a description of the white van and that it was found at two in the morning. He gave details on the description of her "kidnappers" and reported that a ransom request had been sent to the hospital for two million dollars. Krista looked at her father angrily.

"I didn't send any ransom request. If they received one, it was a hoax, but I'm thinking this tidbit is being used as propaganda. God forbid any woman in this country not want to remain an unwilling victim of this asinine forced breeding program. I can only imagine how awful it is to be raped repeatedly for your country."

"It wasn't like that," Krista whispered. Both Martha and her father gave her surprised looks. "I love Braxton Bray. He's the father. I would never have volunteered for this, but it wasn't as if they hurt me."

Her father didn't look happy. "Do you want to stay?"

"No. I know if I went back, they'd just take me away from Brax anyway. It wouldn't be fair to my daughter to stay here and know she'll be sent away to a protection facility in a decade."

Todd nodded. "I know how much it hurts to lose your child, believe me. You're making the right choice."

It didn't feel right, but she knew it was the only one she had. Martha went into the room where the others were warming up around a wood burning stove and returned with sweatpants and a thick wool sweater. She even had wool socks. Krista took the items, gratefully. "Thank you," she whispered.

"You're welcome, Kristannie. Your father has spent years waiting for this day. I've been a pit stop many times. He's helped many young women, but I know he always wanted it to be you."

Krista nodded and went into the bathroom, happy to shed the hospital gown and cut off the plastic identification bracelet. When she returned with it in her hand, Martha took it and opened the round cover on the wood-burning stove. She tossed in the incriminating evidence before replacing the lid.

"Are you hungry? I'll fix you up some nice steak and eggs."

"Oh Martha, you are the perfect woman. If you weren't married, I'd bring you up north with me," Nervous Guy teased.

"Jonathan, you just sit down and stop flirting with me. I'm old enough to be your grandmother."

So Nervous Guy has a real name, Krista thought as she sat down next to him at the table.

She crackled with mirth and shook her head before opening the ancient looking refrigerator and fishing out the ingredients she wanted.

"We really don't have a lot of time," Todd said, glancing nervously at the clock.

"Well, give me fifteen minutes and you can take it to go," Martha said.

Todd nodded. Martha set to work quickly and the heavenly smell made Krista's stomach grumble. The elderly woman packed up scrambled eggs and steak along with some toast. Todd accepted the sack and kissed her on the cheek.

Krista rode in a seat this time, the tinted windows providing a bit of safety for now, but she still sat low and hid her hair under a baseball cap. Mara put her fake mustache on again and Krista was glad they hadn't asked her to wear one. The women's bulky sweatshirts hid their breasts.

They started down the icy, winter road again. Everyone ate the delicious breakfast quietly, until Jonathan cleared his throat. "So one of your boys was the comedian from all those HBO comedy specials, is he really funny in person?" His neck craned around the middle row of seats to see her from the back.

"Yeah, he is." She didn't know why she felt odd talking about Mal. It felt wrong sharing anything personal about the men she'd grown to care for in different ways, as if she was betraying them somehow.

"I saw his last special, not as funny at all." Jonathan snorted. "It felt a bit like he was censoring himself."

"He's funny. Maybe you just have a bad sense of humor." She didn't like this man criticizing Mal and immediately became defensive.

"You care about them?" Mara sounded surprised.

"Yeah, I do. I didn't know if I would, but they weren't cruel to me. I was luckier than most, from the way it sounds. If I'd been sure I wouldn't have been taken away from those particular men, the choice to leave would've been tough."

Krista shrugged.

Mara's mouth parted and she gaped at Krista as if she'd just said the most blasphemous thing possible. "Well, they might've changed after the baby was born. Be glad we saved you. Your father is risking a lot for you. No one even wanted to volunteer for such a high profile retrieval with the two celebrities in your six and the tight security." She sounded bitter.

"Please don't misunderstand me, I'm so grateful. For my daughter's sake, I couldn't stay, but as a woman, I wasn't unhappy with them all the time. It wasn't perfect, but they tried."

Mara made a rude noise. "I'm so glad you liked your gilded cage and life as a sex slave. I suppose not having to work and having a housekeeper and everything you wanted would be hard to leave."

"I wish it was as wonderful as you make it sound. I was very restricted in what I could do. I knew my child would be taken away from me, and yet I had to get pregnant or be forced to endure the awkwardness of forming new bonds with new men. I couldn't even have friends, unless they were hired from a companion service. I appreciate what you're risking for me. I was in love with one of my six, and I'll miss him."

"Stockholm Syndrome, at its finest. You'll get past it once

you have a chance to live without the constant brainwashing. They might have treated you well, but they held you captive against your will. Can you honestly tell me if they'd told you to just leave the protection facility you'd have gone to these men to live your life according to their whims?"

She'd never really thought about it like that before. "I guess not," she mumbled.

"Exactly," Todd said. "You'd have gone on to decide what kind of life you wanted, not just taken the easiest way. Your mother was feisty and determined, I can't imagine you have any less of those qualities."

"I can barely remember her," Krista replied.

"Those traits have nothing to do with memories. You'll get past this feeling for him—them. I've seen other girls deal with guilt and false love too. You need to find your anger and hold it tightly. Don't forget what they've done to you and made you endure. I'm grateful they didn't beat you, but as far as I'm concerned the bastards are monsters."

"They didn't have a choice. It's not as if they had a way to go out and meet women. If they wanted a woman in their life, they had to sign up for the lottery." Her voice rose as she defended them. Her father kept his eyes on the road, but she noticed he held the steering wheel in a white-knuckled grip.

"It's the damn government that's to blame ultimately, but

if the men— the rich, healthy men that Uncle Sam wants—
grew a spine and started to refuse the lottery, there'd be some
real and positive changes for women in America."

"I can't blame them," Krista whispered.

"I have to have someone to blame for all the years I've
missed, muffin. They are the face of my anger, the flesh and
blood for me to hate, don't be sad. I know a wonderful
physiologist who's helped other girls with Stockholm
Syndrome, and he'll help you too. Everything will be better
once we get you across the border."

Krista frowned. She didn't like her father acting as if he
knew her better than she knew herself. The man hadn't seen
her since she was a toddler for goodness sake! "So what makes
this place in Winnipeg 'female-friendly'?"

Mara reached over and squeezed Krista's hand. "Listen, I
know you *think* those men had your best interests in mind, but
even they don't have the final say in your fate. You know that,
right?"

Krista shrugged. She did, but this wasn't any of their
faults. She could've had it worse. "I get it, but you didn't
answer my question."

"In Canada, women are allowed to choose, and
communities that want their females to stick around work hard
to keep it safe. No one comes in or out of our gated sanctuaries

without identification and a reason. Men work very hard to protect their wives, and marriage is still a beloved institution. Life can almost be—normal. Women can work, but most aren't willing to risk it. I won't lie, there are abductions and rapes, but at least you get to live as you please."

Krista could accept the risks; she knew there were plenty of them in America too. She hated leaving, but staying was just too unpredictable. A tear trickled down her face. "I love Braxton."

Her father glanced up at her in the rearview mirror. "I'm sorry," he said quietly.

"Me too," she muttered. "I'm grateful, really I am. I know you're all risking your lives for me. Every state has instituted the death penalty for what you're doing for me, even Minnesota."

"I sat in my cell, watching democracy die with a whimper instead of a bang. This country represented freedom for hundreds of years, and here we are now, escaping tyranny. I'm sorry you can't have the man you love, but you will find someone to care about again."

His statement piqued her curiosity. "Did you remarry?"

"Yes, you're sitting next to her," he said, chuckling.

Krista glanced sharply at Mara. The woman wasn't much older than she was. "Huh, are you going to be an evil stepmother like in the fairy tales?" Krista teased.

Mara rolled her eyes and shook her head. "I've never been a step-mother so I have no idea, but the idea I'm a step-grandmother is really freaking me out."

A bubble of laughter rolled out of Krista. It felt good to laugh. She hadn't done it in far too long. "I guess we all get to feel freaky. Belated congratulations to you both. How long have you been married?"

"Three years last week. I'm a lucky man." He glanced up at Mara in the mirror this time, grinning.

"You'll be safe with us, Krista, I promise. We'll protect you both. May I?" Mara moved to put her hand on Krista's belly. Krista nodded and Mara rested her hand on the baby bump. A moment of feminine camaraderie passed between them, and Krista realized how much she'd missed having a woman in her life.

"Do you think I'll be able to find my friend Cina? She fled to Canada months ago."

"We'll do our best to help you reconnect," Mara replied.

For the first time since the ordeal in the hospital began, Krista let herself feel true hope. Her heart filled and she bit her lip to keep her tears at bay. Mara put her arm around her, and gave her a quick hug. "You aren't alone, Krista."

Those words were the most perfect ones she could ask for.

"Thank you," she whispered.

"Aww, you don't have to thank me, it's what evil step-mothers do."

Krista giggled until she snorted. She covered her mouth. Her father and Mara exchange amused looks in the mirror.

"You people are making me sick with all this lovey-dovey family reunion stuff, but for Todd I'll deal," Jonathan said. Krista could see he was teasing from his expression, but his voice was serious.

"Thanks for helping me, Jonathan. What made you come with them?" She was genuinely intrigued. He didn't seem to be the self-sacrificing type.

"Your dad saved my daughter from a man who was trying to rape her. We've been buddies ever since. I tell you, this guy is one-of-a-kind. I never thought I'd trust an ex-con, but hell, your dad is more of a man than most."

His words renewed her interest in her dad's past again. "We have time now. Tell me your story, Todd...ahh...Dad."

He looked at her in the mirror again. She noticed sadness in his eyes. Guilt made her look away. "Don't worry about it, muffin," he said, as if he could read her mind. "This whole father-daughter bonding stuff will feel right eventually." He paused and took a deep breath. He wasn't looking at her in the mirror anymore. "We were young, your mother and I. Money was tight. You came along and it got tighter, then I lost my job. I panicked and a friend of mine talked me into making the biggest mistake of my life. I never should have participated in that robbery. I wasn't there for your mother when you two needed me. I sat in the jail cell with another two years on my sentence worrying after news of what was happening outside got out. Everything was a mess, my lawyer was a woman and she died too. I ended up spending an extra eighteen months in there because of the chaos. When I got out, you'd have been six. I immediately tried to find out what happened to you and your mother. I had nothing. I stood next to a mass grave a broken man."

"Where am I from?" Krista asked, looking at him again.

His eyes widened. "You don't remember?"

"No, and they never told me. I guess they didn't want me to have any ties to family or my past. Jared tried to help me by searching old records, but they sealed everything about me up tight. I couldn't even access my own birth certificate."

"Bastards." Todd growled. He huffed out an exacerbated sigh. "I'm so sorry, muffin. Your mom and I were living in the Wisconsin Dells area when you were born. We spent a lot of time on the river. Those were some of the happiest days of my life. When we get home, remind me to show you the few pictures I have. There's a great one of you on a little ride at one of the amusement parks. Your mom and I took you there a month before I lost my job. It was our last family outing."

"I'd love that. I had a scrapbook from my days at the protection facility. I wish I could've brought it with me. I'd love to have shown you the book."

"Ask Mara about my fixation with cameras. We'll never miss another memory."

Mara slapped her thigh. "Heaven help us! He's terrible, everything is photographed. I swear I can't do the dishes without him taking my picture. And he never gets my good side."

"All your sides are your good side," Todd said, and Krista could see he meant it. She was glad her father had found someone to love again. She knew how he felt. She wished she had a picture of Brax, anything to hold on to her memories.

Krista turned and gave Mara a quick tight hug. She squeaked with surprise. "Thank you," she whispered in the other woman's ear. They both burst into tears. She saw Jonathan and her father exchange horrified looks, Mara noticed too and they pulled away, trying to compose themselves.

"These rescues are always emotional, but this is just ridiculous," Jonathan grumbled.

"Music. That'll fix this road trip," Todd announced, and he flipped on the radio. Oldies rock from the 1990s blared, and they all sang along to Nirvana. Krista loved classic rock, they just didn't make music like that anymore.

Before long, her father pulled the SUV over. There was a car parked on the road. Krista got out when directed, but she was confused. An elderly man waited. He shook her father's hand enthusiastically. "Thanks, Stan," Todd said as he exchanged keys with the stranger.

"You know you never have to thank me for this. I'm glad you found her." replied the man named Stan. He gave Krista a strange look. "You have your mother's eyes."

"You knew my mother?" she asked.

The man looked at Todd, raising his eyebrow. Then he turned back to look at Krista. "I knew her since the day she was born. I'm your grandfather, Kristannie."

She'd never imagined having a grandfather.

"I'll come up north to see you, once everything is settled. I'm glad your daddy kept his promise to me." She saw the man wipe his eye before rushing away toward the SUV without another word or another look.

They piled into the small sedan; Krista sat in the back seat. She watched the SUV pulling away. "Why don't I remember him?" she asked Todd.

"He didn't like me much when I married your mother. Our love caused a major strain between them. He was right, I wasn't good enough for her," her father said gruffly. He looked away. Mara made a disgruntled noise, but said nothing. "They weren't speaking when she died. I found him after I got out. I expected you to be with your grandparents. They didn't know your mother had died. Your grandmother died shortly after your mother did, and with all the tragedy, he never thought about the little girl he'd never met. When he realized you'd survived, he tried to get you back, but the protection facility had you and he was as shut out as I was." Todd pulled the car onto the shoulder of the road. "He regretted that your mother died alone and that you were lost. He's the one who helped me get on my feet, and when I found this underground network of like-minded people, he supported my choice to work against the government. We've developed an understanding over the years."

She'd spent so many years feeling alone. The revelation she had people who loved her and missed her felt strange. She didn't know how to feel about all this new family. "I feel better than I did in the hospital, but I'm worried about my baby. How long will it be until we reach Winnipeg?" she asked her father when he glanced up to look at her.

"About another hour. I wouldn't be surprised to learn that the doctor was causing your issues so they'd have a reason to change your placement. It's well known, to most folks at least, that they use this tactic to avoid couple bonds forming. Your doctor may have noticed you had special feelings for your Braxton."

Hearing his name sent a shaft of pain through her heart. The idea that the doctor may have done something to cause her so much anxiety filled her with white-hot rage.

They hadn't seen any police, and she was both relieved and worried. Everything seemed too easy. They remained silent. The radio played, but much of the joviality had dissipated.

Suddenly, Krista heard sirens. She unhooked the seatbelt and slid down to the car's carpeted floorboards. Mara pulled her baseball cap lower and touched the fake mustache, adjusting it quickly. Her father pulled over and the police car sped past. Everyone let out audible sighs of relief.

"We'll be going through a few towns soon. I hate to do this, but I think you'll need to ride in the hidden compartment in the hatch, muffin."

Krista hated the idea of it, and with her condition, she feared what effect this journey was having on her baby. She and Todd got out. The temperature was even colder than before. She reminded herself it was only another hour or so and crawled into the gaping darkness with her father's help. They hadn't brought the blankets from the SUV. Todd gave her an apologetic look then shut the door carefully. Krista lay in the darkness as the car pulled away from the side of the road. Her mind couldn't help conjuring up an image of Brax. If things were different, she'd have him in her life, and only him. Crushing loss weighed on her, and tears filled her eyes. A broken sob escaped and before she realized it, she was crying harder than she'd ever cried before.

Epilogue

Winnipeg, Canada. Three Years Later

Krista pushed Addy, Alicia Denyse, her daughter, in the swing. Grandma Mara had traded for it recently. Krista loved Winnipeg. The natural beauty wasn't so different from home, but here she could enjoy the world with relatively few restrictions. Her father hadn't lied. The community was amazingly protective, and any man who tried to kidnap or rape a woman didn't live very long, so she felt as safe here as she had in the compound or the protection facility.

Addy giggled. She was so beautiful. Her dark hair was the exact same shade as her father's. Braxton. Even after all this time, Krista missed him. She couldn't help wondering what kind of father he would have been. Her six would've been good to Addy, and she'd probably have had another baby already.

She'd resisted Mara's many attempts to set her up with men. She just wasn't ready yet, maybe she never would be. She'd checked the email account a few months after her flight from Minnesota and there were messages. Hundreds of messages from Braxton, his soulful longings poured out day after day. She still checked every single evening, but it'd been months since he'd written. Krista never replied, not even once, out of fear. She wanted him to know so many things, but she just didn't know what to say or how to tell him she hadn't left because she didn't love him. She missed those messages.

Her father and young stepmother were wonderful. She adored them and so did Addy. She was glad she'd had the courage to run, and knowing her daughter had a much brighter future than she'd had as a child made her loneliness worthwhile. Addy was her life.

"Hello, Kristannie," a deep, male voice spoke quietly.

Krista froze, afraid to move. She feared her constant longings had finally made her snap. It couldn't be...Brax?

She turned to look in the direction the masculine voice had originated from. A small gasp escaped her and she turned around toward her daughter again. Momentum kept the giggling toddler moving, but Krista wasn't pushing her child because her hands were covering her own face. She wasn't willing to believe what she was seeing. *Great, now I'm going crazy and seeing things. Wonderful things.* She closed her eyes and took a deep breath. *When I look back, if he's not real he'll be gone.* Slowly, she turned and dropped her hands, but her eyes remained tightly shut. Cautiously, she gathered the courage to open her eyes. As beautiful and real as ever, Braxton Bray stood in her father's backyard.

"Brax?" She breathed the question quietly.

"She's perfect," he uttered, gazing with wonder at their daughter. Then his eyes moved to Krista's face. "I was so angry and scared. I didn't know if you'd gone by choice. I hated you for a little while."

"I know. I read your messages," she whispered, looking away. The raw emotion on his face was too brutal and real. "How did you find me? I'm not going back, and neither is Addy."

"Addy?" His eyebrow rose.

"Alicia Denyse," she explained as she gauged his reaction.

"Thank you for using the name. Your father found me a few months ago at a book signing. He slipped me a note and walked away. He took a hell of a risk."

"What did the note say?"

"It was cryptic. He wrote, 'She still loves you. If you want her, move to Winnipeg. She and the child are well'. I dealt with a few things and looked into the process for becoming a Canadian. I'm here on a provincial nomination now. I asked around about where a woman who'd fled from America might be. I received defensive responses, but one man I spoke to contacted the gentleman who heads the security program in your gated community. He spoke to your father and here I am. I'm not going anywhere, Kristannie, unless you don't want me to stay."

She ran forward. She gazed into his face and his lips descended. She wrapped her arms around his neck and kissed him as if her life depended on it. The hungry demand of his lips left her stomach twisted in knots. Desire and shock battled for control of her brain.

Addy gave an angry scream and Krista pulled away. The swing had stopped and the girl sat reaching for her mother. Krista went and unbuckled her, picking her up. Brax put out his hands, but Addy shook her head, burying her face shyly into Krista's shoulder. Guilt twisted inside of her. "Addy, this is your daddy," she whispered into the girl's ear. Addy looked over at Brax curiously.

"It'll take time for her, for all of us. I want to be a family with you, Krista. I didn't tell the others where you were, I'm selfish. I was worried one of them would come and try to convince you to love them and only them. That's what I want for me, your love."

She thought of the others, alone, and felt terrible. If any of them had come, it wouldn't have been the same. "That's what I want too," she whispered. "I love you, Brax."

A look of pure joy lit his face. "You mean that?"

"With all my heart, it was always only you."

"I want to marry you, Krista, as soon as I'm a citizen and can. I love you, more than I thought I could ever love. I want to get to know my daughter, and take care of both of you."

Krista swallowed around the lump in her throat, the cold, empty hole inside of her heart warming and filling. She'd been content, but suddenly she realized she could be happy again. "Yes," she replied.

Brax chuckled. "Well, I guess I'd better learn to like hockey." He put his arm around her, and for the first time in her life, she knew what it was to have real freedom. The invisible chains of pain and sadness fell away. The two ton stone she'd carried metaphorically on her heart disappeared. Tears filled her eyes. Addy looked at her curiously.

"Everything will be wonderful now, baby. Daddy's home," she whispered into her daughter's hair, hugging the child tightly. In that moment, she realized Winnipeg suddenly felt like home because Brax was here. "Thank you for coming for me, Brax."

"Thank you for agreeing to become Mrs. Bray. Without you, nothing has been right. I love you so damn much."

"Language...we have an impressionable toddler," Krista scolded teasingly.

A look of love filled his face. "I can't believe I'm really looking at you, Kristannie, or our child. I thought I'd lost you both forever." His voice cracked.

Krista handed him his daughter, and he held her

awkwardly at first. Then he pulled her close to him and kissed the top of her head.

"Mine. Ours. I'm actually holding her. Thank you for giving me a child."

Krista didn't know why his words pleased her as much as they did. A sob shuddered out of her. She covered her face with her hands as she sucked in a deep breath and fought for control.

Mara opened the back door and came out. She handed Krista a box of tissues, which meant she'd been watching the reunion from the house. "We have plenty of supper, and if Todd doesn't still want to kill you, I'd be delighted if you'd be our guest until you figure out what the two of you want to do about living arrangements. I assume you'll want him to stay in your room?" She wiggled her eyebrows suggestively and grinned at Krista.

"Meet your meddling mother-in-law," Krista teased, chuckling.

"I'll stay as long as Kristannie will have me," he told Mara, but his eyes never left Krista's.

"I hope you packed everything you need, because I'm never letting you go again," Krista replied, grinning.

"Everything I need is standing in front of me. You're all I ever wanted and all I'll ever need. I love you, Kristannie. Even if there were a million women and I was the last man alive—

I'd want you. You were all I could think about, and not just sex—you. When you left, you ripped a hole in my heart. At first, I was terrified you'd been hurt. I had nightmares…terrible images of you in pain, it felt like I was suffocating all the time, but I couldn't die."

As cheesy as his words were, she could see the honesty in his eyes, and her heart physically ached as the bitter shell of self-doubt and pain cracked inside her soul. She'd felt so ridiculous for not being able to just live—everyone told her she was better off without him, but she wasn't. He hadn't abused her or forced himself on her. She'd loved every minute in his arms, especially when he'd dominated in a way none of the others had. He hadn't been cruel or rough, just in charge, and it had filled a need in her that the others left empty. As she looked into his eyes, she saw something that made her breath catch in her throat. Love.

He moved to Mara and passed her the little girl. Addy clung to her step-grandmother. Mara cradled the child tightly. He turned back to Krista and cupped her cheek in his hand. Love. That look on his face made her want to start bawling all over again.

"Brax, I love you. I'm glad you didn't die. I've been just existing, and now I know why. I was waiting for you."

He wrapped his arms around her and pressed a kiss to the

top of her head. "I never knew what it was to live. When you came into our—my life, it was the first time I really felt like I had a reason to take my next breath. You've saved me. I want to save you back every day. I'm going to deserve you—someday."

She clung to him, desperately trying not to cry again. She knew he meant the words, and she knew without a doubt that he would do what he said.

Brax had picked her up without giving her any warning. Krista cried out. He turned to Mara. "You'll watch the baby, right?"

Mara flushed. Her eyes were bright with unshed tears. "Right, I have her. Todd won't be home for a few more hours. I was thinking about taking a long walk. Come on, Addy. It's a beautiful day, let's find the stroller."

Krista watched her go until Brax began walking toward the house. His domineering way didn't bother her a bit. Her emotions were on such a crazy rollercoaster ride. She couldn't stop herself from trembling in his arms. He looked down at her and she bit her lip.

"Do you want me to put you down, Kristannie?"

She loved the way he said her full name. She'd missed hearing it. He was the only one who ever said it in that special way. The way he uttered the word was like a powerful spell, binding her to him. Reminding her she belonged to him. Even if no piece of paper made her his, she was. Something more powerful than law wove them together now.

"No, never again," she whispered.

He smiled and lust darkened his beautiful eyes. "Where is your room?"

"Up the stairs, first door on the left. Addy sleeps in the room on the right. Todd and Mara sleep downstairs."

"Todd?"

"Dad, um, it's still a little weird calling him that."

Brax nodded his understanding. "I'm sorry you've been through so much."

"I'm not," she replied.

He flinched, surprise evident on his face.

"No matter what, all this hell has brought me here and has *given* you to *me*."

His lips touched hers and she sensed his frantic need, even as he kissed her slowly. Her arms wrapped tighter around his neck. She could feel the muscles in his back under her hands. She wanted his shirt off—now.

He rushed into the room and set her on the bed. She watched him close and lock the door as he quickly stripped off his clothing. She began pulling her shirt over her head, but he stopped her.

"Let me," he whispered.

She paused and he gently finished removing her shirt. He reached around her and unhooked her bra. Her now ampler breasts fell free. Brax sucked in a breath.

"Fuck. You're beautiful, woman. I've fantasized about you so much, but even my imagination couldn't see how perfect you are."

He dropped to his knees in front of her and took one of her nipples into his mouth. He sucked her softly, then hard, and then softly again. Her back arched. A moan slipped from her lips. His hands caressed her bare back tenderly. Her eyes fluttered closed. If this was another dream, she didn't want to wake up. She'd missed sex, but most of all, she'd missed Braxton. Her fingers slipped into his soft hair and she held him to her breast.

"I love you so much. I wish you'd been my first, my only," she murmured. There was a sad hitch in her voice.

He pulled away and looked up into her face. "As you know, you were my first and my only. If you'll trust me, I'll give you pleasure in a way no one ever has before."

His words excited her. She'd thought she'd been pleasured every way possible. She nodded. "I'm yours. I trust you."

He grinned. She loved seeing him happy. He had lines on his face that hadn't been there three years ago, but when he smiled they went away.

"I suffered without you. I never want to let you go again." His mouth found her other breast and she cried out.

Her body was hypersensitive. His every touch scorched her. He pulled away and the cool air made her nipple pucker tighter. He gave it another tweak with his fingers. She groaned. He pushed her back onto the mattress and she looked down to see him undoing her fly. He pulled her jeans and panties to her ankles in one motion. Then he pulled off her shoes and socks. A moment later everything was off. The air touched her pussy and she felt it pucker.

He inhaled sharply. "Damn, you smell good."

He knelt between her legs and she opened them for him. Brax began sucking on her clit, nibbling it. Then he lapped passionately at her. She jerked, bucking against his mouth. Her back arched again. Krista came loud and hard. She was glad no one was home. When her body had settled down to nothing but phantom spasms, her pussy squeezed, desperate for some cock.

Brax stood. "Turn onto your stomach for me."

She loved his tone. That deep, sensual voice made her shiver. The dominate quality in his sexual intensity only made her hotter. She rolled to her stomach without a word. He pulled her closer to the foot of the bed, and pushed her hips up just a little to raise her ass in the air. His fingers began swirling in her wetness. She sighed. Then he plunged his cock into her hard, pumping her twice. She cried out, squeezing her eyes tightly with the pleasure. She hadn't had a man inside of her in over three years. The joy that shot through her womb was mind-blowing. He withdrew quickly. Krista whimpered. She wanted him inside of her again.

"Do you trust me?"

She nodded, not trusting her voice. Her body was nothing but sensation and primal need. Words were beyond the de-evolution he caused in her brain. The smell of his cologne wafted to her nose. She inhaled the scent of Brax and sex. Her pussy tightened. She wiggled her ass, wanting more. He gave her a hard, albeit it playful, slap. She wiggled again, wanting his hands on her as she craved his control.

His thumb and forefinger pinched and rolled her clit as the fingers of his other hand entered her pussy. She whimpered. Her body was on the precipice of another release. Then he rubbed her wetness against her virginal anus.

"Relax. Trust me. Let go completely."

She did. The tone of his voice made it easy. She wanted to give him her body so completely he'd never doubt her love—or that she was his. She'd waited for this man...pined for Brax until she'd made herself sick. He was here and her hormones were on overdrive. She'd known lust and pleasure in his home, but nothing like what she felt now. Here, she could belong only to him and it sweetened her desire. This was love, not duty. There was no guilt that he was her favorite. Everything that had been wrong with her desire for only him was gone, and now the rightness of it hit her with the force of a speeding train. She was helpless. She'd given him her soul, and it was good to be reunited with all her missing pieces.

He slid his damp fingers inside her ass. She forced herself to relax, reminded herself he wouldn't hurt her. At first it was odd, and then the sensation became good. His fingers never stopped rubbing her clit. She was so wet, the proof of her desire running down her thigh.

"Do it! Do anything," she cried out in her animalistic fervor.

Another finger stretched her. There was no pain. She leaned into him, wanting him deeper. Krista grunted, half-crazed with her excitement.

When he withdrew she gasped. "No." Her wail didn't even sound like it belonged to her, but it did.

Then something larger nudged her there. She stiffened, then relaxed. Giving in to his body filled her with a twisted joy. She closed her eyes and rested her forehead on the mattress. Her body was teetering on release, and she clutched wildly at the sheets, pulling them off the mattress with her writhing, grasping restlessness.

The head of his cock entered her ass. It felt gigantic. His prick wasn't small, but right now it seemed like the biggest dick in the world. She grunted. He rubbed her back softly.

"Shh, baby. Relax and this will be so good."

She forced her body to still and took a deep breath in through her nose. She let it out with her mouth. Her ardor grew. He rubbed her clit harder. He pushed inside of her, and her body slowly gave way to him. When his balls slapped against her ass cheeks she knew he was all the way inside of her. Brax was taking her in a way no other man ever had. She closed her eyes, relishing the feeling. Now, he was her first. The beauty of knowing it made her eyes water.

"Are you okay?"

She didn't respond, too overcome with emotion.

"Damn it, Kristannie, are you okay?"

She heard him speaking through gritted teeth. It made her smile. "I'm fine, Brax. I just love you so much."

He was still. His cock stretching her, he leaned down and kissed the center of her back. She shivered. "You are the most incredible woman—beyond anything I'd imagined could exist. I'll never deserve you, but thank God you're letting me try."

His words touched her. He rubbed her pussy harder and moved slowly inside of her. She came. The orgasm hit her with unexpected force. She growled out her pleasure. The scream sounded almost painful. She bucked against his cock, frantic for him to come inside of her. He pulled out and she turned her head to look at him. He was still erect.

"Lie on your back and wait for me. Play with your pussy, Kristannie. I want to see you touching yourself."

She obeyed immediately, without question, desperate to make him as happy as he made her. Even having come, she was still hot. She wanted him again.

There was a private bathroom adjoining her room and he rushed inside. She heard the water running. He was out in just a moment. Her hand was still between her legs because he wanted it there. He leaned against the door and watched her fingers with intense interest. Then he crawled onto the bed and spread her legs as wide as they would go. He rested his hands on the mattress, framing her head, and leaned down to kiss her. She kissed him back, opening her mouth for his tongue.

His cock filled her needy pussy. She wrapped her legs around him. He pulled back to look into her eyes.

"I'm so fucking close, but I don't want this to be over," he whispered.

"It doesn't have to end now. Forever." The last word came out in a moan as she arched her back once more. It seemed surreal, but she came again, and just as hard. His hips slammed into her with bruising force a few more times before he stiffened.

"Kristannie." Her name slipped out of him in a reverent whisper as he released inside of her.

Her pussy milked his cock and she enjoyed the sensation of the spasms, even after she'd come off her euphoric endorphin high, and the pleasure ebbed.

He flopped down on the mattress and rolled onto his back, pulling her to rest on his chest. His arms came around her as if they were iron bands.

"This is a small mattress."

"Yes," she replied and cocked her head to the side, her eyes narrowing with confusion. "Do you want to sleep somewhere else?"

"Never, I want to hold you close. I like the idea that you'll be snuggled right up against me all night."

She chuckled and rested her head on his damp chest. The wiry hair tickled her cheek.

"I'm going to love you until the day I die," he declared.

She closed her eyes and sighed. She hoped that day was decades away, but she liked his long-term goal.

The sound of the front door opening made her sit up.

"Crap, my dad is home. We'd better get dressed. He doesn't exactly like you."

Brax grinned. "I can't blame him. I want to do wicked things to his daughter." He wiggled his eyebrows.

She slapped his shoulder playfully. "I'm serious."

"So am I."

He kissed her again. All thoughts of impropriety fled. Nothing mattered but the man who held her. When Brax let go she was love-drunk with the taste of him.

She quickly put on her clothing. He also dressed, but at a more casual speed. Krista rushed out of the room and flew into her father's arms.

"Thank you so much. Todd—ah Dad, you are the best! I can't believe you reached out to him for me." Tears dripped onto her warm cheeks.

He pulled back and looked at her. She knew what he saw. Her face was flushed, her hair was a mess; she looked like she'd been doing just what she'd done. A slow grin spread across his face.

"He's here, huh?"

"Yes."

"So, Mara and Addy gave you both some catch up time?"

"Yes."

"Are you happy? Is he really what you want? If he's not, I'll throw his ass out of here now."

"Don't you dare, but just…" She threw her arms around

her father again. "Thank you, Dad." For the first time, the words really felt right. He was really her dad. He'd put her first, risked so much for her. Her heart swelled with love.

Her father patted her back awkwardly, but she could feel his love for her. "I just don't want you to hurt any more, muffin. It's your turn to be happy."

Brax came cautiously down the stairs. The men looked at each other, sizing one another up.

When Brax extended his hand, her father shook it firmly. "Thank you, sir," Brax said.

"Take care of her, of them both, and we're good. Mess up and I kick your ass back down south."

"Understood."

Krista glanced back and forth between the men in her life and couldn't stop her smile. The sound of the back door made her turn. Mara walked in holding Addy. They paused and Mara surveyed the scene.

"Are we good or should I cover the baby's eyes?"

Todd scowled. "We're good." His expression didn't match his words, but Mara smiled anyway. Addy reached out toward her grandfather. He took the little girl from his wife.

"I have a roast in the oven. It should be ready. It will be nice to have the whole family together," Mara said, looking into each of their faces.

Krista couldn't agree more. *The whole family...* Her story finally had a happy ending.

About Ashlynn Monroe

Ashlynn Monroe has been dreaming up stories all her life. She started to put them on paper at thirteen, but it wasn't until she was thirty that she decided to share them with others. She's a busy mom with a full time job, fantastic friends, and a unique sense of humor. She's just a regular girl who's in love with the idea of happily-ever-after. She's honored to be multi-published by some of the best electronic publishers in the industry. Ashlynn survives each day by dreaming up her next tale of romance. She loves her readers and can't thank them enough for the wonderful support they give her.

Ashlynn's Website:

www.ashlynnmonroe.com

Reader eMail:

authorashlynnmonroe@gmail.com

CPSIA information can be obtained at www.ICGtesting.com
Printed in the USA
BVOW070027120413

317976BV00001B/10/P

9 781937 325626